Proving Paul's Promise

by Tammy Falkner

Night Shift Publishing

Copyright © 2014 by Tammy Falkner

Proving Paul's Promise
First Edition
Night Shift Publishing
Cover art by Vladimirs Poplavskis - Fotolia.com
Cover design by Tammy Falkner
ISBN-13: 978-1500218928

*For all of you who have done what's in the best interest of your children.*

# Friday

I've heard that the best way to get over one man is to get under another. With that said, I doubt this is what the speaker had in mind. A hand squeezes mine tightly. It was pretty stupid of me to allow them to be in the room with me for this part because I'm feeling terribly exposed, despite the fact that my lower half is draped with a sheet. There's just something about having my legs up in stirrups and the top of a woman's head visible between my thighs that makes this all awkward.

It should be beautiful, and really, it is. It's just…odd.

I have Cody on my left and Garrett on my right. They lean toward one another to kiss over my head, and Garrett uses his free hand to wipe a tear from Cody's cheek.

The doctor looks up from her perch down below. "You doing okay up there?" she asks.

I squeeze my eyes shut. "Fine," I say.

Garrett leans down and kisses my temple, his lips lingering there. "Thank you for doing this," he whispers vehemently, and emotion swells within me.

"Thanks for letting me do this," I say back. I tip my face up, and he presses a soft kiss to my lips. There's no passion in this kiss whatsoever. There's only emotion and gratitude and a type of affection like I've never known.

Cody squeezes my shoulder. These guys make the cutest couple. They have been together for about twelve years, and after three failed adoptions, they wanted more than anything to have a kid. They didn't even ask me. I volunteered to be their surrogate. I'm healthy, I'm young, I'm in love with the type of love they have for one another, and I wanted to give them their own baby.

We used a donor egg and a mishmash of their sperm. The donor egg is so I could stay as far removed from the situation as possible. The mishmash is so they won't know who the father is. They'll both be fathers. All I know is that I don't want to be a mom. But I'm willing to let the little guy cook in my uterus for nine months or so. Then I will gladly hand him over to these wonderful men, and they will be able to raise their own child.

I wince as the doctor cranks the speculum down and pulls it from my vagina. She lifts my feet from the stirrups and rolls her chair back. "Friday," she says. That's my name. Friday. Like the day of the week. It's not the name on my birth certificate, but it fits me better than that old relic of my former life ever did. "In about ten days, I want you to come in for a blood test."

Cody rubs his hands together. He's so excited that I get all teary again. That could be the hormones they used to get me on a cycle similar to that of the egg donor, but either way, I'm much more emotional than on a normal day. "Ten days until we find out if we're going have a baby!" Cody squeals.

A grin tugs at my lips as Garrett helps me sit up. I feel a lot better with the gown covering all my girly bits, instead of having my hoo-ha up in the air for everyone to see.

"I can go to work today, right?" I ask.

She nods her head. "The only thing you can't do is have an orgasm."

Heat creeps up my cheeks, so I slap my palms against them. "Oh no!" I cry. "What am I going to do without my daily orgasms?"

Garrett holds up two fingers. "Twice on Sundays."

"Don't do any heavy lifting or any strenuous exercise. And no warm baths," the doctor says. She looks at the tattoo on my knee with keen interest. It's a spider web with a baby rattle in the middle. "Interesting," she says, more to herself than to me. Hell, she already saw the one on my inner thigh.

I cover my knee with my hand, and she jerks her gaze away. I have tattoos all over my body. I love them, and each one tells a story. I drew most of them, and they all mean something to me. I know people with tattoos have a lot of stigmas attached to them, but I just like art, and I like to wear art on my body. Judge me if you want to, because I don't care.

"I have to get back to work," Cody says, and he leans over to kiss Garrett on the lips. Then he kisses my temple and leaves, his smile big and bright.

Garrett hangs out with me while I change clothes behind the curtain. I can hear his feet hitting the side of the exam table he's sitting on. He's like a giddy little kid with his feet swinging back and forth. "Where do you have to go when you leave here?" he asks.

"Work," I say as I pull my dress down over my head. I like vintage clothes, and today is no different than any other day. I wonder how I'm going to be able to pull off the vintage look when my belly is big and round. I am not sure vintage-inspired maternity clothes will be easy to find.

"Don't you want to take the rest of the day off?" he asks. "We could go shopping. Buy some baby stuff."

"Tempting," I say. Honestly, it sounds like hell. "I'll leave that to you and Cody, if you don't mind."

"Fine," he tosses back harshly, like he's annoyed, but I know he's not. "Let me buy you lunch, then. And I'll walk you back to Reed's."

Reed's is the tattoo parlor where I work. The idea of him walking me there makes me surprisingly joyful. "Will you be sure to kiss me before you leave?" I ask. I grin as I put on my delicate shoes with the tall heels that I love so very much. They match the dress.

"Why?" he asks, instantly suspicious. He jerks the curtain back as I pull my hair from the neck of my dress. He grins. "Which of the Reeds are you hoping to make jealous?" He narrows his eyes at me.

I start to tick them off on my fingers. "Logan is married and has a baby on the way. Pete is with Reagan. Matt is married and knocked up his wife. With twins!"

"So that leaves Sam and Paul." He appraises me shrewdly.

Kissing Sam would be like kissing my brother. Paul, on the other hand...

"Mmm hmm," Garrett hums. "It's the big one, right?"

"He's not that big," I mutter to myself.

"Are you kidding?" he shrieks. "He's fucking huge." He grins. "I bet the rest of him is just as big."

Sometimes having a gay man as a really good friend has its advantages. Because a straight man would never wonder how big Paul Reed's dick is. "I wouldn't know," I murmur. His baby mama would, though, because he still sleeps with Kelly. That part makes my gut ache.

"Does he still walk you home at night when the shop closes?" Garrett asks.

I shrug. "One of them does."

"Does he still try to kiss you?" Garrett sings. He's like a damn woodland creature with his giddiness. I expect him to break out into song any second.

"That only happened once," I say. It was the kiss that rocked my world, though. I pick up my purse and step out into the room.

"And?" He makes a rolling motion with his finger as he opens the door for me and we walk through the hallway. He checks us out, pays the bill, and we step into the sunshine.

"And what?" I huff as I put on my sunglasses and pretend like I don't know what he just asked.

"The man laid one on you and you still have to see him every day, Friday. How's that going?" He takes my hand in his and threads his fingers through mine as we wait for the subway. The baby doctor's office is on the good side of town. And Reed's is not. It's in the area that I love more than anything.

"Fine."

He gapes at me, his mouth hanging open. "That's all I get? Fine?" He points to my belly. "You might have my baby in your uterus, and that's all you're going to tell me?"

I cover his mouth with my hand. "You don't get any say over any part of my body except for that baby that may or may not be growing in there."

"Oh, that was cold," he says. But I have quite effectively changed the subject.

He talks about nurseries and bottles and clothes and all the things I don't even want to know about until we get to Reed's. When we get there, he stops in front of the shop, cups his hands around his eyes, and looks through the glass into the room.

"Yep," he says with a grin. "It's showtime!" He takes my hand and opens the door. The grin falls off his face, and he replaces it with a look of aloofness. It's uncanny how he can do that. He minored in theater many years ago, though, so I guess it makes sense. He's a teacher now.

I drop my bag behind the desk at the front, which is where I usually work. I design the tattoos, and sometimes I do the actual tattoo part. I'm still learning how to do that, but drawing is my thing. That is where my skills lie—I'm an art major at NYU, after all. Or at least I was until I graduated two weeks ago. Now I'm just a possibly-knocked-up soon-to-be-homeless person. Oh crap. I haven't told Garrett and Cody about my living situation yet.

Paul looks up from where he's doing a tattoo on a guy's shoulder, and he frowns. "Morning," he says, looking from me to Garrett and back. Garrett swells up in size. Honey, no matter what you do, you will never look as big or as tough as Paul Reed.

"Morning," I chirp back.

Logan is here, too, and he smiles at me and waves. Logan is deaf but can speak, and we all learned how to sign many years ago. I wave back.

*Who's that?* he signs at me and points to Garrett.

I put my hand on Garrett's shoulder. "Garrett, this is Paul, and the quiet one there is Logan."

Logan stands up and shakes Garrett's hand. Paul just grunts.

"Nice to meet you," Garrett says. He turns to me and tips my face up. He leans down close to my ear and says, "I bet he's fucking huge." I laugh and try to turn my face away, but he just holds me there with his thumbs beneath my chin and his fingers splayed toward my ear. Then his lips touch mine.

He's actually a really good kisser, and I kind of envy Cody a little bit, because if he goes after sex the same way he's going after this fake kiss, Cody's getting it pretty good.

The only thing about it…there's no spark. Not a single one. It's just warm, wet lips sliding across mine, and a really quick touch of a tongue. I pinch his side, and he laughs against my lips and pulls back. He drags his nose up and down the side of mine.

"Cody is going to love it when I tell him about this." I stab him in the side with my index finger, and he bends over, trying not to laugh.

"Remember what the doctor said," he tells me, facing me and speaking quietly. "No orgasms. Not even ones offered by great big studly tattoo artists that make you sweat." He waves a hand in front of his face like a fan. "He makes me sweat a little bit, too."

I hear a clatter behind us as Paul throws down his tattoo gun and stalks toward the back of the shop. He pulls the privacy curtain closed behind him.

Logan looks up at me, grins, and just shakes his head.

Garrett kisses my forehead, lingering there for a second. "In ten days, you might be my baby mama," he says, his body rocking against mine as he chuckles.

I punch his shoulder and point toward the door.

Next time he fake kisses me, I have to remember to tell him not to use tongue. I wipe the back of my hand across my mouth and watch him leave. He waves and blows me a kiss.

Logan throws up a hand to get my attention. *You're playing with fire,* he warns. He jerks his thumb toward the curtain. *He's pissed.* He must not want Paul to hear him or he would be talking instead of signing.

I wave a breezy hand at him. *He'll have to get over it.*

He looks toward the curtain. *You should go talk to him.*

*Why?*

*Because he still has a client out here, and he had to leave because you were sucking face with the other guy.*

Crap. Paul walked away with a client in his chair. With a half-finished tat. *He has no right to be angry.*

Logan's brow arches, and he shakes his head.

*Well, he doesn't.*

*Quit being a baby,* he signs. He jerks his thumb toward the curtain again. *Go talk to him.*

I heave a sigh and go to get Paul out of his snit.

# Paul

I can't fucking believe she brought that man here. To my shop. Where I work. Hell, it's where I *live*.

I lean against the counter and balance myself on my palms. My forehead rests against the upper cabinet, and I force myself to take a deep breath and count to ten. It was all I could do not to jerk him off her and show him the door. With my foot up his ass.

One of my brothers left shit on the counter that should have been put away, so I clean up and slam the cabinet door. That feels a little better, but not much. I can just imagine that douche in the front of the shop. He's probably got his hand all the way up her shirt by now.

I slam another door.

The curtain rattles behind me, and a breeze tickles the back of my neck as someone walks into the space. "Not now," I grind out.

"Then when?" she tosses back.

Great. It would be her that came to get me. I knew it was her. No one else makes the hair on my arms stand up or gives me fucking chills. Not to mention that the perfume she wears gets to me before her voice does. It reaches across the room, creeps up my nose, and wraps itself around my heart. I lower my head and grit my teeth. "Go away, Friday," I say.

"You have a client waiting," she says, as though I don't know.

"I'm aware."

"Then what the fuck are you doing?" she asks.

Friday is the only one who talks to me like that in my shop. She calls me on my shit, and she has since the day she first walked in here. She was eighteen years old, and she had just started at NYU. She walked in looking like she was lost, and I hired her on the spot when she told me what was wrong with the tattoo on the side of my neck. She told me how she would change it and that any good artist would have known that it was placed wrong. She pulled out a sheet of paper and drew a quick sketch of a new design.

"Want a job?" I'd said.

"Yeah," she'd replied. "But only if you'll fix that fucking tattoo so I don't have to look at that monstrosity every fucking day."

I'd grinned. Hell, the thought of it still makes me grin. Logan had fixed the tattoo that day, and she'd started working for me. That was four years ago. Four fucking years of looking at her beautiful legs and red lips. Every. Single. Day. Four years of watching her and wanting her. Four years of lusting over Friday. Four years with her busting my chops.

"I'll finish in a minute," I say. I heave a sigh and drop heavily into a chair. Friday wears me the fuck out.

She puts her hands on her hips and glares at me. "Why?"

"Why what?" I force myself to look at her face instead of her rack. She has the most beautiful rack I have ever seen, and I've been looking at it long enough to know.

"Why are you back here instead of out there working?"

Because I couldn't watch you sucking face with that douche. "I told you, I'm taking a break." I give her a what-the-fuck look. If I let her think she's gone mental, I can blame it all on her, right?

"But why?" she asks. She stomps that little foot of hers, and it immediately draws my attention to her feet, and then up her legs, and then… God. I swipe a hand down my face. "Why, Paul?"

"Who's the douche?" I ask, instead of telling her how I'm feeling.

"What douche?" She still has her hands on her hips.

"The one who had his tongue down your throat." I glare at her. But she doesn't back down. She never does.

"His name is Garrett," she mumbles. She is suddenly really interested in looking at the magnets on the fridge.

"Garrett is a fuckwad. Tell him to keep his dick in his pants the next time he comes in my shop."

She blows out a breath and raises her finger to point at me, and I can tell she's about to ream me a new one.

"Weren't you fucking somebody else last week, Friday?" I blurt out. I want to take it back immediately because it hangs there in the air between us like a bomb about to explode.

"What?" she asks, and her voice goes soft.

"Last week it was a different guy who took you to lunch." I grumble to myself and get up, pretending to clean the counter.

She thinks it over. "You mean Cody?"

"How many are there?"

She blinks hard. What the fuck? Friday never cries. Ever. I take a step toward her, and she steps back, putting her hand up like she's going to push the air around me back. "How dare you?" she breathes. A tear falls over her lashes, and she swipes it away and then looks down at the back of her wet hand like she doesn't know what the fuck a tear is.

"Friday," I say. I step toward her again. I soften my voice because I have no idea what to do. I have never seen this Friday before. I have only seen the one who can eat my balls for lunch. Hell, she'll feed *my* balls to *me* if I piss her off enough. And make me like it. Four years and I have never seen her shed a tear.

She turns around and runs into the bathroom, slamming the door behind her. I lean my ear against the door and listen, but I can't hear anything over the sound of the fan. I knock. She doesn't answer.

"Dammit," I swear. I lean my forehead against the door.

"Leave her alone," I hear from behind me.

I turn around because Logan is talking. "I can't," I say to him. I knock again, but she doesn't answer.

"Just leave her the fuck alone," he says again. He's pissed, I can tell. "You have a client." He waves toward my customer like he's Vanna Fucking White. "Work to do. So, you might want to get to it."

I heave a sigh and look at my client. "Just a moment," I say.

"Take your time," he says with a grin. He's loving the show, apparently.

I pull my keys from my pocket and fit the key in the lock. I hesitate long enough for Logan to notice.

"You shouldn't," he warns.

I know I shouldn't, but I am.

I turn the key and let myself into the room. I find Friday washing her face.

"What the fuck, Paul!" she cries. She turns back to the mirror and dabs beneath her eyes. She looks at me in the mirror. "Get out."

I close the door behind me and lean against it. "Why are you crying?"

"I don't know," she bites out. But another tear slides down her cheek. "Fucking hormones," she says as she swipes it away.

All this because she has her period? I know better than to say that out loud. "Oh," I say instead.

She turns to face me, hitching her hip against the sink. She crosses her arms beneath her breasts, which pushes them up and makes little pillows over the top of that low-cut dress she's wearing. My God. I look up at her face. She smirks at me. I like a smirking Friday a lot better than one who's crying because I don't know what do with tears. Not from her.

"I didn't mean to hurt your feelings," I blurt out when she just glares at me.

"Yes, you did."

"No, I didn't."

"Yes, you did."

"Fuck me, Friday," I breathe. I swipe a hand down my face again and growl to myself.

She faces the mirror and starts to put on her lipstick. "I tried to do that and you didn't want to," she says. She purses her lips and kisses toward the mirror. The move shoots straight to my dick. "So, you, Mister I Am Jealous, don't get to tell me who I can and can't sleep with." She looks directly into my eyes in the mirror. "So, I can sleep with Garrett. I can sleep with Cody." She throws up her hands. "Hell, I can sleep with both of them at the same time, if I want." She glares at me. "And you don't get to have any say-so about it." She walks toward me. "You can't say a word because you didn't want it." She gestures toward the front of her body. "You said no to all this, so you don't get to have an opinion."

"I didn't say no," I mumble.

"You kissed me and then you tried to take it back!" she yells.

Okay, I like Friday yelling. I like it so much more than Friday crying. "I didn't try to take it back!" I slap my palm against the wall, but she just looks at my hand, smirks, and rolls her eyes. "I just... Never mind."

"Just what?" she asks.

"It doesn't matter. It's over and done with."

"Yep," she says, letting her lips pop on the *P*. "Over. Done." She dusts her hands together. "So you don't get to go all Neanderthal when someone else kisses me."

"I just..." I shake my head. "I had something I needed to take care of."

"Don't you mean somebody?" She smirks and shakes her head. "Was it Kelly you had to take care of? Heaven knows Kelly needs to come more than I do."

Did she just say *come*? I shake the thoughts away. They're not going to get me anywhere.

Friday tolerates my daughter's mother, but I don't think she's ever really liked her. "It actually was Kelly I needed to take care of," I say. I may as well lay all my shit bare. Friday cried, for God's sake.

She lets out a heavy breath. "You kissed me, and then you went and got some from Kelly?"

Her voice is soft. She's… What is she? Is she hurt?

"No, I didn't *go and get some* from Kelly. I went and broke things off with Kelly." I take a step forward until I'm towering over her and she has to tip her head back to look at my face. "I had to go and tell her that I kissed you and that you rocked my fucking world."

She freezes, so I take a chance and put my arm around her, pulling her against me.

"What?" she breathes. She turns her face up to mine.

"I haven't slept with Kelly since before I kissed you. I don't want to sleep with Kelly. I have you on my fucking mind, and I can't get you out. So, I went and broke things off with Kelly. Completely."

She blinks her brown eyes at me. Blink. Blink.

"Then I came back to see you, but you were pissed. You wouldn't let me in. You said 'no fucking way, you stupid son of a bitch.' And you told me to go home. So, I went. Alone."

Blink. Blink.

"Kelly and I weren't dating. We were just friends with benefits. Or parents with benefits. Whatever. Now we're just Hayley's parents."

Blink. Blink.

"I went and told her that we couldn't do that anymore, and she understood."

"You told her?" she whispers. "That you…what? What did you tell her?"

"I told her that I can't stop thinking about you." I brush her hair back from her forehead. I kissed Friday that one time when I walked her home and she invited me inside, and we both knew what she was offering, but I don't think I've ever just held her in my arms. I like it. She lays her palms flat on my chest, like she needs to steady herself.

"I have a thing for you," I admit. I wince inwardly because it sounds so lame.

"A thing?"

"A big thing."

Her gaze drops.

"Not that thing." Although now that she's looking down at it, it's ready to rise to attention. Fucking attention whore. I tip her chin up. "But," I say.

"But what?"

"Then you showed up with that first douche. And then that second douche. And I had just changed my whole life for the possibility of you. But you had moved on. Quickly." I drag my fingertips up and down her bare arms, and chill bumps rise. She shivers. "So, yeah, I'm mad. Sorry."

"You don't sound sorry."

"I'm not."

She laughs, and the sound of it shoots straight to my heart.

"Am I too late?" I ask. I wait, with my heart in my throat.

She steps back from me. "Paul," she says. Her voice cracks. "I'm so sorry."

I don't need to hear any more. I go out and start my machine up and get back to work. I hear her move around in the shop, and I glance up at her every once in a while, but she gets busy with clients, drawing tattoos, and she ignores me. She doesn't look in my direction. Not even once. Not for the whole rest of the night. And when it's closing time, Logan volunteers to walk her home. I let him.

# Friday

I didn't even sleep last night. I just tossed and turned and thought about what Paul said to me yesterday. He basically asked me if I have feelings for him. I have lots of feelings for him. Some are easier to define than others.

Sometimes he drives me up the wall, particularly when he sulks. Other times, he makes me laugh until my stomach hurts. And the way that he loves his family... That makes me ache inside. All those Reed boys together—they embody everything that I would want if I had been lucky enough to have a family. I watch Paul with his daughter and I almost melt into a puddle on the floor, because I know there's nothing that Hayley could ever do to make him not love her. She could dance naked in the street. She could fall in with the wrong crowd. She could discover drugs and alcohol. Okay, so he would wring her neck for that, but he would still love her. She could even get pregnant at fifteen, and he would still love her. He would stand by her no matter what. That's something I never had.

I walk into the shop and wince when the bell over the door chimes. Paul comes out from the back of the shop wiping his hands on a towel and stops short. He looks everywhere but at me. "Morning," he murmurs.

"Good morning," I say back. I drop my bag behind the counter and smooth my skirt with my hands. Paul's gaze drops to my legs, and then he looks away. I'm glad he's the only one here, because we really need to talk.

He turns to go back to the rear of the shop, and I call his name. "Paul." He stops, and I see his shoulders tense.

He answers without looking back at me. "What?" He heaves a sigh.

I walk toward him and lay my hand on his back. He tenses more, his muscles bunching up beneath my fingertips. "I'm sorry," I say. "Please don't be angry at me."

"I'm not angry," he bites out.

I force out a laugh, but there's no merriment in the sound. "You are so angry."

He turns around and looks down at me. "I'm jealous," he says. "And, yeah, that makes me angry."

"You don't have anything to be jealous about," I tell him.

"Keep your boyfriends out of here and I won't be."

"They're not my boyfriends."

He growls. "I don't even want to know what they are." He holds up a hand to stop me when I open my mouth. "Shut it," he says. "Don't even bring them up. I don't want to discuss it."

I bite my lip to keep from talking and play with my lip piercing with my tongue. His gaze drops to it and stays there. I force my tongue back in my mouth.

I toy with the hem of my dress. "Did you really break things off with Kelly?" I ask quietly. My voice is little more than a whisper, but I know he hears me because he swears under his breath.

"Yes," he grits out. "I did."

"So, are you going to go back now?" My cheeks are so hot I probably look like a clown.

"Go back where?"

"To Kelly."

"No, that's over. It should have been over a long time ago. It was just easy to let it keep going."

"Oh. Was she okay with that?"

I follow him into the back room and he makes himself busy putting ink supplies away in the cabinet. "She's getting married, so yeah, she was fine with it."

"She's engaged?" What the fuck?

"Yes."

"Did you know?"

"Yes."

"Are you heartbroken?"

"No."

"Are you going to answer with more than one word?"

"When you ask me something that's even remotely your business, I might." He glares at me over his shoulder.

"How much longer are you going to be a dickwad?"

"For as long as it takes for you to leave me alone about Kelly." He smiles at me. "Quit being so nosy." His fake smile falls away, and he glowers some more. "You don't even like Kelly."

"I like Kelly," I protest.

"No, you don't."

"Yes, I do."

"I'm not stupid, Friday. You clam up every time she comes in here."

I sit down across from him in a rolling chair. My skirt slides up my thighs and his eyes land there, but I don't care. I'm wearing fishnet stockings. He runs a hand through his blond hair and jerks on it when he gets to the tips. Then he closes his eyes and takes a breath.

"I don't *dislike* her," I say.

"Mmm hmm," he hums.

"Did you tell her about the kiss?"

"Yes."

"In detail?"

"No."

"Why not?"

"Because I don't know how to talk about that."

"What do you mean?" I am so confused.

"Do we really have to rehash this?"

"Yes."

"For how long?"

"Until we're done with it."

"I'm done with it now."

"Fuck you."

He chuckles. *Finally.* "Fuck you," he tosses back. "Look," he says, "I didn't mean to ruin everything. Let's just go back to how it was before."

"Before what?"

"Before I kissed you."

"If I remember correctly, I kissed you."

He grins. "Yeah, you're right."

"I thought I was wrong once, but it turned out I was mistaken." I shrug my shoulders.

"Friday," he growls, but at least he's laughing now.

"What?"

"You're not going to make this easy, are you?"

"Probably not."

He goes back to unloading the box and putting the ink away.

"So, what did you tell Kelly?" I ask quietly.

"I told her that I couldn't fuck her anymore."

"That's all it was? Fucking."

He looks up at my mouth and stares at it until I start to squirm in my seat.

"What?" I ask.

"It tears me up inside when you use dirty words. You should do it more often." He grins at me.

"Like you could stop me." I snort. Everyone knows I have a colorful vocabulary. My mother called it a potty mouth. When I'm around Paul's daughter or Matt's kids, I have to work really hard not to use bad language.

He rolls his eyes.

"So…" I say really slowly, rolling out the O.

He quirks an eyebrow. "So?"

"So, about fucking Kelly."

He tosses a bottle of ink a little too hard. "I don't want to talk about fucking Kelly."

"Was it fucking Kelly or was it making love to Kelly?" I wince because I know that sounds stupid. "That's a dumb question," I murmur.

"No." He shakes his head. "That's actually a good question. It was scratching an itch. It was easy. You get used to one person because you know what she likes and how to get there. And she knows what you like and how to get you there." He shrugs. "It was easy."

"Do you still love her?"

"Nope."

"How do you know?"

Suddenly, he grabs the edge of my chair, falls to his knees, and rolls me into him. With one gentle hand on each of my knees, he parts my thighs and wiggles until we're chest to chest. My breath stalls. He's an inch from my face when he speaks, and his breath becomes mine. "Because you're all I can think about. I wake up with you on my mind and go to sleep with you in my dreams. I wouldn't be having these intense thoughts about you if I were in love with anybody else. I'm not that kind of guy." He kisses the end of my nose. "I know you already know this about me. I'm a stand-up man, Friday, and I'm loyal."

"I want to tell you I feel the same," I say. I close my eyes, and he startles me when he places a kiss on each of my eyelids in turn.

"What's stopping you?"

"That guy I was with yesterday," I say. I put a hand on his chest to push him back, but I don't want him to go anywhere.

He leans back on his heels, but he leaves his hands on my knees. I close my legs, because without him there, I just feel...empty.

"Is he your boyfriend?"

"No."

"Then why was he kissing you?"

"So, I could make you jealous," I blurt out. I cover my face with my hand because I'm mortified to admit that.

"Well, fuck. It worked."

Why doesn't that make me feel good? "I thought you kissed me and then crawled back into bed with Kelly," I admit.

"I can see how you'd think that."

"But that's done?"

"Done." He dusts his hands together. "You want to have dinner with me tonight?" he asks. He brings my fingertips to his lips and regards me over the top of my hand. He lingers there long enough for his warm breath to tickle up my arm and shoot desire straight to my girlie parts.

"Um, well," I say.

"What now?" he asks.

"Cody and Garrett," I start. I don't even know how to tell him this part.

"The guy from yesterday and the guy from last week?"

"Yeah."

"Who are they to you?"

"Well," I say. I close my eyes and steel my heart for the next part. "One of them might have gotten me pregnant." I open my mouth to tell him about the surrogacy. But he interrupts before a sound can move past my lips.

"Fuck!" he swears as he gently shoves me back from him. My chair rolls backward until it softly bumps the wall. He jumps to his feet.

"I didn't know you had feelings for me at the time!" I yell.

The bell over the door to the shop tinkles, and Paul yells, "Out!" at the top of his lungs. I see Sam back out the door, with Logan behind him. Sam is explaining to Logan why they're leaving when they just got here. At least as well as he can. He probably has no idea.

"I won't even know if it's positive for nine more days!" I yell.

"You let me pour my fucking heart out when you were fucking those two guys?"

My gut twists. "You think that highly of me, huh?" I ask.

"What else am I supposed to think?" he yells. Paul never yells. He has this quiet way of leading.

"Nothing!" I yell back. "You're supposed to think nothing!"

I get up and smooth my dress. Paul just glares at me. Then he looks at my stomach. I lay a protective hand over it.

"I didn't know you had those kinds of feelings for me," I say.

"I liked it better when I thought you were a lesbian," he says.

"Yeah," I toss back. "Me too." I jerk a thumb toward the door. "You had better go let your brothers in." All of them are pressed against the front window with their hands wrapped around their eyes so they can see in, even Matt, who must've showed up while we were yelling.

"You go let them in," he says. And he stomps toward the back of the shop.

# Paul

It was so much easier lusting after Friday when I thought she liked to eat pussy as much as I do. I could put my arm around her and pretend like the scent of her didn't shoot straight to my dick, since I couldn't do anything about the attraction anyway. But now all I can think about is putting my arm around her and having her perfume shoot straight to my dick. Then I think about kissing her again. Then pulling her on top of me and letting her ride me until we're both sweaty and satisfied.

Fuck, fuck, fuck, fuck.

I have rotten luck. And even worse timing, apparently.

Friday could be pregnant. That means she's been getting it on with one or the other, or both, of those bozos. She's been having a great time while I've been wearing my hand out to thoughts of her.

I get a bottle of water from the fridge and tip it up, closing my eyes as I drink it gulp after gulp.

The privacy curtain I pulled shut makes a clinking sound, and I keep drinking with my eyes closed. I know it's not her because my skin doesn't start to sizzle. When I open my eyes, I find Matt leaning against the counter with his arms crossed. He has a smirk on his face that annoys the hell out of me.

"What the fuck are you doing?" he asks.

I hold up my water bottle. "Drinking water, numbnuts. Why?"

"You know that's not what I mean." His foot starts to tap.

"None of your business," I murmur. I hate it when Matt does this. He's so gentle and quiet. He's pretty much the opposite of me in every way, except for our looks. And even in that, he's thin and wiry, but strong. And I'm…not thin or wiry.

He points toward the front of the store. "Friday is all of our business," he hisses quietly. "She's family, Paul."

"I know," I breathe. "Another reason why it's best to keep things the way they are." I throw my bottle into the recycling from across the room.

"Well, you've already fucked up the atmosphere," he says. "What are you going to do about it?"

"Nothing," I say. "I'm going to do nothing."

Friday has been a part of our circle for four years. But almost all of that time, I thought she was a lesbian. The five minutes when I didn't is when the trouble started.

"It didn't look like nothing when we got here. You were kissing her eyelids and she didn't seem too put out by it."

"She's not in the right position for what I want," I say. I can't tell him about her being pregnant. It's not my story to tell.

He grins. "Well, what position did you want her in?"

"Shut up," I grouse.

"If she's in the wrong position, flip her the fuck over." He throws up his hands. "Hell, turn her upside down if you have to."

"It's not that easy."

His gaze softens. "Nothing worth having is easy to get."

If anyone would know, it's Matt. He battled cancer and thought he would never get married or have a kid, and now he has three with twins on the way. He fought, and he won.

"Is she worth having?" Matt asks.

"I don't know." I shake my head.

"Do you want to find out?"

"I don't know." I drag a hand down my face.

"I never took you for being a quitter."

I heave in a breath. "I've never quit anything on purpose. But this fight might be more than I want to take on."

"Hell, you knew she had baggage. Layers. You told me you wanted to find out everything about her. Find out why she doesn't have a family. Find out why she's all alone in New York. Find out why she's living in Pete's spare room until tomorrow."

I spin to face him. "She's living with Pete and Reagan?" I didn't know about that. "Why?"

He shrugs. "She had to move out of the dorm after graduation. They had an empty room. But Reagan's parents are coming to stay for two weeks, so she's going somewhere else."

"Where?" I ask quickly.

He shrugs. "Does it matter?" But he's grinning.

Fuck yeah, it matters. "Is she going to stay with one of the douchebags?"

"What douchebags?" Matt scratches his head.

"Never mind," I say. Hope swells within me. I shouldn't let it, but it does. I get out a piece of paper and write on it in magic marker:

ROOM FOR RENT
PRICE NEGOTIABLE
ONLY BEAUTIFUL LITTLE
BOMBSHELLS NEED APPLY
PREFERABLY ONES NAMED FRIDAY

I walk out of the back room and go to the bulletin board. I stick a thumbtack in the "advertisement" and walk away.

I hear a snicker from behind me and turn to grin at Logan.

*You're a d-o-o-f-u-s*, he signs, fingerspelling the last word because there's no sign for something so stupid.

*I know*, I sign back.

He looks a little worried for me, but I don't care. I can't get where I want to go if I don't take a first step. Regardless of whether or not she's pregnant, she needs a place to stay and I have two empty rooms. And she's family, for Christ's sake.

I've never wanted to eat out a member of my family, though. I scratch my head. I should probably stop thinking like that.

I whistle to myself as I walk to my office. I have some paperwork to do before my first appointment arrives. And I need to give Friday time to find my ad.

# Friday

I've been working on a particularly tricky tat for a client, and I can't quite get it right. I motion Logan over to take a look.

"What do you think?" I glance up at him. He pinches his lips together and shakes his head. "What?" I ask, throwing up my hands. "Use your words."

Instead, he takes my pencil and spins the paper toward him. He draws on it for a second and then shoves it toward me. He hands my pencil back and grins.

"I hate you," I say, when I see that he just added two lines and made my drawing perfect.

"I love you, too," he says. He leans over quickly and kisses my forehead. I squeeze my eyes closed and let him.

He makes a noise and goes over to the bulletin board. He starts to draw little hearts around the edges of a posting. I tap his shoulder so he'll look up. "What are you doing?"

"Adding hearts," he says, like I should have guessed.

I tap him again so he'll look at me. "Why are you doing that?"

He shrugs. "It needed hearts."

"What needed hearts?" I ask. I lean closer so I can read the paper.

My own heart thuds. "It doesn't need hearts," I say. It needs condoms. Well, that is, if I'm not already pregnant. I look up at Logan. "He doesn't know what he's doing, does he?" I ask.

He squeezes my shoulder. "Go easy on him, will you?"

"Why?"

"He quit Kelly for you, Friday." He glares at me. "Like, cold turkey. He quit her. He's been fucking Kelly for years. And he broke things off with her."

"How do you know all this?" I ask.

"We talk." He gestures toward his brothers, who are all draped around the room like furniture. Really big, good-looking furniture.

"Of course, you do," I say. I pull the thumbtack from the ad and take a deep breath.

"Go easy on him," he says again.

"Fuck that," I reply.

He grins and shrugs. "I can't say I didn't try." He takes my shoulders and turns me toward Paul's office. "Go Friday on his ass." He slaps me on the butt while Pete and Sam snicker and high-five one another.

I walk to the back of the shop and knock on Paul's office door since it's closed. That usually means he wants to be left alone. "What?" he calls.

I open the door and stick my head in. "Do you always answer the door like that?" I ask.

"Yes," he says. He has the phone balanced between his shoulder and his ear. "What do you want?"

"Are you on the phone?"

"On hold, Friday. What do you want?"

I slap the paper down on his desk and hold my flat palm over it. "What the fuck is this?"

He looks down at it. "That was a perfectly good invitation, until somebody fucked it up with hearts," he growls.

I look down at it. "I kind of like the hearts," I admit.

"Next time, I'll use hearts," he says. He smiles.

"You're looking for a roommate?" I ask. I toy with my lip piercing until his gaze lands there, and then I force myself to stop. "Since when?"

"Since I found out you're homeless," he says.

"I'm not homeless," I protest.

"Where are you living after today?" he asks.

I'm not at all sure about that, but he doesn't need to know it. "Shut up," I say instead.

He pushes the paper toward me. "I have an extra room. You need a place to stay. Let's not make it more than it is, okay?"

"That's all you'd expect?" I ask, hating how quiet my voice suddenly gets.

"You could be pregnant, Friday," he says. "What else would I want from you?"

My breath catches. He is so right. I have been looking at this like it's all about us, but it's not. It's all about this baby I have to protect for nine months, a baby he's now fully aware of, even if he's not aware of the details.

"How much?" I ask.

"How much can you afford?" he asks.

He knows full well how much money I make; he pays me. But he isn't aware of the money I make doing commissioned portraits and other artwork.

He waves a hand in the air. "Don't worry about what it costs," he says. "Pay me whatever you can. The room is just sitting there empty. And if you live with me, I won't have to worry about you being homeless."

I snort. "Like you'd worry anyway."

His brow rises. "I worry. I worry about you all the fucking time. But if you live with me, I won't have to. So take pity on me and just take the fucking room, dammit."

"Okay."

He looks surprised. "Okay?"

"Yes."

He grins. "Okay."

"Can I come over tonight?" I ask.

He nods and brings the phone back to his mouth and starts to speak. I close his door.

Reagan's parents are coming tonight. I was going to go to Logan and Emily's, but I'd rather not have to hear their bed thumping against the wall all night. Emily is almost nine months pregnant and those two still go at it like rabbits.

Wait. Will I have to hear Paul's bed thumping against the wall? Shit. I didn't even think about that.

# Paul

I try to clean up a little bit since I know Friday is coming over. I toss out all the pizza boxes and put clean sheets on Matt's old bed. His bedroom is right next to mine, and I can already imagine what it's going to be like lying in my bed fantasizing about her naked in hers.

"You're a little bit whipped," Sam says from behind me.

I turn around and scowl at him. "I am not."

"Yes, you are. I think it's cute." He grins at me as he balances himself in the doorway, dangling from the overhang like a monkey. "You have a crush."

"I do not have a crush," I say.

"Oh, you totally have a crush," he sings out.

I can't let him tease me like that, so I chase him out of Matt's old room and down the hallway into the living room. He jumps over the back of the couch, and I go over it after him. I catch him around the waist and knock him to the floor. He's wiry and quick, and I don't remember him being quite as strong as he is now, but I pin him to the floor anyway.

I must be getting old because it's harder to hold him down than it used to be. A lot harder. Sam's a collegiate athlete, and he's even being scouted by a couple of pro teams, so he's in peak physical shape all the time. Unlike me. Thankfully, I have size on my side.

A knock sounds at the door. I yell, "Come in!" without letting Sam up. He grunts and shoves at me, but I sit on him. The door opens and a man walks in carrying a box. I freeze, because he looks familiar.

"Get off me, you big fucker," Sam says. The man raises his brow at us and looks back at Friday, who is dragging a suitcase.

I let Sam up, and he swipes the hair back from his brow. He's sweating. I'm not. But I also wasn't the one trying to scramble up from the floor.

"Looks like my kind of party," the guy says. He grins at Friday, and I hate him immediately.

Friday rolls her eyes at us and walks inside. "Are we too early?" she asks.

"Too early for what?" I reply. I don't like it at all that she brought this fucker to my house. Not one bit.

"Too early to move in."

I look from her to him and back. "Beg your pardon?" I say.

She points to the dickwad and then to me. "Garrett, you remember Paul. Paul, Garrett. The one who got pinned is Sam. Sam's a pussy, but he can't help it because he's never been loved enough." She laughs, and the tinkle of it hits me in the gut.

Garrett sticks out his hand to shake. I take it and squeeze it hard enough that he winces. I can't believe he came to my house. "Good to see you again," I say.

"You, too." He twists his hand out of my grip.

"How long are you staying?" I blurt out. I can't help it. I'm a guy.

He grins and looks down at Friday. "We're having dinner, right?" he asks.

She nods. "Come and help me put my stuff away," she says.

I get the feeling she's talking to him since he follows her into her new room and they close the door. Then she sticks her head back out and asks, "Will you call us when the pizzas get here?"

I nod because I can't get any words past the fist she just shoved into my gut.

"That's fucked up," Sam grunts.

Yeah, I know.

I flop into my lazy chair and flip through the channels until another knock sounds at the door.

# Friday

"Damn, he's smoking hot," Garrett whispers vehemently. "Just wait till Cody meets him. I'll get laid because he'll be fantasizing about your man."

I snort. "He is so not my man."

I motion for him to lug my suitcase onto the bed, and I unzip it, then start hanging up my clothes. I really don't have much, because I don't need much. But one thing I do have is clothes. With my love for all things vintage, I buy stuff at secondhand shops most of the time. It's pretty much all I wear.

"Oh, honey," Garrett says as he flops back onto my bed and fans his face. "He so has the hots for you."

I keep hanging up clothes. Garrett snags a thong from my suitcase and twirls it in the air on his index finger. "Someone has a kinky side."

"Thongs are not kinky," I scold.

"Mmm hmm," he hums. He laughs. "I bet Paul is one kinky motherfucker."

My face flushes.

He sits up suddenly. "When you finally find out, will you give me all the details?" He looks like a puppy that's sitting up begging for a treat. He even pants like one.

"Shut up," I say, but I laugh, too.

"So, how's this thing going down tonight?" he asks, sobering suddenly.

"When will Cody be here?" I ask.

"He's stopping to get the beer and pizza, and then he'll be here. Do you want me to lay one on him when he walks in the door or wait?"

I shrug. "Do what comes naturally." It's not like Paul's not going to know immediately when he sees Cody and Garrett together that they're a couple. A happy couple that has been together for a really long time.

Someone knocks on my door. "Come in," I call.

Garrett sits up on his elbow as the door opens. Sam sticks his head in. He scowls at Garrett. "Your pizza's here," he says.

"Showtime," Garrett says, and he rubs his hands together, excited. He gets to his feet and follows me into the kitchen.

Paul is watching TV, and he doesn't bother to get up. I go sit on the couch as Garrett lets Cody in. The two of them stand in the doorway and whisper to each other for a moment. Cody scowls at Garrett and shakes his head. Garrett reaches for him, but he dodges and walks toward us, lowering the pizzas to the end table.

Cody bends over and kisses me on the forehead.

Paul makes a noise that sounds a lot like a growl. He picks up the remote and flips the TV off. "I'm going to bed," he says. "Good night."

"Don't go," I say. I really, really need for him to meet Garrett and Cody so he'll understand.

"I'm tired," he says. He gets up and fakes a stretch, but a strip of his belly shows under his shirt. Garrett makes a noise, and Cody elbows him in the side.

"You didn't meet Cody," I say.

"I don't need to meet anyone else." He's kind of cute when he pouts. And kind of annoying.

Cody sticks out his hand, and Paul takes it reluctantly. Cody holds out a beer next. Paul shakes his head. "No, thanks. You guys have fun."

He goes to his room and shuts the door.

"Well, fuck," I say.

Garrett talks around a mouthful of pizza. "You should go get him." He waggles his brows at me. "Bring him back so he can play with us."

I walk down the hallway past Sam's room and stick my head in. "There's pizza," I say. He nods at me. He's on the phone.

I knock on Paul's door, and he calls out, "What?"

I open the door a crack. "What the fuck is it with you and that greeting?" I say.

"Did you want a soliloquy?" he asks. He's lying back on his bed tossing a ball toward the ceiling.

"I want you to come back out and hang with me and the guys."

"No."

That's all I get? "Why not?"

"Why should I?"

"Why shouldn't you?"

"I don't particularly care to watch you with your boyfriends." He keeps tossing the ball.

"They're not my boyfriends, dumbass," I say. I shove his legs over and sit down on the edge of his bed. "If you'd come out here and spend some time with them, you'd see that."

He sits up and moves to the other side of the bed. "I can't believe you brought them to my fucking house."

"Would you zip your fucking mouth before you dig yourself a bigger hole?"

"It's my house. I can dig around in it as much as I want."

He sounds like a two-year-old, and it makes me laugh. Then I snort.

"Which one is your baby's father?" he asks quietly. He stops tossing the ball.

I shrug. "It could be either one of them."

He tenses. I can see it in the lines of his body. He's solid as a rock, all of a sudden. "I don't like that. Not at all."

"You don't understand. If you'd come out there, you'd get it."

Suddenly, he hooks an arm around me and drags me to lie on top of him. I rest on my elbows on his chest. "I don't like the idea of you fucking them."

"I didn't fuck them," I say. I move like I'm going to get up.

"I'm jealous as hell, Friday, and I don't like it. I don't like it one bit. So, go and play house with them. Leave me out of it."

"They're gay," I blurt out. I really wanted him to come to the knowledge by himself so he would understand.

"What?"

"They're a couple. I'm their surrogate." I lift my fist and knock playfully on his forehead. "Earth to Paul," I say. "Are you still in there?"

"They're a couple?" he asks quietly.

"Yes."

His arms tighten around me, and then he flips us over until he's hovering over me. He brushes my hair back from my face. Then he does something I never would have expected. He chuckles. It's a deep belly laugh, and he buries his face in my neck, his body rocking, he's laughing so hard.

"They're married," I say. "And they wanted a baby." I point down toward my belly. "I wasn't using my uterus for anything, so I told them they could borrow it." I lay my palm on the side of his face and bring his blue eyes to meet mine. "Now can you stop being so jealous and come and have dinner with us?"

"You never slept with them?" he asks. His eyes search my face, like he's looking for the meaning of life.

I shake my head. "I don't think they're into vaginas," I say. "And I kind of have a vagina."

He grows hard against my belly, his breath blowing hot across my lips. "I kind of like that you have a vagina," he says. He laughs again, and his nose sweeps back and forth against mine.

"Well, it's been so long since it's seen any action that it might be broken."

"I'll fix it," he says quietly. He's so fucking intense that I can barely think.

"And there might be a baby in there."

"When will you know?"

"Nine more days."

"And if you are?"

"They're going to be the happiest men on the face of the planet."

"How do you feel about it?" He's so quiet and direct that it's almost unsettling.

"It's like having an empty apartment in the city. Someone should get some use out of it." I try to laugh, but he's not laughing with me.

"Do you want kids?" he asks. "Your own some day?"

"No." I don't need to think about it; I already know the answer. I do not and will never, ever want kids.

"So, I suppose I should let you up to go meet the men who got you pregnant." He laughs. "That sounds so wrong." He kisses my cheek. "All I want to do is kiss you, though," he says quietly.

"What's stopping you?"

"There's beer and pizza," he says as he lifts himself off me and holds out a hand. I let him pull me up, and I adjust my dress where he messed it up. He motions for me to precede him out the door, but at the last minute, he tugs my elbow and draws me back. "Friday," he says.

"What?" I ask, breathless with how close he is to me.

"I…ah…I don't know what to do with all these brand-new feelings for you," he says quietly.

"Okay," I breathe in response.

"They scare the shit out of me, but they make me feel hopeful, too."

"Why me?" I ask.

"Because you're you," he says, looking at me like I've lost my mind.

And therein lies the problem, Paul. I'm me. And that's all I'll ever be. The real me—the one he hasn't met. He'll probably never see her because it has been a really long time since I've seen her myself.

# Paul

I can't fucking believe that I ever thought she screwed either of these guys. I reach out my hand to take Cody's, and he grips mine tightly and looks into my eyes. "If you hurt her, I'll have to take you out," he says quietly so that only I can hear him.

It startles me for a second. I'm not sure how to respond. He's not nearly as big as I am, but he's serious and I have to respect that he's trying to take care of her. "I'll keep that in mind," I murmur, looking for Friday to come save me from his gaze, but she's sitting on the couch beside Garrett, her head on his shoulder.

I twist my hand to pull it from his grasp, but he holds tightly. "I might not be able to kick your ass," he says, and he jerks my arm, pulling me forward until we're chest to chest. "But I *know* people," he goes on to say.

Okay, now I'm annoyed. "If you find someone big enough and there's just cause, you should go for it," I tell him. I squeeze his hand tightly until he winces, and I let him go. He steps back.

"Now that we have that ugly discussion out of the way," he says, "it's really nice to meet you." He grins.

"You, too," I grunt out. I still can't fucking believe he just tried to manhandle me in my own living room. I brush a hand through my hair, casting furtive glances in his direction.

Garrett smirks. "I thought you were going to teach him the two-step there for a minute," he says, talking around a mouth full of pizza.

Cody's eyes rake up and down my body. "He looks more like a swing dance kind of guy."

Friday snorts.

"Shut it," I murmur at her, but I can't keep from grinning as I take the beer that Garrett offers me.

The room goes quiet for a second, until I can't stand the silence anymore. "So, you knocked her up, huh?" I suddenly blurt out.

Friday's face colors, and she looks everywhere but at me. "Paul," she whines, closing her eyes tightly as she winces.

"Well, we hope so," Cody says as he goes to sit down on the other side of Garrett. He takes Garrett's hand and pulls it onto his knee. They're so damn cute together they make my back teeth ache. "We've been trying to adopt for a long time, but it hasn't worked out."

"What are the chances this won't work?" I ask. I might as well know what I'm up against, right?

Cody holds up his hands like he's weighing something. "We have no way of knowing. Not until next week."

"Chances are good, though?" I ask.

They nod.

"I hope it works out for you."

They cast questioning glances toward Friday, and I can't help but wonder what they're thinking. I'll ask her later, after they've left, I guess.

Sam comes out of the bedroom and stops, looking from Cody and Garrett to Friday and back. "Hell yeah," he finally says. He lifts his hands like he's praying to God and says, "Thank you for small miracles. And for putting Paul out of his misery." He shoves my shoulder. "Glad they finally told you."

I choke on my beer. "You knew?" I croak out.

"Well, yeah," he says. "If you weren't looking at them through that red haze of jealousy you got going on, you'd have seen it, too."

I throw a wadded napkin at his head, but he just laughs.

The door opens, and Emily waddles into the room. Emily is married to my brother Logan, and she's almost nine months pregnant. She's so damn adorable with that pregnancy waddle that I can't help but grin. Sam isn't quite as smart as me. He laughs out loud.

Emily walks up behind him and threads her hand into his hair. She gently yanks, tilting his head back and looking into his eyes. "Are you seriously laughing at the pregnant chick?" she asks.

He holds up his hands as though he's surrendering to the cops. "Not me," he says.

She kisses him quickly on the forehead and shoves his cheek gently, and he makes room for her on the couch. She drops down beside him and sits back, blowing out a heavy breath. Sam lays a hand on her belly. "How's my niece doing in there?" he asks. He leans down and talks to her belly, and she giggles, shoving him away with a hand to the side of his face.

"She's fine. Still cooking." She lays a hand on her basketball-sized belly and smiles.

Friday introduces Cody and Garrett, and Emily helps herself to some pizza.

"You want some water?" Sam asks.

"Yes, but I don't want to get up," she says. She bats her lashes at him.

He groans, but he gets to his feet and goes to get her a drink.

"Can you turn the TV on?" Emily asks. "They're doing a news report on that band I played with last week."

I flip the TV on and go to the channel she tells me to. She leans forward as she sees the lead singer of the band being asked questions.

"Turn it up," she cries.

She listens intently while they talk with the lead singer. She's pretty in a dead-of-the-night sort of way. It makes me want to wash all that dark makeup off her face to see what's underneath. Kind of like I want to do with Friday. I'd love to see what Friday looks like without the red lipstick and the heavy lashes. I'd kind of like to see what she looks like without her clothes, too. Heat creeps up my cheeks when I catch Cody smirking at me. Apparently, I looked at Friday's legs a little too long.

A grin tugs at my lips, and I shake my head.

"Busted," he sings out.

Friday looks from him to me and back. "Who's busted?" she asks.

Cody opens his mouth to answer her, but Emily saves me by butting in. "They asked me to record with them," she says as she takes the remote and turns the volume back down.

That takes my attention off Friday. "Seriously?" I ask.

She nods. "I'm still thinking about it. They want me to tour with them, too, but I told them no."

Sam shoves her shoulder, and she grunts and points to her belly. "Um, helloooo?" Emily sings. But she's grinning, too.

The door opens, and Pete walks in. Damn, it's like a revolving door tonight.

"I can't believe you turned them down," Sam says.

"Who turned what down?" Pete asks. Sam and Pete are identical twins, but anyone who knows them can tell them apart.

Sam points to the TV. "Em got an offer to tour with the girl band, Fallen from Zero."

"Shut the fuck up!" Pete cries. He throws himself over the back of the couch so that he lands with his legs across Sam's lap.

"Watch the belly!" Emily yells as she covers it with her palm. He's far from hitting her, though.

"That drummer is hot," Sam says. He's still watching the footage with no sound, since we play the TV with subtitles for Logan all the time.

"I would have thought you'd like the lead singer best," Emily says, watching his face.

He shakes his head. "Not my type."

"Not enough ass," Pete tosses out. "He's not into skinny chicks." Pete looks over at Emily. "No offense, Em."

Emily rolls her eyes and points to her very pregnant belly.

Sam shoots Pete a look and shoves Pete's legs out of his lap.

Pete makes a move like he's grabbing and squeezing. "Sam likes a girl he can hold on to."

Sam's face goes pink as he shrugs. "I like curves," he says. "I can't help it."

Pete shoves him again. "He wants tits *and* ass," he says, making that squeezing motion again.

"And a brain," Sam says, holding up his finger.

"And an appetite," I add.

Sam raises his brow. "I like to cook. So I like a girl who likes to eat. Go figure."

Emily laughs.

Sam must feel the need to explain himself because he goes on. "I hate taking a girl to dinner and having her order a salad. Or having her tell me she can't eat one of my famous cupcakes because she's on a diet." He shivers like he's repulsed by the very idea of it. He draws an hourglass figure in the air with his hands. "I'll take tits, ass, and thighs, please," he says, as though he's ordering dinner. "And, dammit, if there's icing that can be licked off places, I want her to be able to partake without thinking about calories."

"TMI, Sam!" Emily cries, covering her ears.

Sam laughs, so I throw a remote at his head. "Act like a gentleman," I warn, because I feel like I should. But that shit's funny as hell.

"I could introduce you to that drummer," Emily suggests.

He pulls his lip piercing into his mouth and toys with it. "Let me think about it."

The door opens again, and Matt and Skylar walk in, along with Logan. Matt is the next oldest brother, after me, and Skylar is his wife. She's pregnant and almost as big as Emily since she's carrying twins, even though she's only seven months along. Their three kids walk in behind them. The little girls run to Hayley's room to play, and Seth, their sixteen-year-old, pulls a chair from the table and turns it around backward, straddles it, and folds his arms over the back so he's facing us.

I glance down at my watch. Hayley has been with her mom this week, but Kelly should be dropping her off soon.

I get up, and Sky sits down in my chair. Matt sits at her feet and takes the beer that Garrett passes to him. I sit down at the end of the couch by Friday and press my shoulder against her leg. I look up at her, and she looks down, appearing somewhat startled.

"You okay?" I ask quietly.

She nods. As long as she's all right, I'm all right.

She's kicked off those four-inch heels she wears, but she's still wearing the fishnet stockings. I slide my hand around the back of her ankle and tickle the inside of it with the tips of my fingers. Her toes jerk, but she doesn't move her foot away. She spreads her thighs about an inch and presses more tightly against my shoulder, and I can feel the air around her move as she takes in a deep breath.

So that's what it's like… Now I get how Logan, Pete, and Matt felt when they met the women they'd spend the rest of their lives with. Because I'd rather sit here and touch her ankle than I would fuck any other woman in the world.

We listen to Pete tell a story about a boy he met at work and how he's helping him through the system. Pete started a local buddy program, hooking ex-cons up with juvenile offenders. It gives the ex-con something to look forward to and someone to be better for. Many of them never had families, or they lost what family they had, so it builds a support network. Plus, it helps the kids hopefully stay out of future trouble. I am so proud of Pete that I could bust sometimes. But I know I can't take any credit for him being the awesome man he's become.

Suddenly, Emily shoves Sam's shoulder. "Seriously?" she squeals. "Did you seriously just do that?" She covers her nose and holds her breath. "That is just foul."

Sam grins. "I don't know what you're talking about."

"Sam," I warn, trying to keep my voice firm. But it's hard. "There are women here."

He looks around like he's looking for them. "Where? All I see are Emily, Friday, and Sky, and they don't count as girls." Sam gets up and goes to put his hands on Sky's belly. She smiles and lets him. He glances up. "Did you feel that?" he asks, and he grins.

"Oh, I feel all of them," Sky says with a sigh. "Four feet and four hands. And two rear ends sitting on my bladder." She motions to Sam so he'll move back, and she holds out her hand. "Pull me up so I can go pee."

He laughs and helps her lumber to her feet, her belly coming up out of the chair before the rest of her.

Matt gets up and takes Sam's seat on the couch, and Emily leans into him. "You doing okay?" I hear him ask her. He brushes her hair back behind her ear. Matt and Emily bonded when they first met, and he cares so much about her. And she feels the same way about him. I'm just glad Sky's not jealous of the amount of care he takes with Emily.

"I'll be better once she gets here," Emily says. She lifts her feet onto the coffee table. "Look at the size of my ankles." Matt turns her so that her feet are in his lap and starts to rub her instep. She smiles and closes her eyes. "I'll give you ten minutes to stop that," she warns playfully. Matt laughs.

Friday wiggles her toes, and I realize I've been sitting here rubbing the inside of her ankle for about ten minutes. I pull my hand back, kind of chagrined that I let it go on that long. Matt raises his brow when I catch his eye, and he grins at me. I flip him the bird.

Gentle fingers slip into the collar of my T-shirt and start to tickle the back of my neck. I lay my head on Friday's knee and close my eyes. It feels good having her touch me. It hits so much more than my dick, which is where girls usually strike me. This time, it reaches deep inside and wraps around my heart so tightly it steals my breath away. I hope she never stops.

But then the door opens again and Pete's girlfriend Reagan walks in, with my ex right behind her. Kelly freezes in the doorway when she sees Friday touching me, and I get up and go to her, although all I want to do is have my daughter launch herself into my arms while Friday stands beside me. I don't want the feeling of being near Friday to ever go away. But now Kelly's here, and it's over.

Kelly lays her hand on my arm and says, "Can we go somewhere and talk privately?" She looks at the full room, which has all my brothers and Friday's friends in it, and turns up her nose.

"About what?" I ask.

She purses her lips and nods toward my bedroom, so I heave a sigh, take her by the elbow, and lead her in that direction.

She closes the door behind us, and I flinch. I have an immediate need to open it back up, but I'm hoping she just wants to say something she doesn't want Hayley to hear.

But then she opens her mouth.

"I don't want my daughter to walk in and find you in bed with Friday," she says, blowing a lock of hair from her forehead with an upturned breath.

"What?" I ask. How dare she?

She crosses her arms in front of her chest. Once, that would have immediately drawn my gaze to her boobs but not anymore.

"I mean it, Paul. You can fuck her all you want, but don't involve my daughter in it because we both know she won't be around tomorrow. They never are."

I hitch my hip against the dresser and lean back, trying to look relaxed, but I'm anything but calm. My heart is beating as fast as my tattoo gun does, and I don't know where I might find my next breath. "You're getting married," I remind her. "Why do you care what I do?"

"I don't care who you do. I only care if you involve my daughter in it." She tosses her hair over her shoulder.

"What's this really about?" There's more to this than she's telling me.

She bites her lower lip, and for once, I don't want to pull it free and kiss her teeth marks away. She shakes her head. "It's nothing."

"Tell me, Kells," I say. "We've never had secrets from one another before." I motion from her to me and back. "That's why this thing between us works so well."

Suddenly, she buries her face in her hands and waits. When she lifts her head, her eyes are shiny. "I've never seen you with that look on your face, not when it's not for me."

"Oh," I say. I scratch my head. "What look?"

She jerks her thumb toward the living room. "When I walked in, you had your head on Friday's knee and you looked so peaceful."

Friday makes me feel anything but peaceful. "So you were jealous?"

She nods, nibbling on that lower lip again.

"You're getting married, Kells," I remind her again. I push off my dresser and walk toward her, then take her in my arms. I pull her gently against me and hold her. But this time, holding her isn't about heat or passion. It's about friendship. It has been weeks since we've slept together, and holding her this close to me doesn't even make my dick get hard.

Kelly wraps her arms around my waist and holds on tight for a minute. I stroke her back until she steps away from me.

"You okay?" I ask.

"I'm jealous," she says, and then she sniffles. "Sorry."

"Don't be. We're still us. We're still Hayley's parents. We always will be." I look her in the eye. "Don't mess up a good thing, okay?"

"You have a house full of people tonight," she says. She rocks back and forth on her heels like she's uncomfortable.

"I know." I smile. "Isn't it great?"

She shivers. "It's torture," she says. "Too noisy, too smelly, and too many Reeds all in one place."

That was the problem with me and Kelly. All the things I loved...she didn't love them back. She didn't like having my family around, and she didn't want to have much to do with them. "I love every minute of it."

"How does Friday feel about it?" she asks.

I shrug. "She seems like she's at home. She just got here today. She's renting a room."

Kelly nods. "I get it."

"What do you want from me, Kelly?" I ask on a heavy sigh.

"I guess I wanted everything to stay the same," she says. But then she grins. "I know it can't, though. I'm getting married."

"You want me to walk you down the aisle?" I ask. I'm only half joking.

"Maybe," she says. "That would be pretty fitting."

"I'm open to it."

She smiles at me. Finally. "We'll always be friends, right?" she asks.

"The best kind."

Suddenly, my door opens, and Hayley runs into the room. I reach down and scoop her up. She has icing all over her fingers and smears it across my shirt. I grab her hands and hold them out. "Has Sam been feeding you cupcakes?" I ask.

She shakes her head and grins. "He said to tell you no, it wasn't him."

Kelly snickers.

"Not funny," I say to her, but I'm grinning, too. I put Hayley down and pop her gently on the bottom. "Go wash your hands." She runs out of the room.

"I didn't love you enough," Kelly says. "I hated the noise and never getting to be alone."

"I know."

"I'm glad you didn't let me break you guys up," she says.

"I couldn't." They're all I had until her. And they'll be here long after she's gone. I knew it then, and I know it now. What we had couldn't last. But we got a wonderful daughter out of it. "I'm sorry," I say.

"Sorry I freaked out," she says quietly.

"It's okay," I say, even though it's not. "We'll find our way."

She points to my shirt. "Hayley got you dirty."

I pull a clean T-shirt from a rack in my closet, and Kelly walks out of my room. I lift my shirt over my head and put the new one on, still tugging it down as I walk out of my bedroom.

"You want to stay for some pizza?" I ask Kelly. I do like her. Just not the same way I used to.

She shakes her head. "Not tonight. Some other time?" she asks. She winks at me.

"Anytime," I say.

She kisses Hayley good-bye and waves to my brothers. They don't really like her so they barely give her the time of day. She doesn't care.

When she's gone, I look over and see Friday on the couch. I walk over to sit down at her feet, just like I was before, but she looks me in the eye and says, "Don't even think about it."

She looked so peaceful before Kelly got here. Now she's not. Now she's not peaceful at all. I'm afraid to push it because I get the feeling that if she got her fingertips near my neck now, she'd use those hands to choke me.

What the fuck did I do?

# Friday

I am not a fan of Kelly's. Never have been. Probably never will be. And I like her even less when I see her coming out of Paul's room while he's still pulling his clothes back on. Fuck her.

I look away from Paul with a huff in my breath. He leans down next to my head from behind the couch like he's going to whisper in my ear. But I put up my hand and push against his nose with the flat of my palm.

"Oh!" Pete cries. He jumps to his feet. "That counts! That so counts!" He points at me and then to Paul's nose. "She just hit you in the fucking nose, man," he shouts. He high-fives Sam, who's grinning like an idiot.

He rubs his nose. "She didn't hit me in the nose."

"Trust me," I say, "if I hit him, he would know it." He shoots me a glare.

Paul leans toward me again. "You could tell me what I did wrong," he says quietly, while his brothers are still placing bets and catcalling about my little shove to his nose.

I lean closer to him and sniff. I expect to smell sex on him, but I just smell fresh, clean male. Fresh, clean, hot-as-hell man. Hmm.

"What did I do?" he asks. He leans his elbows on the couch, hanging over my shoulder. I can feel his warm breath on the side of my neck, and a shiver runs up my spine.

"Nothing," I say.

"Nothing is always something in girl code," he says. He smells like Michelob Light and Paul.

"What girl code is this of which you speak?" I ask.

"The one where you're right and I'm wrong no matter how we look at it." He grins. "Talk to me, Friday." He leans closer, and his lips touch the shell of my ear. "What did I do wrong?"

I grunt and cross my arms.

"That's it, then," he says. "You forced me to do it."

He stands up, stretches, and cracks his knuckles.

"Forced you to do what?" I ask.

"To take matters into my own hands," he says. He reaches down and scoops me up in his arms.

"Paul!" I screech. "Put me down! Right now!" But all I can really do is grab his neck because he's moving faster than I thought possible.

"The drawer!" his brothers all cry at once. They're laughing like hell and high-fiving one another.

"Fuck the drawer," he says.

"What drawer?" I ask. I am so confused.

"The drawer!" they yell, all pointing toward it. He stops and looks back at them.

"We're just going to talk. Where the fuck do you think I'm going to put it?" he asks. "On my tongue?"

Pete looks at Sam and shrugs. "I've heard dumber ideas," he says.

"Seems like overkill to me," Sam replies. He shrugs, too.

Paul shakes his head and bumps his door open with his shoulder.

"That's what they all say," Matt calls. "Get a condom out of the drawer!"

"You have a condom drawer?" I ask.

"In the kitchen, yes."

I must look dumbfounded because he goes on to explain.

"I raised four teenaged boys. I had to be creative about getting condoms in their hands. And on their dicks."

Paul sets me down gently on his bed. Then he turns around and closes and locks his door behind us. "Let me out of here," I grit out. I scurry across the bed like a crab.

"Not until you talk to me." He starts to pace from one side of the room to another.

"I can't fucking believe you brought me in here right after you brought her in here," I bite out. "Of all the fucking nerve, Paul Reed." I stand up and brush the hair from my forehead. "If you think you're going to get me between your dirty fucking sheets, you have another think coming!" I point my finger at him. "Fuck you, Paul." My breaths are heaving as though I ran a five-minute mile. He comes forward and traps my wrists in his fists. He's strong. I knew it, but I have never really felt it. He holds me tightly.

"I didn't fuck her," he says. He jerks me gently, which makes me fall into him. "Look at me," he says. He's still holding my wrists, with my front plastered against his.

"I don't want to," I pout.

He chuckles, so I try to strike out at him, but he still holds my wrists. I could get free if I wanted to. I know that much about him. But I *really* don't want to. Mainly because I'm starting to think my perception of what happened was wrong.

"Stop laughing," I say.

"I didn't fuck her. She wanted to read me the riot act because she was jealous. That's all. We talked. She sniffled a couple of times, and I hugged her. That's it."

"Then why were you pulling on a new shirt?"

"Because Hayley smeared my other one with icing."

"Kelly was jealous?" I ask. My voice is so quiet I can barely hear it. But the tight fist of my own jealousy that was wrapped around my heart eases a little bit.

"She was."

"Why?" My voice is still small.

"Apparently, when I had my head on your knee, I looked peaceful."

"You felt peaceful," I murmur.

"Yes, I did," he says. "I like having you close to me. I like it a lot." He heaves in a sigh and says on an exhale, "Probably more than I should."

"I like it, too," I say.

He lets my wrists go and brackets my face with his hands. He tips my chin up with gentle thumbs and looks into my eyes. His are blue, so blue they're almost gray. They're like a cool pond on a hot summer day. I could fall into them and stay there forever.

His breath brushes across my lips. "I really like you," he says.

I grab his wrists this time, because if I don't hold on to something I'll fall over. My knees never wobble like this. "I like you, too," I whisper again. I look from his eyes to his mouth and back, hoping he'll just shut up and kiss me.

"Do you trust me?" he asks.

"I don't trust anyone," I admit.

"Why not?" His thumbs sweep back and forth over my cheeks.

"Because most people aren't trustworthy." My gut clenches when his eyes flash. That leaves him with questions, and they're not questions I want to answer.

"Will you tell me the story about why you feel that way sometime when we're alone?" he asks. He's still staring into my eyes.

"Probably not."

He chuckles.

"Paul," I say quietly.

"What?" he whispers back.

"Are you going to break my heart?" I look into his eyes because I think I might find the truth there, if there is such a thing.

"No," he says. His voice is strong and clear.

I hear a voice through the crack in the door say, "Ask him if he promises!"

"What the fuck?" Paul says, tossing his head back. He opens the door, and Pete and Sam fall into the room. They land on top of one another.

"Don't you have better things to do?" Paul asks, staring down at the two of them in a heap.

They look at one another. "Not really." They start to lumber to their feet, and Paul walks out of the room.

Sam wraps his arm around my shoulders. "Ask him if he promises," he says.

"What does that even mean?"

"When Mom died, we asked Paul if it would all be all right and he promised it would. It was," Sam says.

Pete goes on to say, "And when Dad left, we asked again if it was going to be all right, if we'd make it by ourselves. And we did...because Paul promised we could."

Fuck. My gut clenches. "I wouldn't want him to waste a promise on me." I try to laugh it off, but they don't think it's funny.

"Sometimes, all you need is a promise so you can keep going," Sam says. "If you need a promise, ask for it. He'll say yes or no."

"I don't need a promise."

"Yes, you do." Sam stares at me.

I break free of him with a shove and walk back out into the living room. Cody and Garrett are side by side, talking to Matt and Sky. Their daughter Mellie runs through the room, and Matt sticks out and arm, scooping her up and flipping her upside down as she squeals. Her shirt falls down, showing her belly, and Matt blows a raspberry there. "Daddy!" she squeals.

Matt visibly melts every time he hears that word. He grins and hugs her so tightly that she squeaks.

I look at Seth, but he just smiles and shakes his head at their antics.

I sit down beside Garrett, and he leans over and presses his lips to my forehead. "You okay?" he asks.

"Yeah," I say, leaning into his kiss. "I'm fine."

"That was kind of hot," Garrett says. "I might get Cody to reenact that carry-you-off scene with me later."

Cody shakes his head. "Something tells me it wouldn't have the same effect." He grins.

Probably not. He'd have to be a tatted-up, sexy blond hunk of man meat named Paul Reed to make it work. Paul settles at my feet and pulls my foot into his lap. He spends the next hour picking on his brothers while he draws tender circles on my inner ankle. I have never felt such an intimate touch. I've had sex with men and not felt this close to them. What the fuck is that about?

# Paul

I like Cody and Garrett. I don't particularly like that their baby could be growing inside Friday, mainly because it makes me jealous as hell, but I like them as people. They're funny and kind and so obviously in love. They're going to be good parents. Would it be terrible for me to admit that I hope the insemination didn't take? It probably would, so I keep that to myself.

On the one hand, I am really happy they have a chance at building their family. But on the other, I wish it were my fucking baby inside her. I want to see her get fat and cranky with my child growing in her body. I want to share those moments with her, and I don't know if I can do that when she's pregnant with somebody else's kid. I doubt there are any rules around that, no book I can read to tell me what's right and wrong. I want to win her, but I don't know if I can play the game while she's growing a life.

Cody and Garrett shake hands with me at the door, and Garrett pulls me into his chest for a quick man hug and a thwack on my back. "Take care of her, okay?" he whispers.

"You got it," I say back. I want to take care of her every day. All day.

He hugs Friday and says to her, "Remember, no orgasms."

What? I look from him to her and back, and her face colors.

Garrett just smiles, and he leaves hand in hand with Cody.

"Did you like them?" she asks as the door closes behind them. She leans against it for a second and takes a deep breath. My brothers all left one by one with their girls, except for Sam, and he just went to bed. Matt and Seth had to carry Joey and Mellie to the car because they fell asleep in Hayley's bed.

Hayley pops her head out of her room, scrubs her eyes, and toddles over to me. She looks up at me, sleepy-eyed. She's so damn cute in her frilly jammies that it makes my chest ache sometimes just to look at her. I force myself to stop and take mental pictures of her so I won't forget these moments. I stop time in my head—click!—and try to remember the frame for a while. She won't be this little forever.

"You going to tell Friday good-bye, too?" she asks.

I shake my head. "Friday is going to spend the night."

"You having a sleepover?" Her little brow furrows. She blinks her big blue eyes at Friday and grabs on to my leg.

"Friday is going to stay here for a while. She's going to sleep in Matt's bed, since no one is using it." I run a hand down her silky blond hair. "That okay with you?"

She nods but looks up at me skeptically. "She's not going to sleep with you?"

Friday laughs but bites her lips together when I look up at her. *Sorry*, she mouths.

"She's going to sleep in her own room, in her own bed, with her door locked."

Friday's eyes open wide. *I am?* she mouths. I nod, and she looks down at Hayley. "I am!" she says as though she's excited about it.

"You going to tell her a bedtime story?" Hayley asks.

# Friday

Paul swipes a hand across his smile. "Probably not."

Hayley slides her hand into mine and says, "You can come and listen to mine." She tugs my fingers so I follow her into her bedroom. I stand there, not at all sure where I'm supposed to go.

Paul sits down on the bed with his back against the headboard. "Which book?" he asks.

Hayley points to one, and I look around the room. I don't know where to go because she doesn't have any furniture aside from her bed and her toy chests, so I sit down on the carpet beside her bed and lean against it. My head is near Paul's knee and his feet are crossed, pointed toward the end of the bed. He's taking up a lot of space, and Hayley snuggles into her covers with a stuffed rabbit in her arms.

Paul opens the book and starts to read about a bull named Ferdinand. It makes me smile, hearing him read to his daughter. He loves her so much that I'm a little bit jealous. Not because he loves his daughter, but because I feel like I missed out on having anyone love me like that.

His voice gets softer and softer, and he stops when he's about halfway into the book. "She's asleep," he says, and he closes the cover.

"You can't stop now," I protest. "I have to find out what happens."

He grins, opens the book back up, and continues to read. He turns pages with one hand while the other strokes down the length of my hair. My eyelids grow heavy, so I lean against the mattress and let them fall closed. His fingers dig deeper and start to massage my scalp. I finally look up when I realize he has closed the book and all his attention is on me.

I get up on my knees and lean on my elbows, looking at Hayley snuggled and safe under her blankets. "She's beautiful," I whisper.

"Yeah, she is," he says. He brushes my hair back over my shoulder. "So are you."

My heart stutters, and I force myself to take a deep breath through my nose. But all I can smell is him and the little-girl scent that's all Hayley.

"Did you ever want this?" he asks, jerking his head toward his daughter.

I nod. "Once upon a time, yes," I whisper. "I wanted it. More than anything."

"What changed?" he asks. His blue eyes stare into mine.

"Everything," I say. Regret hits me like a truck smashing into my body. I push to my feet and walk to the door. I turn back to look at him. "Are you coming?" I ask.

He shakes his head. "Sometimes I just like to watch her sleep."

"Okay. Good night," I say softly.

He looks up at me and smiles. "'Night."

I go out to the kitchen and clean up a little. The pizza boxes go into the recycling and so do the beer cans. I load the dishwasher and wipe off the counter.

I startle when I see Paul with his hip hitched against the counter. "You don't have to clean up," he says. He's quiet, probably because he doesn't want to wake Hayley.

"I don't mind." I wipe my hands with a dishtowel and smile at him. He looks at me. He really looks at me, and it makes me want to squirm. "We never did talk about how much I'm going to pay you for the room."

"I thought we'd just take it out in trade. You know, sexual favors?"

I snort and toss the wet towel at his head. He catches it. "Have you ever paid for sex?" I ask.

This time he snorts. "Never had to." He grins, and it's so damn sexy I could drop my panties right here and not even feel bad about it.

"Women come easily for you."

He smiles even more widely. "Some come more easily than others."

He knows that's not what I meant. "You and Kelly…you weren't exclusive, were you?" I ask.

He shakes his head. "We were before we had Hayley. Then we weren't."

"And that was okay with both of you?" I go sit down on the couch, and he follows me. He sits beside me and takes my hand. Heat shoots from his palm to mine, and a tingle spikes up my arm. I shiver.

"It was okay with us," he says quietly. "I like that you shiver for me," he adds, his voice so soft and rough I can barely hear it.

I take a deep breath, and he watches my chest rise and fall and licks his lips. "I can't have an orgasm," I blurt out.

He sits back a little. "What?"

"I…um…I can't have an orgasm. I can't come. I can't get off." Fuck, I should have stopped at *orgasm*. I groan inwardly.

He chuckles and scratches his head. "Well, that's a challenge. But I feel sure we can get past it." He leans down until his lips are almost touching mine. "I'm sure I can make you come," he says. "I'm a hard worker."

"That's not what I meant," I squeak, pushing him back with a hand on his chest.

He sits back. "Talk to me."

"Since the insemination, I'm not allowed to orgasm. Not until after my checkup. It'll lessen the chances of the baby taking root."

His brows rise. "Really?"

I nod.

"Oh, so on a normal day, you don't have a problem with orgasms? Getting off? Coming?" He adjusts his jeans, tugging on the zipper, and I can see his manhood pressed hard against it. He doesn't touch it or do anything inappropriate, and I wouldn't even know how affected he is if he wasn't so fucking big. God.

My cheeks are on fire. "No, normally not an issue. Although it has been a really long time."

"How long?" He turns to face me and rests his elbow on the back of the couch, and drags his fingers through my hair.

"A really long time," I repeat. I let my head fall back and groan to myself. "I know you're not used to waiting…" I let my voice trail off.

"I've been waiting for you my whole life," he says. "I can wait as long as it takes."

"You're so not what I expected, Paul," I tell him.

"What did you expect?" His hand stops moving in my hair and starts to trail slowly up and down my arm.

"Sex on a stick," I say quickly. I want to bite the words back as soon as they fall from my lips, but now they're out there.

He chuckles. "I thought the same thing about you." He tweaks my nose. "I've been fantasizing about you for years."

I roll my eyes. "But your fantasies included me and another chick." He did think I was a lesbian, after all.

He shakes his head. "No, it was just you in my head. All you, all the time." He gets quiet for a second, but it's not uncomfortable. "When you kissed me, you shocked the shit out of me."

I wince. "Sorry."

He holds up both hands. "Oh, please don't be sorry. I loved it. But then I knew I had to make some changes if I wanted anything real with you. So I did." He shrugs.

"Why me?" I ask.

"Because you're you."

"You don't know the real me."

"I know. That's why I wouldn't sleep with you right now even if there was no medical issue with it."

I shove his shoulder. "Liar."

He shakes his head. "I want to know everything about you." He lifts my wrist and looks at my tattoos one by one. I have lettering up my inner forearm, and he starts to read it, but I twist my hand before he can finish. "You have these all over, right?" he asks. "Just like me."

I nod.

He grins somewhat sheepishly. "I want to explore them all with my tongue." He chuckles.

"Changing your mind about sleeping with me already?"

He shakes his head. "Nope. Exploring your body would give me just about as much pleasure as fucking you, Friday. I want to know everything."

"There are some things I'll never tell you." I know this about me. He should know it, too. That way, he won't have any unmet expectations. "I don't think I can go that deeply. Not with anybody. I'm sorry." I start to fidget because I don't know what to do with my hands. "So after my little *medical issue* is over, I still won't bare my soul to you." I lean forward and take his face in my hands. I swipe my fingers beneath his eyes, back and forth in gentle sweeps. "I'll sleep with you, though. On my terms."

"I don't like to share," he says.

"Neither do I."

"I won't share," he clarifies.

"Neither will I."

He smiles. "You're not going to make this easy, are you?"

I shake my head. "Probably not."

"I have a feeling we could be really good together."

"You always keep your promises, right?"

He nods. "I try to."

"Promise me that you won't break my heart."

He heaves a sigh. "Friday," he says.

"Paul," I say, mocking his tone.

"You'd have to hand me your heart before I could break it."

I nod. That's true. "Okay."

"But if you ever do trust me enough to give it to me, I promise not to harm it. Is that what you want to hear?" He shakes his head. "I don't even know why this is an issue when you just plan to use me for sex." He chuckles then raises a hand. "I volunteer as tribute!" he cries quietly.

I laugh. The bad thing is that if anyone could get me to hand my heart over, it's him. Because I've had him in my head for so long that I don't even know where to compartmentalize him anymore.

"Want to be my girlfriend?" he teases.

I shake my head. "Let's just start with roommates."

He nods. "I'll take whatever you'll give me."

He gets up and holds out a hand. I take it, and he gently tugs me to my feet. He walks with me to my doorway, where his fingers pull from where they're wrapped up in mine and fall away. "Lock your door," he says.

"Why?"

"So Hayley won't wake you up in the morning. She's nosy. And she gets up at the ass crack of dawn."

I laugh. "I wouldn't mind."

"Lock it so I won't come to you in the middle of the night. I'm nosy, too."

"I'll take my chances," I whisper as I close my door. I hear his footsteps creak across the floor as he walks away. I fall back against the door and finally allow myself to breathe. God, what have I gotten myself into?

# Paul

I know Friday is pregnant before even she does. She's been here for just over a week, and she's woken up sick for the past two days. Is it bad that I kind of wish she had a virus? I crack the door to the bathroom and ask her if she needs anything.

She grunts and heaves. "Go away," she growls.

I don't open the door because we haven't established that kind of intimacy yet. So, I just talk through the crack. "Want a wet cloth?" I ask.

"Yes," she says quietly.

I open the door and find her leaning against the wall with one knee raised, her elbow resting on it. She's wearing a T-shirt and panties, and I can see the elastic of the leg. I look away and get a washcloth from the cabinet, get it wet, and wring it out. I pass it to her, and she slaps it onto her forehead.

"Thanks," she says.

"Want me to help you up?" I hold out my hand to her.

She burps into her closed fist. "Not yet," she says, then she's suddenly bent over the toilet again, heaving her guts up.

I just woke up so I get out my toothbrush and brush my teeth. I don't want to leave her like this, but I can't stand here and do nothing, either.

"When do you go to the doctor?" I ask.

"Tomorrow."

"They're going to be two happy motherfuckers," I say. That part makes me grin. Garrett and Cody are going to be over the moon.

I reach down, and this time she takes my hand and lets me pull her up. She reaches for her toothbrush and sticks it in her mouth, but even brushing her teeth makes her gag. I rub her back gently, and she glares at me in the mirror.

"Go away," she says around her toothbrush.

"Nope." I cross my arms and lean my rear end against the counter. "I kind of like watching you get ready for the day."

She pulls the shower curtain back and turns on the water. "You sure you don't want to leave?" she asks, her eyes glinting in challenge.

"Not if you need me."

She shrugs and then pulls her T-shirt over her head. She tosses it into the hamper, and suddenly she's wearing nothing but a pair of pink panties. I can see the expanse of her naked back, and she has a large phoenix tattoo that I would have never guessed she had, along with a few others that are smaller.

"That is so not fair," I say. She's facing away from me toward the shower.

"I did warn you," she taunts over her shoulder.

She hooks her thumbs in the hips of her panties and drags them down her bottom. She has these two adorable little dimples at the small of her back. And her ass, it's just as round and perfect as I imagined in my wet dreams.

I turn to face the door. "Jesus Christ, Friday," I grit out.

She makes a noise, but I can't tell if it's a laugh or if she's still feeling sick. "Next time, you should give me some time alone when I'm in the bathroom," she yells over the noise of the water.

"Can I go to the doctor with you tomorrow?" I call back. I wince. Why the fuck did I ask her that?

She jerks the curtain back and glares at me. "Why do you want to go?"

I shrug and look everywhere but at her. "I just do."

"Ten o'clock," she says, and she jerks the curtain closed.

I want to pump my fist in the air because I feel like I finally won a battle with Friday. All this week has been one fight after another. She fights to pick up after Hayley. She does the dishes and the laundry when she knows I'm planning to do them. She made dinner for me and Hayley twice this past week. Even Sam liked it when he finally dragged his ass home.

I'm not used to having anyone take care of me, and I can't figure out if I like it. I have been taking care of everybody around me for a long time, but Friday has come in like a steamroller and changed my whole fucking life.

"Hey," I say. "I want to take you somewhere special with me."

"Where?" she asks over the rush of the water.

"My dad used to take me to this old movie theater. It's closed down now, but it's my favorite place in the whole world. We would have to break in, but the last time I did it, the projector still worked. We would just have to turn it on."

She sticks her head out of the curtain. "I've never heard you say anything nice about your dad before."

I shrug. "It's just a movie theater."

"No, it's not," she calls back. "I guess we could go one day. Is it the one with the old ticket booth out front."

"Yes."

"I'd like to go there."

My heart warms. "Good."

Her voice jerks me out of my thoughts. "Can you pass me a towel?" she asks.

I open the cabinet and get out the biggest and fluffiest one I can find. It must be hers, because none of what I have is this nice. She reaches around the curtain, her skinny little tatted arm waving impatiently at me. God, she makes me laugh.

That's the best thing about Friday. She makes me laugh. I don't know why, but just seeing her can get me out of a funk.

"Do you remember that guy who was at the shop last week when we were arguing?" I ask as she scrubs the towel over her hair. I can see it moving over the top of the shower curtain.

"Which time?"

I grin. We argue more than we agree, and I fucking love it. She's the only person who ever tries to put me in my place. "When you cried and went into the bathroom."

"Yes," she says. She jerks the curtain back, and I realize that she's wrapped the towel around her naked body and tucked the end of it between her breasts. "Stop looking at my tits," she says. But she smiles and shakes her head so I know I'm not really in trouble. "What about him?"

"He called me yesterday. He wants to come in and do a pilot for a reality TV show based on the shop."

Her gaze jerks up to mine. I realize suddenly that she has the cutest little freckles across the bridge of her nose. I don't usually get to see her without makeup on. I like it. I like it a lot. I drag my fingertip down the bridge of her nose.

She scrunches up her face. "Why would he want to do a show based on the shop?"

"Well, there are five of us and apparently people have a thing for tattoos right now. Not to mention that Emily is recording with Fallen from Zero and now Sam is being scouted by the NFL." I look away.

"What else?"

I grin. "What makes you think there's more?"

"Because you're awful at evasion."

"Well, they really like Matt's blended family, and the work Reagan and Pete do with the boys in the prison program excites them."

Her brows arch. "And?"

"And apparently they thought you and I had chemistry."

She snorts. "Chemistry?"

"Chemistry," I repeat.

She looks at me in the mirror as she runs a comb through her hair. "How do you feel about that?"

She reaches around me for the medicine cabinet. The front of her body grazes mine, and she steadies herself with a hand on my chest as she reaches for a bottle of lotion. She squirts it into her hands and raises one foot to rest on the top of the closed toilet lid.

"Paul," she says, jerking me from... Where was I?

"What?" I ask.

"How do you feel about the reality show?"

I shrug. "It's a lot of money."

"How much?"

She lifts her other foot and starts to rub lotion up her other leg. "Paul," she coaxes.

"Enough that they could all get a good start in life."

"What about you?"

"What about me?"

"Would it help you?"

"That's not important. I just want to see them all settled and happy."

She nods and steps up onto her tiptoes, kisses my cheek really quickly, and then sinks back down onto her heels. "You should talk to them about it."

I nod. "I will." I let my eyes scan her face. "I like your freckles," I say.

"Good." She grins. "Do you feel like going somewhere with me today?" she asks.

Logan, Matt, Sam, and Pete are all working today, so I don't technically have to go in. I narrow my eyes at her. "Where?"

"It's a surprise." She smiles mischievously. "You're not scared, are you?"

I scoff. "Of you? Never."

I'm only scared of her every fucking day. She makes my gut wrench and my heart skip and my head churn. And she does it without even touching me. One day, she's going to want to touch me and I'll get to touch her back. But I kind of need for her to take the first step. I'm terrified of loving her because I know loving her won't be easy. But I also know I don't want to miss the chance.

# Friday

It's the end of May, and there's a big fundraiser today for the homeless shelter in the park. The shelter I volunteer with has set up tents for the weekend, and each one has a different event going on at it. Mine is body paint. I'll be doing henna tattoos and painting faces for kids all day. Anything that can be painted, I will paint.

I pull my hair back into a ponytail. I don't usually do much volunteering, but this event is kind of my thing. I owe this rescue mission my life: they took me when no one else would. My life spiraled out of control, and they helped me find my footing. They don't know the new me, so I have to go as the old me, and it's the me that Paul has never seen. I am not wearing makeup, and I have on shorts and an old T-shirt that says *Will work for change*. And I will. I'm willing to put my money where my mouth is when it comes to fundraising for this group. I'll take dollars, I'll take change, I'll take checks, and I'll take credit cards. If I can get one girl off the streets, I've done a good thing and I can sleep easier.

I put on a baseball cap and pull my ponytail through the back of it. I sling my backpack, which has all my paints in it, over my shoulder. The rest of my stuff is waiting at the tent in the park.

"We're going to be late," I say as I run out of the room toward the front door.

"Jesus Christ, Friday," Paul says quietly when he sees what I'm wearing.

I look down and fidget with my jean shorts. "What?" I ask.

He shakes his head. "I've never seen you look so...normal."

"Is it bad?" I ask.

He closes his mouth. "No," he says. He smiles. "It's good. Very, very good."

I usually wear my vintage clothes and heels when I'm working at the shop, and it's what people have come to expect so I keep doing it. I get a lot of attention that way, and that's what the shop needs. "You ready?" I ask.

He is wearing jeans and a T-shirt with the Reed's Tattoo logo on it. "Are you going to be okay getting that dirty?"

He looks down at what he's wearing. "I don't see why not." He stops and grabs my elbow. "You're not going to have me rolling in mud or anything, are you?"

"Nothing quite that sophisticated," I say.

He rolls his eyes and follows me out the door. When we get to the street, he takes my backpack from my shoulder and puts it on his, and then he takes my hand. My heart skitters. I never would have taken Paul for a touchy-feely kind of guy, but he totally is. He never touched Kelly much in public, or any of the other girls I know he slept with, but with me, it's like he can't get enough contact.

He squeezes my hand. "This okay?" he asks.

I nod and grin at him. He has the most adorable dimples, and he gives me a crooked smile, showing them off.

"Aren't you afraid someone will get the wrong idea about us?" I ask.

"What idea are you worried about?"

I shrug. "That they'll think we're a thing."

"We are a thing," he says. He starts to swing my hand in his between us. "We are totally a thing."

When we get to the park, I see that there's already a line at my booth. I do this every year and people come just to get some of my art put on their faces.

"What are we doing?" Paul asks.

I grin at him. "We're painting," I say, rubbing my hands together with glee.

I motion the first person forward, and he has a little girl with him. She hops up onto my stool.

"What would you like to be?" I ask her.

"An ice cream cone!" she says.

Her dad teases her. "She didn't ask what you want to eat. She asked what you want to be."

"A butterfly!" she cries.

I get out a brush and start to paint, and Paul watches me closely. In less than a minute, I have a butterfly painted around her eyes that looks like mint chocolate chip ice cream. Paul looks at me. "It's really good," he says.

I grin. "I know."

I point to the stock art that's pinned to the fake wall behind him. "You can do the stock art ones. The baseballs and the glittery flowers."

"Okay," he says, and he sits down. He motions a man forward, and he brings a little girl with him, as well. She hovers between her dad's legs. Paul holds out the brush to her. "Would you like to try out my paint?" he asks. He sticks out his arm. "Right here," he instructs.

She takes it and makes a swirl on his arm, and he makes a big deal about how awesome it is. She grins and hands the brush back. "Your turn," he says as he sets her on his stool and starts to paint.

A few minutes later, he helps her down, and I see that he turned her into a tiger. And it's pretty fucking awesome. I knew he would be good at this. His job is art. The permanent kind. Of course, he rocks at it.

The kid's dad shakes Paul's hand, and one of the volunteers comes forward to take his money and lead someone new up to the stool.

A few kids later, I look up and find that our line is wrapping around our tent and down the row, and the end is way past where I can even see it.

Paul picks up his phone and makes a call. "Hey, Matt," he says. "I want you to close the shop and come to the festival in the park. We need some help." He talks for a second. "Bring everyone," he says.

Paul grins at me, and I shake my head. He seems happy to be here. And I'm happy to have him with me. There's not much I'm passionate about, but I am about art. And the Reed family. Put the two of them in the same place, helping out a charity I love, and I might as well be in heaven.

A cheer goes up when his four good-looking brothers show up and set up work stations. Logan brought Emily, Matt brought Sky, and Pete brought Reagan. They all get busy helping to take money and form lines for each of the tables.

The boys grin and settle in for the day. I hear giggles, and I realize that our line is no longer made up of only kids wanting their faces painted. There are teenage girls and even older women in line now, too.

"You guys are drawing a crowd," I tell Paul. His face colors, and he shrugs. The man is seriously sex on a stick and he still blushes when he gets attention? I step up onto a chair and wrap my hands around my mouth. I call out to the crowd, "Attention, please," I yell. "I think it's getting hot out here, so they should all take their shirts off! What do you think?"

A cheer goes up, and I see people who aren't even in our line stopping to watch.

Sam grins and yanks his shirt over his head. These boys have nothing to be shy about, I'll say that for them. I fan my face and look at the crowd. "Just one of them? I think they need some encouragement!" I hold out the money jar, and people come up to put cash into it. I look down and mentally count. "There's enough in here for one more of you to strip."

Reagan looks at Pete and rolls her eyes. Then she motions for him to go ahead. Very slowly, Pete hooks his elbows in his shirt and draws it up over his head. The cheering from the crowd gets even louder.

Sky looks at Matt and motions for him to go next. "What?" she asks, throwing up her hands when he glares at her. "I am proud of my husband." He pulls his shirt up high enough for the crowd to see the frog on his lower belly, but then he lets it drop.

He shakes his head and sits back down. "Not enough money in the cup," he says.

"I have a thousand dollars for the three of you to do it!" someone yells from the back of the crowd. A lady walks forward, and we all laugh when we see that it's Emily's mom.

"That's cheating," Matt says. But he pulls his shirt off. Several women nearby sigh out loud.

Sky points to her round belly and says, "He has three at home already and two more on the way." That makes me laugh, her feeling like she has to tell them that. But he just became the most wanted man out of the five because who doesn't want a man who takes care of his responsibilities? Matt leans over and kisses Sky's belly.

Logan strips his shirt off next. I hear some excited shouts and a few frustrated moans move through the crowd.

Paul is the only one left who is still wearing a shirt. "Your turn, big guy," Mrs. Madison says. She fans her face, and the crowd goes wild. Paul stands up, turns to me, and says, "What do I get if I do this?"

I motion to the mass of people waiting. "Crowd approval?"

"Not enough." He shakes his head and sits back down.

I lean over his table, resting on my palms, and ask, "What more do you want?"

The grin falls off his face. "I want everything," he says. "But I'll start with a kiss."

# Paul

Friday has paint smeared across her forehead and all over the side of her face, and I've never seen her look more beautiful. She leans over the table, and for once I can't see her cleavage because it's covered up by that T-shirt. Yet she's so fucking sexy she takes my breath away.

"You want a kiss?" she asks. She sits back and puts her hands on her hips.

I nod my head. "I want a kiss."

I watch her throat as she swallows so hard that I can hear it. "If I give you a kiss, you'll take your shirt off?" she asks.

I stand up. "I'll do just about anything you want me to do for a kiss, Friday."

"Off with it, then," she says. The crowd starts to chant, led by my brothers.

"Traitors," I say to them. They laugh and rev the crowd up.

I reach behind my back, over my head, and grab my shirt with both hands. Then I pull it forward the way men do, slowly pulling it over my head. Friday's gaze slides up my body as my shirt goes up, and I feel like her eyes are touching me all the way from my belly button to my shoulders.

The crowd goes wild when I throw the shirt down at my feet. Then I take a step toward Friday. "Time to pay up," I say.

She giggles and turns like she's going to run away from me. I hook an arm gently around her waist, pull her back to me, and turn her so that her front is touching mine from top to bottom. I slide my knee between her legs, and hitch her higher with my hands under her bottom. I squeeze her ass and lift her up toward my waiting mouth.

Her eyes meet mine, and I freeze. At the last minute, I kiss her on the cheek with a loud smack and set her back from me. She wobbles on her feet, so I steady her with my hands under her elbows. "You owe me," I tell her.

"I owe you nothing," she teases. "You just forfeited."

I lean down close to her ear. "When I finally kiss you, it won't be in front of a crowd full of people. It'll be me and you and no one else." I kiss the corner of her lips, and she shakes her finger at me. I grab her finger and pull it against my chest. "And it will rock your world."

"Prove it."

I nod. "When we're alone, I will."

"Believe it when I see it," she taunts.

Since the five of us Reed boys have our shirts off, Friday, Reagan, Sky, and Emily redirect the lines so that the kids go to Friday and the adults come to us. I'm fine with that. I deal with overly amorous women daily, albeit I don't usually do it with my shirt off.

A woman who has to be in her eighties toddles up on her walker. She lays her hand on my chest and stares at my nipple piercing. Then she shakes her head and reaches for the top button of my jeans, unbuttons them, and stands back and laughs. "Now, he'll earn some tips," she says.

Friday snickers, and she suddenly can't take her eyes off my stomach.

The older woman sits down, and I give her angel wings on her upper arm with her late husband's name below it. She tells me the story of how they met, fell in love, and went on to have eight kids together. When we're done, she sticks a twenty-dollar bill in the waistband of my jeans and winks at me. "Don't let her get away," she says, nodding toward Friday.

"I don't plan to."

"She's going to give you a run for your money."

I laugh. She already is.

# Friday

The volunteers came around with water bottles and Paul sent Sam to get us all lunch in the middle of the day, but by five o'clock, I'm starving. The boys put their shirts back on when it starts to cool off, and our line starts to dwindle. We weren't even supposed to be here this long, but we couldn't turn down the people in line. They were all waiting so patiently.

Paul dips his paintbrush into a cup of water and rinses it out. "I think I'm ready to be done for the day," he says.

"Me, too," his brothers echo.

Everyone helps clean up. Emily bends over to pick up a piece of paper she dropped, and her shirt slips up her belly. I shake my head because Logan has painted a big basketball on her stomach. It looks like the real thing but even bigger. Once she's down there, she can't get back up.

"Logan!" she cries pitifully.

But Logan is looking the other way, and he can't hear her. Paul rushes over to her and offers her a hand, but as she stands up, she scowls and grabs for her belly. "Uh oh," she says. She looks down at the water that has splashed all over the pavement and Paul's shoes. "Sorry."

Paul looks everywhere but down. "Either you just spilled your water or that baby's ready to make an appearance."

She holds up a full bottle of water that still has the cap on it. "Sorry about your shoes," she says. She sits down, clutching her belly like the baby might try to crawl out her belly button. "Can you get Logan for me?"

Sam smacks Logan on the shoulder and points to Emily. Emily crooks her finger at him. "I think it's finally time," she says.

"Holy shit," Logan says as he runs his fingers through his hair. He drops down in front of her. "Are you serious?"

She smirks at him. "Either that or I just peed all over Paul's shoes. And I kind of think I'd never be able to live down the latter, so I'm hoping it's the former."

Reagan jingles her keys at them and says, "Take my car." Logan pulls his keys from his pocket. "Ours is at our apartment. Go get it if you need it." Reagan takes them, but I know she won't use them. She's going to be just like the rest of us who will be sucking up space in the hospital waiting room.

"We'll meet you there," Paul says, but Logan is focused solely on Emily. He doesn't even see Paul's comment.

Emily waddles to the car with Logan holding her elbow.

I grab Paul's arm. "You don't think she overdid it today, do you?" I ask.

He leans down and kisses the bridge of my nose. "I think it's just time for the newest Reed to make an appearance."

"Is her mom still here?" I ask. I look around, but she must have left after she made the big donation that made all the boys strip.

"She's gone. Logan will text her."

"Should I call her?" I ask.

He smiles and lifts the brim of my baseball cap. "I think this is Logan's show. We should let him ask us for help when he needs it. He will. Eventually. When he can think again."

Paul's phone buzzes in his pocket. He pulls it out and smiles when he reads the text. "He wants one of us to go to their apartment and get Emily's bag with her clothes and stuff in it."

He was right. He knows them so well.

Reagan holds up the keys Logan already gave her. "We'll go."

Paul nods. "We'll meet you at the hospital."

Sky drops down in in a chair. "Oh fuck," Matt says, squatting down beside her. "Not you, too," he says.

It's too early for Sky. Way too early. "No," she says. "I'm just tired."

Matt looks up at Paul like he's waiting for assurance. "This is a first baby," Paul says. "It could be awhile. You should go home and sleep for a couple of hours. Take a nap. I'll call if things go faster than that."

Sky shrugs. "We need to go check on the girls and Seth anyway."

Matt nods. "Call us if anything goes wrong. Or faster. Or just goes."

Paul takes my hand and pulls me toward the exit. The volunteers have agreed to dismantle our tables and hold on to our tips from the day. I already counted it twice, and we made just over eleven thousand dollars with tips and a few very generous donations. It was a good day.

"You should be very proud of yourself," Paul says as we go down the stairs to the subway. "You made a lot of money for the charity."

He squeezes my hands, so I squeeze his back. "*We* made a lot of money. Not me," I correct. "Couldn't have done it without you."

"That's what family is for," he says. He watches my face closely as we get on the subway. There are no seats, so he stands up, grabs one of the handles, and wraps his free arm around my waist. He pulls me against him, and I am so close that I can feel the beat of his heart against my chest. "Where's your family?" he asks me quietly.

"Right here," I say. I look up at him, and his blue eyes are clear and bright. And curious. But not in an intrusive kind of way. In an intimate kind of way.

"I like that answer," he says, and a chuckle moves through him and into me. "But before us, who did you have before?"

"No one," I say. I look everywhere but at his face. I lay my head against his shoulder so I don't have to look into his eyes. Because he might find the truth in them, and that's the last thing

I want Paul to know. He cherishes his family, and if he found out that mine gave me away, and then that I did the same thing, he might hate me. I really don't want him or his brothers to hate me.

"One day, do you think you could tell me?" he asks. He turns me in his arms and leans down by my ear.

I don't want to answer him, so I step onto my tiptoes and press my lips against his instead. He freezes, and I immediately think that I have made a huge mistake. But then a growl vibrates against my lips, and he kisses me back. He licks across the seam of my lips, and feeling like I have never been kissed before today, I tentatively reach out my tongue to touch his. His hands bracket my face, and he makes little noises as he kisses me. I can feel him all the way to my toes. I grab his T-shirt in my fists and lift myself up higher, pressing against him as I try to crawl inside his heart.

A loud cough jerks us apart. I startle, and he looks into my face. His eyes search mine, and I'm worried that he'll find my fears there, all my anxiety about my past, and then I worry even more that he'll find my feelings for him shining back at him. Then he'll know too much. And he could use it against me. I don't ever want him to be able to go that deep.

"Damn," he grunts.

A grin tugs at the corners of my lips. "Something wrong?" I ask.

"I like it when you kiss me, but I don't like it when you use your kisses to evade my questions," he says quietly. He squeezes me in a gentle hug.

"I wasn't evading," I choke out. But I swallow hard trying to get past the lump in my throat.

"Yes, you were. And I don't hate it." He chuckles softly. "I might even understand it, if you'd let me in. But don't use my feelings for you as a smoke screen for what's really going on between us, okay?" He squeezes me again.

"What's going on between us?" I ask, my voice cracking only slightly.

"I'm getting to know you," he says, very matter-of-factly. He tips my face up with the gentlest of touches. "I want to know you," he says directly. "Everything."

I shake my head. "You wouldn't like what you find out." He would hate me. Family is everything to him and I gave mine away.

"Try me," he says.

I hold on to his waist—he still has his arm around me—as the subway comes to a stop. He looks down at me for a second too long, long enough for me to see his brow furrow and the little vee form between his eyebrows.

"What are you hiding?" he asks.

"Everything," I whisper. But I say it more to remind myself than to tell him anything he doesn't know. I'm hiding everything.

I pull him out the door and into the station, and we race to the top of the steps. "Friday," he calls when I'm a few steps in front of him. "You have to at least give me a chance."

I pretend like his voice gets caught on the wind, but it doesn't. It sinks deep inside my heart, and hope blooms. Hope blooms in a place where no light has lived in a really long time.

I thought it was difficult being on the subway and having Paul ask me so many questions, but that was nothing compared to the memories that swamp me when walk into the maternity ward.

# Paul

I let Friday walk ahead of me into the hospital because I feel like she needs to take a break from my probing. Don't get me wrong. I want to know everything about her. But I don't think she likes my prying.

I feel as though I'm opening the plastic top on a brand-new can of coffee grounds. I open it and the sweet essence of what's inside seeps out and makes everything smell nice, but then someone comes along and slams it shut again. The bad thing is that Friday is the one who keeps slamming her own fucking coffee can lid closed. I get one second of the essence of her, and then she slams it shut again. Then the wonderful smell of her is gone, and all I can see is this really pretty can. The can is full—I know that much. But opening the can and having it stay open… That's going to be a lot harder.

We meet Pete, Sam, and Reagan on the way into the hospital. "Did you just get here?" Pete asks. He has a bag filled with what I assume are Emily's things over his shoulder.

"Just walked in the door," I tell him, and I clap him on the shoulder. "We need to find out where they are."

But Friday nibbles her thumbnail and motions us toward an elevator. We follow her and go up to the floor she punched. We get out, and there are pictures of babies on the walls and nurses walking around in scrubs with pacifiers and rattles on them. And dogs. And cats. Lots of cats. But I'm pretty sure we're in the right place because pregnant women are walking by us pushing IV poles.

We stop at the desk and she asks, "Emily Reed?"

The nurse smiles and motions us forward. We follow her to a small room, where Em is sitting on the edge of the bed wearing a hospital gown. She jerks the rear of it closed, and Logan walks around behind her to tie it. He smiles, but she doesn't really look that happy to see us. I hand Friday the bag and motion for Pete and Sam to follow me. Reagan and Friday walk into the room, and the door closes behind them.

"Why can't we go in?" Sam asks, looking like a kicked puppy.

"Because she's going to have a fucking baby, numbnuts," I tell him. I shove him into the waiting room. A minute later, Logan comes out, wringing his hands.

"She kicked me out," he says.

I swipe a hand across my smile. "Why?"

He glances toward her room. "Reagan and Friday are getting her dressed." He paces from one side of the room to the other. "And they're washing the basketball off her belly."

I wave my hands wildly so he'll stop long enough to look at me. "What did the doctor say?" I ask, when I finally have his attention.

"Oh," Logan says, scratching his head. "Four centimeters." He holds up four fingers. "One hundred percent effaced."

"What the fuck does that mean?" Pete asks. "Is something wrong with its face?"

Logan goes and sits on his lap and bounces on top of him. "No, dumbass," he says, when he finally stops. Pete is moaning and making funny noises from below him. "It means her cervix is ready."

Pete shoves him and says, "Eww. I don't want to talk about Emily's cervix."

Reagan sticks her head into the waiting room. "Paul," she says, crooking her finger at me. "Emily wants to talk to you."

"What about me?" Logan asks.

Reagan waves him off impatiently. "Not yet," she says. Logan's face falls.

"Do you mind?" I ask him, pointing toward the room where she's waiting. She's his wife, after all.

He shrugs and goes to the window to glare out it. There's nothing but a cement wall outside that window, so I know he's not enjoying the view. He's hurt.

"Come on," Reagan says, waving at me impatiently.

"Holy hell," I mutter to myself.

I open the door cautiously and stick my head in. "Did you need something?" I ask. I try not to even look at her. But she barks at me.

"Get in here," she says.

I walk in, my feet tentative against the floor, barely making a sound. I jab my hands in my pockets and wait.

"I need for you to take care of Logan," she says. "I don't want him to miss anything, so wherever he is, can you try to stay with him? Translate. Don't let him miss a word. I will do as much as I can, but I'm afraid I'm going to get busy."

That's all she wanted? "Okay." I scratch my head again. "You don't mean I have to be in the room, do you?"

"Not for the actual birth, no," she says, blowing out a breath. "But if anything goes wrong, you have to promise to stay with him. Promise you won't leave him."

That's a given. "I promise."

"You're going to stay the whole time, right?" she asks.

You couldn't pry me away with a tire iron. "Yes."

Emily's face tenses, and she takes in several slow breaths.

"Is there anything I can do for you?" I ask.

Her face relaxes after a moment, and she looks up at me. "Go get Logan."

"Thank God," I say as I turn around and go get my brother.

But I have to give her credit. Even when she's hurting and scared, she's thinking about my brother and what he needs. My gut clenches. I want that for myself. I want it now.

Logan shoulders his way past me and glares at her. "I'm not leaving again," he says to her.

She nods. "I know."

"No matter what you say," he goes on.

"I just needed to do something. I wanted it to be a surprise." She holds her hand out to him. "I meant to do it later, but time got away from me, and then I realized that I hadn't done it yet, and I was almost out of time. And so Friday helped me with it." She motions for him to take her hand again. "But first we had to wash that stupid basketball off."

A grin tugs at the corners of my lips when she lifts her hospital gown and I see that the ball is gone. She's wearing a pair of Logan's boxer shorts for now, but her belly is huge and she looks like the timer on her chicken has popped. Across her belly are the words, "My name is Catherine. And I'm my daddy's girl."

"You finally picked a name?" Logan asks. He puts his hand on her belly and draws out the letters. It's made like his tattoo that says, "My name is Emily." It's the one he got when he found out her real name.

"That name was your favorite, right?" she asks.

I know it's more than just his favorite. Catherine was our mom's name.

He nods, and I see him swallow really hard. "Kit," he says.

"Kit," she repeats. Her voice cracks. There's so much history between them with regard to that nickname.

Oh holy fuck. They're going to make me cry.

I look around, and I don't see Friday in the room. "Hey, where did Friday go?" I ask.

They don't even look up at me. Logan pulls Emily into him and presses his lips to her forehead, holding there for a long beat. Then he sets her back and looks into her eyes.

They're not concerned with where Friday has gone, but I am.

# Friday

They wouldn't let me hold him after he was born. They said it would be easier that way. But none of it was easy. I remember sneaking from my room and going to the observatory window where all the little bassinets were safe behind the glass. There were so many babies in the nursery that night. All of them had names on the front of their bassinettes except the one I assumed was mine. I can still see him in my head sometimes. I never got to hear him cry. I never held him in my arms. But he looks like me with his dark hair. I know that much.

The baby in the window in front of me kicks his feet and turns a brilliant shade of red. I want to go in and hold him, but a nurse comes forward and picks him up. She gently coos to him and tucks him into the crook of her arm.

An arm slips around my waist, and I turn to look up into Paul's face. I wipe the tears from my eyes that I didn't even realize were there. My whole face is wet. Paul offers me his sleeve, and I shake my head. I wipe my eyes with my fingertips, sluicing the water from my face like windshield wipers.

"I love the belly art," he says as he looks through the window at the babies with me.

A grin tips the corners of my lips. "It was her idea."

"You did a good job."

He doesn't say more. He just looks at the babies.

"Do you remember the day Hayley was born?" I ask.

"Like it was yesterday. Kelly got pissed and kicked me out, and then she begged and pleaded for them to find me. Sam and Pete were at home because they had school the next day, and Logan was watching them. But Matt was here. He kept me steady." He looks down at me and smiles. "Who kept you steady?" he asks, his voice quiet and soft.

I flinch. I don't mean to. I can't help it. "I don't know what you're talking about."

"Okay," he says. He goes back to watching the babies. But his question lies there like a barrier between us, even though his arm is still around me and he's so very close to me.

I heave a sigh. "Can you respect my decision and let it go?" I ask. "Please?"

"I can and do respect your decision, but I can't let it go," he tells me. "I'm sorry, but it's such a big part of who you are."

"It's not, though. It's just a blip in time."

"It's not a blip, Friday," he says. His voice grows a little louder. "It's part of you, and it always will be. I'm not going to pry it out of you. But I'm here if you ever want to talk."

"Are you going to let it come between us?" I ask.

"Are you?" he tosses back at me. Then he sees Matt walking down the hallway with Sky and their three kids, and he shows them to the waiting room.

He leaves me standing there watching the babies. Only I don't feel completely alone. Not like the last time I was here.

I heave a sigh and stand there until the baby from earlier is back asleep. He smacks his lips together and dreams.

I had dreams once. Dreams of a family of my own. One that would stand by me no matter what. But no matter how strong my grasp, I just couldn't hold on to it.

# Paul

Logan lays his ear on Emily's belly and swears he can "hear" Catherine's heartbeat. Emily laughs and threads her fingers into his hair. The doctor gave her an epidural about an hour ago, and she's a lot more comfortable now than she was before. She was in a lot of pain. She has been laboring for about five hours and hasn't gotten very far until now.

The nurse dashes into the room, gives her a quick exam while I look out the window, and calls for the doctor. "It's time," she says.

Friday goes to Emily and whispers something to her, and Emily's eyes fill with tears. I want to ask her what she said, but I suppose it can wait. The doctor rushes into the room, and the nurse leads me and Friday—the only ones who were allowed to be in the room with them—back to the waiting room. The only reason we got away with staying as long as we did was because Logan told them he needed a translator. He doesn't. He does fine without one. But it worked. And Friday got to stay, too.

Logan had me run Emily's parents out of the room a couple of hours ago. They were just too excited and too worried for Emily to be any help.

Logan doesn't need me for this part, but it's really hard letting him grow up and be a man all on his own. I fucking raised him. And I don't think I'm ready to be done yet.

Friday takes my hand in hers, and we walk into the waiting room. Pete is asleep in a recliner with Reagan tucked into his side. He's snoring, and I think she is too. Sky is awake, and she's drawing circles on the back of Matt's hand while he talks softly to her. His hand lies on her belly, and there's something so beautiful about it that I can't look away. Their girls are asleep on a blanket at the their feet. Joey and Mellie found out the baby was on the way and there was nothing Sky and Matt could do to keep them at home. Seth is standing by the window drinking a soda.

Sam is asleep on the sofa. His feet are up on the back of it, so I sit down in the empty space that's left. I motion for Friday to sit in my lap. She perches on the arm of the couch beside me instead.

Emily's dad leans forward. "What's going on?" he asks.

I grin. "It's time," I say. I can't stop smiling.

Mrs. Madison claps her hands together. "I can't wait!" she cries.

Matt rolls his eyes behind her, and it makes me grin.

Friday threads her fingers in my hair, a lot like the way Emily did to Logan a minute ago. I close my eyes and enjoy the fact that she's touching me. That she wants to touch me. It means something to me. Especially when I feel like my guts are hanging on the outside of me because I'm so fucking nervous for Logan.

I reach out and pull Friday into my lap, and she settles her head against my chest. She nestles into a spot, snuggling with me, and then she tilts her head back and looks up at me.

"Wait!" Sam says, lifting his head.

"What?" I ask. I force myself to look up at him.

He motions from Friday to me and back. "Are you guys a thing now?"

I grin and look down at her. She worries her lower lip with her teeth. "Are we a thing?" I ask her.

"We're a thing," she whispers to me.

My heart trips a beat. I press my lips to her forehead and linger there, and she makes a soft noise. It's almost like a purr, and I find that I really, really like it.

I tip her face up and press my lips to hers.

"God," Sam complains, "it's so fucking weird watching you two be a thing. You make me want to throw up."

I smack his leg. "Watch your mouth," I say. I move my eyes toward Emily's parents, but her dad just shakes his head and laughs. He likes us a lot more than he used to.

"Sorry," Sam grumbles.

"Kids," Mrs. Madison says, commiserating with me. "What can you do? Mine ran away from home, fell in love, and made a wonderful life for herself."

"They're happy," I say. Friday yawns, and I feel her hot breath through my shirt. I sit up a little so I can draw her even closer.

Suddenly, Logan runs into the room. "She's here," he says, signing at the same time. But he's so fucking excited that his hands are flying wildly. "Eight pounds, two ounces, and she's twenty inches long. And she's perfect." He stops to take a breath. "I just cut the cord, and it was disgusting and awesome all at the same time."

His eyes are shiny with tears, and he dashes his hands across his cheeks. He leaves to go back to Emily, and the door shuts with a *swoosh* behind him.

I swallow hard because my heart is in my throat.

"You did good," Friday says quietly. She tips my face down and kisses me. "Really good."

"I didn't do anything," I say, surprised to hear how gravelly my voice is.

"You did everything," she whispers, and I feel her tears against my shirt. I hold her to me because I have a feeling this has a lot more to do with her past than Logan's present. "You did everything they needed."

"Can I be what you need, too?" I ask.

I feel her nod against my chest. And my fucking heart takes flight. She can keep her secrets if she needs to. But I'm here to take her burden if she wants that, the same way I take theirs. Because she's family. My family.

# Friday

Is it terrible that I don't want to hold Catherine, aka Kit? I watch as Mellie and Joey both take a turn holding her, with Matt bracing both of them in his strong arms. He's so gentle with his daughters, a lot like Paul is with Hayley. Seth waves the baby away, though he does present Emily and Logan with a coupon book for a dozen diaper changes that can be used in the future.

"Preferably before she starts to eat solid food," he says with a laugh.

Logan shoves him, and then he pulls him in for a hug. Seth has become a part of the family. Sky takes the baby next, and she props her up on her big belly and looks down at her. "She's so beautiful," she breathes.

"My turn," Reagan cries. She takes her from Sky like she's a football and holds her up so Pete can help her support Kit's head. Kit's eyes are wide open and she stares into Reagan's face, and Kit grabs hold of Pete's finger and holds on tight.

"She's got one hell of a grip," Pete declares.

"Let me have a turn," Sam says, and he takes her next.

"All these blond men," Emily's mom says. "She's not going to know who's who."

Kit's eyes wander over to Logan, almost like she's looking for him, and he smiles, his arm still around Emily as he sits beside her in the hospital bed. Emily looks tired, but she knows none of these boys are going to leave without holding that little girl at least once.

Matt goes to Emily and kisses her cheek, whispers into her ear, and then ushers his family out of the room. The little girls get one last look at the baby, and then the room empties out just a little.

Pete and Reagan leave next. "Get some rest," Pete tells Emily, squeezing the top of her head. He makes a loud slurping sound against Logan's cheek, and Logan swats him away. Sam passes the baby to Paul and goes out with Pete and Reagan.

"Thing one and thing two," Emily's dad says.

Paul chuckles. "At least they're staying out of trouble."

A lady comes in and introduces herself as a lactation consultant. Paul puts Kit in my arms before I can stop him and wraps his arms around us both. I close my eyes and let the safe sensation wash over me. When I open them, Emily is casting me a curious glance.

"We should all go," I say.

Emily's parents look at one another and nod. They're leaving, too. I was worried we'd have to run them out so Emily could learn to breastfeed her baby in private. I would totally do that for her.

"We'll be back later," Emily's dad says. Emily just lays her head back against the inclined bed and nods.

I put the baby in Logan's arms, and she squirms, her little mouth opening to let out a cry. Logan looks at Emily. "Is she loud?" he asks.

Emily shakes her head. "She kind of sounds like a baby bird," she says.

Logan stares down at his daughter as though she's a thing of wonderment. And she is. She really is.

"Congratulations," Paul says to them both.

Emily winces when Kit's sounds become more like a siren. "Okay, now she's loud," she says with a laugh. Logan passes Kit to Emily, and she looks up at the lactation consultant like she's not sure what to do.

Paul ushers Em's parents out the door, and we follow.

He heaves a sigh and looks down at his watch. "Don't we have a doctor's appointment today?" he asks.

I stop and think. "Oh shit," I say. The sun is up, and it's Monday. And I have an appointment at ten in the morning.

I reach for my purse to pull my phone out, but I realize I left it in the hospital room.

"I'll be right back," I say, and I sprint back up to Emily's room. I knock softly and wait for someone to call out that I can come in. Emily has the baby in her arms and her shoulder is bare. Logan tosses a lightweight blanket over her really quickly.

"It's just me," I say. "Sorry, but I forgot my purse."

I dash over and grab it. But at the door, I have to stop and take one last look. Emily is sitting up in bed staring down at their daughter. Logan has his arm wrapped around them both, and he's holding them close, talking softly to Emily. She turns and kisses his cheek. He smiles at her, and there's so much love there that it makes me ache inside.

They're all wrapped up in one another, so I leave the room much more quietly than I arrived.

But outside the door I stop and think about the way they looked together. Their family is perfect. Is it safe for me to want that, too? Or is perfect something I'll just never have?

Paul looks so damn handsome leaning against the pole outside the hospital that I have to stop and stare at him. He laughs down at his phone. God, that man makes my heart go pitter-patter when he smiles. And when he frowns. And when he does nothing. But mostly, when he smiles, he takes my breath away.

"What's funny?" I ask as I walk up to him.

He holds up his phone and shows me the picture of Emily and Kit that Logan must have just taken. *First full tummy*, it says under it.

"Next he'll send one that says *first full diaper*," Paul says with a chuckle. He hops up onto the curb and walks down it like it's a tightrope, his arms outstretched. He can be so serious and still such a kid at the same time. I guess he should still be young at heart. He's only in his mid to late twenties, although he's been carrying the burden of his entire family his whole adult life. I like this side of him.

I shove him off the curb, and he jumps to the ground. He takes my hand.

"You always this happy in the morning?" I ask.

He points to his chest. "Who, me?" he asks. "I am Mr. Sunshine all the time."

I laugh out loud. "Tell that to someone who doesn't know you."

He looks down at his phone and then throws his head back and laughs. "See," he says. "Told you."

I see the picture of Kit's first diaper change and roll my eyes. "I think it's sweet," I say quietly.

He sobers a little and looks closely at me. Too closely for comfort, so I cross my arms and speed toward the subway.

"You know you're pregnant, right?" he asks my back.

I stop. "I won't know until later," I say. I turn to face him.

He brushes my hair back from my forehead. "You've woken up sick the past two days," he says. "You're pregnant."

"I won't know until later," I say again, and I start for the subway again.

"And if you are?" he calls after me.

I shrug. "Then I am."

"And?" he shouts.

"And what?" I turn around and glare at him.

"And how do you feel about that?" he asks.

I shrug again. "Fine. It's not like I didn't plan for it." I make my eyes go wide and stare at him.

He holds up his hands like he's surrendering. "Just checking," he says.

"It's not like it's mine," I remind him.

"So that means what?"

"It means it's not mine," I say again. "This baby is going to have two wonderful daddies, and just because it's growing inside me does not make it mine." Hell, even the one that does share my DNA isn't mine. I close my eyes.

"I think you'll like being pregnant this time," he says. He takes my hand and pulls me into the subway. He wraps his arms around me like before and talks close to my ear. It's all intimate, even though there's a crowd of people around us. "After this one," he whispers, "do you think you might like your own?"

"No." I don't even need to think about it.

His brow furrows. "Why not?"

"I'm not mother material."

"Fuck that," he says.

"Fuck you," I say back.

He grins. "I wish you would," he whispers, and then he kisses me quickly.

I shove his shoulder. "Shut up."

He lifts my arms and wraps them around his neck, and then he kisses me. He kisses me in the middle of a crowded subway car with people all around us—again—but I feel like we're the only two people in the world.

His phone dings, and he pulls it out of his pocket. He grins and shows me the picture. "First spit up," he says.

# Paul

I know it sounds crazy, and this is totally the wrong time to have thoughts like I'm having, but I want to *be* an ultrasound wand. I try to look at Friday's face as the technician rolls a sheath over the long wand and then puts lube all over it, but it's damn hard not to watch the movements because that stick is about to get all intimate with Friday.

We went home really quickly so she could shower, and we were almost late getting to the doctor's office. Cody and Garrett were pacing the sidewalk as we walked up.

Now they're waiting in the next room while the ultrasound people get Friday ready. The pregnancy test was positive, just like I knew it would be. They're going to do a quick check for a heartbeat, just in case there is one to be seen. They might not be able to find it yet. We'll have to wait and see.

"I'm up here," Friday says as I watch the wand. She laughs. But her hand shakes when I take it in mine.

"I'm jealous of that wand," I whisper in her ear.

She shivers, but I can't tell if it's a sexy shiver or if she's so fucking nervous that her skin is jostling.

The technician warns us that she's about to insert the wand.

"Close your eyes or something, Paul," Friday says, her cheeks growing rosy.

I turn so that my back is to her lower half, and I look at the wall for a minute.

"All set," the technician says. "Should I let the dads in?" She looks at Friday and then at me with a curious expression.

"You could just get a picture for them," I suggest. I know it sounds ridiculous, but I don't want to share this moment with anyone. Then I remind myself that this baby isn't mine. Friday isn't even mine. Yet.

Friday nods her head. "They're the dads," she says. "They deserve to enjoy every moment."

Her lower half is draped with a sheet, and if you didn't see the wand before it went in, you'd have no idea she has something up her vagina that can take pictures.

Cody and Garrett walk in holding hands, and Friday smiles at them. She's still shivering, though, and her teeth start to chatter. I bend over her face and look into her eyes, then drag my finger down her nose over and over until her eyes close. Her dark lashes flutter against her cheek, and then she opens her green eyes and looks into mine.

"Thank you," she whispers. She takes a deep breath.

I kiss her cheek and scoot closer to her, and Cody and Garrett step up beside me. Cody takes her free hand, and they look toward the monitor.

The technician maneuvers the wand and a picture appears on the screen. She squints, and her brow furrows. But then she stops and smiles. "Right there," she says. She points at the monitor. "That little, tiny flutter. Do you see it?" She looks at the dads and I doubt they can even see at all because they're both blinking back tears. She hands them tissues, and they wipe their eyes really quickly. Cody blows his nose. It sounds so much like a foghorn that Friday laughs. The picture on the screen moves, and the flutter stops.

"What happened?" Cody asks. "Is it all right?"

"Just needs a little adjustment," the technician says. The flutter reappears. You can barely see it. It's kind of like the beat of a hummingbird's wings, and it moves so fast that you might miss the action altogether if you blink.

The door opens, and the doctor slips into the room. "Congratulations," she says to Cody and Garrett. She barely spares Friday a glance.

I want to poke her and say, *Notice the vessel, bitch,* but I refrain. I squeeze Friday's hand, instead.

She mouths, *It's all right*, at me. I lean down and kiss her, because I just need to.

I don't know at what point I started needing her. Probably the moment I found out she wasn't a lesbian and I had a chance with her. But now I know it. I do need her. That scares me a little bit, and I am not sure she's ready for what I want.

The doctor sits down on a rolling chair and looks at the screen, takes some measurements, and then scoots back. She pulls the wand from inside Friday and pulls off the sheath. She presses some tissues into Friday's hands and then helps her up. I reach around behind her and pull the pillow closer to her butt because she's naked from the waist down and not wearing a robe. She has a sheet over her lap, but still.

Friday rolls her eyes at me. "They're gay," she whispers dramatically.

"I still don't want them looking at your ass," I whisper back.

"I could be completely naked and they wouldn't care."

"I would care," I grunt out.

"Why?" she asks. Her brow furrows.

"Because," I murmur.

"Because why?" she asks.

I lean close to her ear. "Because it's mine," I say so that only she can hear me. "That okay with you?"

"Yes," she says. "I'm officially pregnant, though," she reminds me. Like I need reminding.

I look at her. "I can wait."

An electrical current passes between us, and my skin does that little sizzle that only she provokes until Cody puts an arm around my shoulders and I have to jerk my eyes from her to look up at him.

"We're having a baby!" he says. He squeezes me really quickly, and I thwack him on the back.

"Congratulations," I say.

They're so damn happy they can barely speak.

"I wonder if they make those candy announcement things that they sell at the baby store for dads? Like the funny cigars and stuff." Friday asks. "Yours would have to say *We knocked up a chick* or something really clever."

Cody puts his hands on his hips and fake glares at her. "Anyone who knows us at all would know we would never knock up a chick."

"But you did," Friday reminds them. She giggles, and I can't bite back my grin.

The guys look at one another. "Yeah, we did," Cody says, and Garrett kisses him really quickly. Cody looks sheepishly at me. "Sorry," he says. "Didn't ask you if you are okay with the PDA."

I look at Friday, and I must have a question in my eyes.

"He's fine with it," she says.

Friday looks toward her clothes and up at Cody and Garrett. They're not taking the hint. I get up and motion them closer to the door. "Let's give her a minute to get dressed, shall we?" I say.

They nod and step outside. They're jabbering at one another and talking about baby names. I smile and close the door behind them.

"And you, too," Friday sings out. She makes a shooing motion at me.

I shake my head. "I'm staying."

"Fine," she says. She stands up and carefully wraps the sheet that was draping her lower half around her waist so that she's all covered.

"Do you need some help?" I ask. My dick twitches in my pants. I can't help it. Her ass is naked under that sheet.

"You want to help me wipe off the goo they just stuck in my vagina?" she tosses back at me.

I let my eyes roam up and down her body until she flushes. "I'll do anything you need if it gets me closer to your vagina."

She lets out a heavy breath. "Paul," she warns. She shakes a quivery finger at me. "Behave."

"Do you still have the piercing?" I ask. No idea what made me think of that.

"Which one?" she asks as she steps behind the curtain. I can hear her shuffling around.

"How many do you have?" I immediately want to go do a quick inventory of all her intimate areas to see how they're adorned.

"Nipples, hood, labia, navel, ears, lip, and tongue," she says.

I sink down onto the edge of the exam table. Damn. "That's all?"

She laughs, too. "I couldn't think of anything else to pierce."

I sit quietly, imagining all the metal in all her most sensitive spots. I want to suck on it, twirl it around, and play with it, preferably with my tongue. "You're going to have to take out the lower ones before the baby gets here," I remind her.

"You don't know that." She shoves the curtain back and pulls her hair from the neck of her T-shirt. I still can't get used to this Friday. She looks so normal. Her hair is hanging loose around her shoulders, and she's not wearing makeup still. I like it. I like her. To me, she's just as sexy, if not more so, when she's dressed like this as she is when she's working at the shop all glammed up.

"Hello," I say. "I'm a professional body piercer."

"So am I," she reminds me. "And I haven't ever been told that."

"Ask the doctor," I taunt.

"I will the next time I see her." She sticks her tongue out at me, so I reach out and grab her by her belt loops and then pull her against me. She falls into me, her hands grabbing my forearms to help her keep her balance. I lift the edge of her T-shirt and lay my palms on her warm skin.

"You always this grabby?" she asks, her mouth so close to my chest that I can feel her hot breath against my skin.

"I'm usually more grabby," I say. "I'm trying not to scare you."

She sucks in a quick breath. "I don't scare easily."

"That's one of the many reasons I want you."

She trembles in my arms, and I fucking love it.

"Did you get all that goop off? Or should I help you with it?" I playfully reach for her zipper, and she swats my hand away.

"That's kind of gross," she says over a laugh.

True. When I finally get to feel her wetness, I'd rather it be because of us rather than an ultrasound wand. But I can't get that wand and where it was off my mind. Yes, I have a dick. Yes, I like to use it. Yes, I'd like to use it on her.

Friday glances down between us. "Umm," she says. She points with her index finger toward my crotch. "I think you're getting a little too excited over some goo and a vagina."

The door opens, and Garrett sticks his head into the room. "Are you guys dressed?" he asks, squeezing his eyes shut tightly.

"No," I say. But at the same time, Friday says, "Yes." She slaps my chest and steps back from me. I adjust the fit of my pants.

"We already checked you out," Cody says.

Garrett waggles his brows at me. "And you too, big guy," he says, like he's a vaudeville actor.

"Quit checking out my man," Friday says, and my heart swells in my chest.

I grab Friday's arm on the way out the door. "What did he mean about me being okay with PDA earlier?" I whisper to her. I don't know why I have that on my mind, but it stuck with me.

"He tried to explain it to me once," she says. "I think it's adorable when they get affectionate with one another, but not everyone feels that way. Even people who 'tolerate,'"—she draws air quotes around the word *tolerate*—"their relationship are sometimes offended by their kissing and holding hands. So, they're careful about who they do it around."

"But they're just two people in love," I say. "What am I missing?"

She steps up onto her tiptoes and kisses my cheek. "You, Paul Reed, are one special guy. Do you know that?" She looks into my eyes.

"In this day and age, they still get judged?" I ask. I just find it hard to believe. What it takes to be a family hasn't changed through the years, but what families look like sure has.

"All the time," Friday says. "He was just being considerate of your feelings. Don't worry about it." She waves a breezy hand in the air and follows Garrett and Cody into the sunlight. She puts her sunglasses on, and I walk beside her.

"We have to get back to work," Cody says. He kisses Friday on the forehead and shakes hands with me. Then Garrett does the same.

"Take care of our baby mama," Garrett says.

I put my arm around her. "I plan to." I want to start with a nap. With her in my bed. Under my covers. Preferably naked.

# Friday

I'm pregnant. My knees are a little bit wobbly, but I'm not sure if that's because Paul is staring at me or if it's because I'm scared shitless of the thought of being knocked up. *It's not mine. It's not mine. It's not mine*, I chant in my head.

"What's wrong?" Paul asks. He tips my face up, and I grab his wrists to pull his hands down. He tangles his fingers with mine, instead, and pulls my hands behind my back, tugging me until my body is flush against his.

I wiggle my fingers in his grip. He's not holding me tightly. He's just loosely gripping my hands, probably to keep me from shoving him away. "Do many of your women find this sexy?"

"Many of my women?" His chuckle rumbles through me. "How many do you think I have?"

"I don't have enough fingers, toes, or freckles to count that high."

"Oh, it's not that many." He kisses the tip of my nose. "You have a lot of freckles." He laughs again. But he's avoiding my eyes all of a sudden.

"I've seen you with the hoochies that come into the shop," I tell him. It bothered me then; it bothers me now. But I don't want him to know how much. "You get around."

"I *got* around. I don't *get* around. Big difference."

I force a little joviality into my voice. "So you're telling me that you're not going to sleep with anyone else ever again."

"If you commit, I commit," he says. "I told you, I don't share. And I don't expect you to share, either."

I twist my fingers out of his, and he looks like a three-year-old who just lost his new toy when I step back from him. If I run, he'll follow and it'll look like I'm playing with him, when I really just need space. Then no one's feelings get hurt.

"Come back here," he says.

I force a laugh and run for the subway. He follows. I can barley hear his running shoes on the pavement, but I know he's back there. His shadow is following me, almost overwhelming mine, much the way he takes me over.

"If you were a man, I'd stick my foot out and trip you," he says to my back.

"If you were a man, you'd be able to catch me," I toss over my shoulder.

He scowls and catches up with me in two long strides. "If I were a man?" he says, dropping his mouth to my ear to growl the words at me. "You doubt it?"

"Prove it, big guy," I tell him.

He shakes his head. "Not yet."

I stop walking and put my hands on my hips. "You're going to let me pick on your manhood and not try to prove it?" I ask. *Take the bait, Paul.*

"If you were anywhere near my manhood, I wouldn't have to prove it." He grabs for a handle as we step onto the subway car, and he pulls me against him. I kind of like having him hold me like this. It's intimate and new. And he seems to like it, too, if the evidence of his desire pressing against my hip is any indication.

I lower my hand to rub him through his jeans, but he intercepts my questing fingers.

"Don't fucking play with me," he warns.

"Whoa," I breathe out. "Where did that come from?"

"Sexual frustration," he says. "Brings out the best in me."

I play with a loose string on his sleeve. "So, what if I want to fucking play with you?"

His arm drops from around my waist. "Then you're talking to the wrong guy."

I suddenly feel cold and alone. I cross my arms in front of me and try to glare at him. But it's hard when I'm feeling this exposed.

"Don't ever use sex as a way to control me," he says quietly. Then his arm wraps around me again. This time, it's me who pulls back. He scowls and follows me when I go to sit in an empty seat. He slides in beside me so I shove myself up against the window. He's big, though, and he takes up all the seat on his side and some of mine. "Don't run from me, either," he says. "I'll always chase. Until you tell me you don't want me to."

I start to tick items off on my fingers. "So, I can't fucking play with you. I can't run from you. And I can't use sex to control you." I throw my hands up. "Why don't you just give me the whole list now?" I ask. "What else can I not do?"

He leans close and pushes my hair back from my nape with gentle fingers. His hand cups the back of my neck, and he talks quietly in my ear. "You can't use sexy tricks to get away from my questions. I asked you what was wrong when we left the doctor's office because you looked like something was bothering you. I wanted to know what it was, and you evaded my question with sexy innuendos and grabby little fingers. Don't get me wrong. I want you to fucking grab every part of me, particularly my dick grabbed by your pussy with you on top." He smiles when the hair on my arms stands up. "But if you can't answer a simple question like 'What's wrong?' then we have bigger problems than I thought. So, let's try again. What's wrong, Friday?"

"What makes you think something is wrong?" I ask, my voice quaky.

"Because I know you. I fucking know you, and I know when something is wrong."

"What's my tell?" I ask. Because now I'm curious.

"Stop it," he growls. "I'm not going to let you change the subject."

I want to say the words out loud. I want to say them so badly. But they get stuck in my throat. "Nothing is wrong," I say. I shove his hand from where it's still clasping the back of my neck.

"Don't lie to me." He doesn't look angry. He looks...hurt? What the fuck is that about?

"I don't know what you want me to say!" I cry. People turn and look at us, and I bring my voice down to a level that won't call dogs from all areas. "I don't know what you want," I hiss.

"Are you happy that you're pregnant?" he asks, sitting back and crossing his arms so he can stare me down.

"Of course, I'm happy," I scoff.

"Not happy for Garrett and Cody. Are you happy to be pregnant? You, Friday. Just you."

Suddenly, tears well up in my eyes, and I blink them furiously, trying to prevent the warm puddles from falling down my cheeks. If they fall, I've failed. I've shown weakness. I can't allow that.

"Fucking hormones," I say.

He chuckles. "You've been pregnant for all of a week," he says. "You had better get used to it."

"I don't cry," I say quietly. "I never, ever cry. Ever."

"Why not?"

Because I don't let people get close enough to make me weak. "Because I don't want to."

"You don't do anything you don't want to do, right?" he asks. His eyes narrow.

"Not anymore."

"When was the last time you did?"

I suck in a breath. My stomach is roiling.

"Friday," he sings.

"Why the interrogation, Paul?"

"Stop doing that."

"Fuck you."

He laughs. "Fuck you."

A grin tugs at my lips. I turn and stare out the window at the graffiti going by. The last time I cried was over *him*. It was over the baby I gave away. And I swore I would never let anyone else make me that vulnerable ever again. But I can't tell Paul that.

"I like being pregnant," I say. I smile at him and force out a giggle.

"Great, now you're going to pretend to be fucking Pollyanna." He throws up his hands.

"Stop prying," I warn. I frown at him. "Stop fucking trying to dig into my psyche. It doesn't like visitors. It likes its solitude. It likes the cobwebs in the fucking attic, so stop trying to clean them up."

"Tell me something true," he urges. "One thing." He holds up a single finger. "Just one."

"That was the truth." I lay a hand on my stomach, and Paul looks down at it. "I fucking love being pregnant. I love that a life is growing inside me. I love that Cody and Garrett are going to be parents and that I get to cook their baby for nine months. It makes me so happy I could spin around and make rainbows from Skittles and shit. Shake the fucking Skittle tree and a rainbow will fall out, that's how happy I am."

"Thank you." He doesn't say anything else. He just crosses his feet in front of him and stares down at them.

"Fuck you, Paul."

"Fuck you, Friday."

"I'm not lying about that," I whisper-shout at him. "I do love being pregnant. I love it this time, and I loved it the last time. I loved it all the way up until I fucking gave him away. Is that what you wanted to fucking hear? Is that what you want to hear, Paul?" I stand up as the subway car slows down. "I love being pregnant," I hiss in his ear. He flinches. "I get to give birth to another baby that isn't mine. Only this time, I can check up on him to be sure he's all right."

Finally, a tear tumbles over my lashes and down my cheek. I swipe it away with the back of my hand. I scoot around him and walk toward the exit. He steps out, and I hesitate. I wait until the very last minute, and when he spins around to see where I've gone, the subway doors close, and I'm still inside. I close my eyes as I pull away because I can hear him calling my name.

# Paul

It's almost eight at night, and Friday still isn't home. Hayley is with her mom this week, so I don't have much else to do except pace and wait for Friday to come home. I can't fucking believe she left me like that on the subway platform. She won. For now. But when I find her, I'm going to get her spill her guts and tell me her secrets. She's carrying an awfully big burden, and I wish she'd let me help her with it.

My phone buzzes, and it's Logan sending me another picture of Kit. This time, she has a piece of paper on her belly that says, *I wonder when my Uncle Paul is going to come and visit.*

I shake my head and grin. Then I grab the keys to my motorcycle and go down to the garage to get it. I won it in a card game, and I can count the number of times I've ridden it on one hand. Logan uses it a lot more than I do. But it's getting late, and I don't want to ride the subway at this time of night. I never get accosted because of the way I look, but I do get a lot of curious glares because of the tats and piercings. People push their children behind their legs, and women put their purses on the other sides of their bodies, like I'm going to steal from them or something. Just because I have tattoos does not mean I am poor, a thief, or in need of their hard-earned cash.

I park at the hospital and go up to the ward where Emily is still waiting to be sent home. I knock softly and open the door. I stick my head in and see Emily sitting in a chair with Kit pulled close to her breast. She rocks and motions me forward. She points toward the bed and rolls her eyes.

"He got tired," she says, shaking her head.

Logan is stretched out in the hospital bed with his mouth hanging open. The best thing about having a brother who is deaf is that he can sleep through anything, so I don't even worry about talking while he's sleeping. I sit down across from Emily, and she just stares at me.

"She was here a few minutes ago," Emily says. She quirks her brow.

"Who?" I ask. I try to look like I have no idea what she is talking about.

She snorts. "Who do you think?"

I don't say anything. Emily pops the baby off her breast with a grimace and fixes her shirt. She does it all under a blanket, so it's not the least little bit weird. Then she hands Kit to me and throws a burp cloth over my shoulder.

"See if you can burp her," she says with a laugh.

"I just happen to be a master burper," I say to Kit. She squirms in my arms like a caterpillar trying to makes its way out of a cocoon. I put her gently on my shoulder and pat her on the back. "When are you going home?" I ask Emily.

"Tomorrow morning," she says.

"Everything okay?" I ask. Kit lets out the sweetest and loudest burp next to my ear, and it makes me laugh. "Good one. You sound like your daddy," I say to her as I lower her in my arms and cradle her close to me.

"Everything is fine." She jerks her thumb toward Logan. "I told him to go home and get some sleep, because we're not going to get much rest when she comes home. But he refused."

"He's smart," I say to Kit, making baby talk. "His mama taught him right from wrong," I say in a singsong voice, talking to the baby still.

"He sounded like Henry, telling me that he can't sleep without me. Without us." Henry is a dear old friend of ours whose wife died recently. He was the doorman in Emily's building when she came back to town, and he's part of all our lives now. Her eyes well with tears as she looks over at Kit. She swipes a hand beneath her nose.

"I'm so glad he found you," I say to Emily. I look directly into her eyes when I say it so that I won't confuse her. I want to be very clear. "You're the best thing that ever happened to him."

"He's the only one who ever accepted me exactly as I am."

"Hey!" I cry in playful protest. "We all accepted you."

She smiles softly. "The Reeds are a special bunch."

"You can blame that on our mom," I tell her.

The room goes silent for a minute, and I take in the beauty that is their daughter. She is asleep already, and she looks so peaceful. She's perfect. "How was Friday?" I finally ask in the silence.

Emily shrugs. "She's Friday."

"Is she coming home tonight?" I ask. I brush my hands along the silken down on top of Kit's head.

"Probably," she says.

I heave a sigh and pinch the skin at the bridge of my nose.

"Keep pushing her," she says.

I jerk my head up. That was the last thing I expected her to say. "What?"

"Keep pushing her," she says again. "She's got a lot of baggage. And you can't help her carry it until she's willing to present it to you. So, keep pushing."

"You know?" I ask.

She shakes her head. "I just know someone who's hiding. I did it myself. I can see the signs. She desperately wants someone to find her. And probably for someone to forgive her for whatever she did, so she can forgive herself." She shrugs. "I'm just guessing, of course. I could be completely wrong."

"I doubt it."

"Don't worry about being gentle. Just be yourself. You know what to say and do." She looks at me with a soft smile on her face.

"Did she talk to you?" I ask. I wince inwardly. I should be asking Friday all of these things.

"About being a surrogate?"

I nod.

"Yeah, we talked about it when she offered to do it."

Well, that surprises me. "I didn't realize you were that close."

"No one is close to Friday," she says. Then she looks directly into my eyes. "Except you."

I laugh, but there's humor in the sound. "I am about as far away from Friday as anyone can get. She's got so many fucking walls that I can't get a peep over them, much less get around them."

"Eventually, she'll open the door and let you walk in."

I look up when the literal door opens. Friday startles and looks at me. "I forgot my purse again," Friday says quietly. She points to a bag lying in the chair beside me. I didn't even see it there.

Emily pushes to her feet and goes to the bed, where she roughly shoves Logan. He jumps and grunts, his eyes flying open. That's exactly the same way I've woken him up since he lost his hearing. It's the only way to get his attention. "Come and take me for a walk," Emily tells him. He stands and stretches.

*Babysitters*, she signs at him.

He furrows his brow at her, and she just nods toward the door. "Oh," he says. "A walk." He looks toward Kit. "Are you sure she'll be all right?"

"I just fed her. Let's go." She takes his hand and leads him from the room. They let the door close behind them.

Friday reaches for her purse, but I stretch out and catch her hand in mine. "Please don't go," I say. "Please."

She nods, biting her lower lip between her teeth. "Okay," she breathes. She sits down beside me and fidgets. I lean over and place Kit in her arms and then press a kiss to her temple.

"Let me love you," I say softly. Then I sit back and I watch her as she arranges Kit in her lap so that she can look into the baby's face.

Silence sinks over the room like a wet, heavy blanket. "He was perfect," she says quietly. "He looked like me. He had dark-blue eyes and freckles and he wasn't but a minute old. Then I never got to see him again. Not close up. They took him from me, and I didn't even get to hold him."

"Where is he now?" My throat clogs so tight with emotion that I have to cough past it.

"He's with a wonderful family that adopted him when he was a day old." She finally looks up at me, and her eyes shimmer with tears. One drops down her cheek, and she doesn't brush it away. "They send me pictures every six months. He's beautiful. He plays baseball, and he loves trains."

"We all do what we have to do to survive," I say.

She snorts. I pass her a tissue because it almost comes out like a sob. "I was fifteen and completely alone." She unwraps Kit and counts her toes and fingers. "She's going to play guitar like her mom," she says. "Look at these fingers." Kit grips Friday's finger in her sleep, and Friday wraps her back up.

I don't say anything because I don't think she wants me to.

"His name is Jacob," she says. She smiles. "I have his footprints and his date of birth on my inner thigh. Pete did it for me."

Fucking Pete. He knew all this time and didn't tell me. "Little fucker," I grumble.

"Pete knows the value of a well-placed secret."

I'm glad she had someone to tell her secrets to. I hope someday, it'll be me. "I treasure your secrets. I'll hold them close to my heart and keep them between us and only us, always."

She smiles. "I know."

She takes a deep breath, and I feel like she's just relieved some of her burden.

"You've never seen him?"

"No. I'm allowed to. It was an open adoption. But I never have."

"Why not?"

"I'm afraid that if I ever get my hands on him I won't be able to let him go." Her voice breaks again. "Or worse—what if I see him and he hates me? I wouldn't be able to stand myself. It's hard enough knowing that he doesn't know who I am. If he hates me, too, I won't be able to take it."

"Thank you for telling me," I say softly.

"I should have told you sooner. I'm very sorry I didn't."

"You're it for me. You know that, right?" I blurt out.

The words hang there like a lit firecracker between us. I can see the fuse burning, and I'm just waiting for it to explode.

"I know you want me to be it. But I'm not sure that I am. I think you can do better."

"I disagree." No doubt about it.

"Can you give me some time?"

"How much?"

She shrugs. "I don't know. I guess I'll know when I know."

"I guess I'll know when you know." I chuckle. But my heart feels so much lighter. I meant to take her burden from her, but I know I didn't because I don't feel any heavier. If anything, I feel lighter, just knowing she shared with me.

The door opens, and Emily and Logan walk back into the room. Logan looks from Friday to me and back, and then he smiles and his chest bellows with air.

"What?" I ask.

"Dude, I'm just glad she didn't kill you. That's all." He makes a scratching like a cat motion with his hands and says, "Meow!"

She fucking kills me every time she turns those green eyes on me. But I'd die a thousand deaths just for one look from her. "Are you ready to go home?" I ask her.

She nods and hands Kit to Logan. He takes her, already looking like he's comfortable with Kit. He's her dad. I guess he should be. Logan kisses Friday's cheek, and I pull Emily to me and hug her. "Thank you," I say in her ear.

Emily chucks my shoulder and doesn't say anything.

We walk out, and I realize that I can't put Friday on the back of my bike because she's pregnant, so I don't even let her know it's there. I flag a cab and get in it with her. I'll get my bike tomorrow. I text Logan and tell him it's there if he needs to use it. He replies and tells me that he'll see to it.

I pull Friday into me, and she lays her face on my shirt. Her hot breaths trickle down my collar and make me feel all warm inside.

"Just give me some time," she says quietly against my chest.

I nod, and the bottom of my chin brushes the top of her head, so she's aware that I've responded. She takes a deep breath and settles into me.

When we get home, I really want to take her to my bed. I want to hold her and be sure she's all right. But she says good night to me at her door, and she closes it behind her. I stand there and feel peaceful just knowing she's safe in my house, close to me. And so are her memories.

# Friday

It has been two weeks since I came clean to Paul, and it's been two weeks since he's kissed me. He holds my hand all the time, so much that I sometimes wonder if I'm going to sprout roots and just be permanently attached to him. But he hasn't kissed me. Yes, we've cuddled on the couch, and I can feel his dick straining against his pants, straining against me, but he still doesn't kiss me. His lips haven't touched a single part of my body. Not even once. Not since I bared my soul to him.

Tonight, I need his help with something, and I'm afraid to ask him so I call Garrett, instead. "Do you think you could come over and help me?" I ask.

"What kind of thing do you need help with?" I can tell he's busy because there's noise and laughter in the background.

"I need to be painted."

I hear a door close and the noise vanishes. "Say that again," he says.

"I need to be painted. Do you remember that contest I told you about? My model dropped out, and I have this kick-ass design I've worked on for the past month. I don't want to miss out. It has a five-thousand-dollar prize."

"And you think I can paint you?" he scoffs. "I have no artistic ability whatsoever. I can't even do crafts. None of them. I'm bad at them all."

"It's just shading. I'll transfer the design onto my skin, and then you just paint like a paint-by-numbers kind of thing." I'm begging. But this design is seriously beastly, and I want to share it with the world. I can win. I know I can. "Don't worry," I plead. "I'm not even going to ask you to paint my boobs. I can do that part myself. I just need for you to do my back. Can you do it?"

"I can't," he says. "We're at an event for Cody's work."

"Oh." I let out a breath.

"Why don't you ask the stud muffin to do it? He's a fucking artist, Friday."

"He's also…like…boyfriend material." I feel heat creep up my cheeks.

"You mean he's, like, totally fuckable."

I laugh. "That, too." I walk out into the kitchen to get a bottle of water from the fridge. Paul is sitting on the couch so I whisper into the phone. "It's just too intimate for us right now."

"He's still withholding the goodies, huh?" Garrett laughs.

I grumble softly and glance at Paul, who gives me a what-the-fuck look. I can tell he's trying to hear what I'm talking about, but he's trying not to let me notice. And I desperately don't want him to hear me talk about him.

"Ask him," Garrett says. "Just do it."

"No."

"Why don't you ask a girlfriend?"

"I don't have any!" I cry. Well, I have a couple. But Reagan is busy and Emily just had a baby two weeks ago, so I can't ask her. My old college roommate, Lacy, is busy, too. I already tried her.

"Go ask him. Then call me later and tell me how it goes." He laughs, and then the line goes dead.

"Well, fuck you very much," I mumble at the phone. I'm incubating your fucking baby.

"What's wrong with you?" Paul asks. He turns the TV off and gets up. His long body gets even taller when he stretches his arms up over his head. I can see that little strip of skin below his T-shirt, and for the first time ever, I see that he has Kelly's name there.

"You have Kelly's name on your belly," I say, pointing like an idiot at his stomach. He tugs his shirt down and scowls at me.

"So what?" he asks.

"So, you have Kelly's name on your belly," I say again. I force myself to shrug. "That's all."

He narrows his eyes at me. "Mmm hmm," he hums. "Who was that on the phone?"

"Just Garrett," I say. Just fucking Garrett who can't help me out when I'm desperate. I take a sip of my water.

I don't know why it upsets me to know that Paul has Kelly's name inked on his skin. But it kind of does. I've seen him without his shirt on before, but I've never noticed it until now. She was and always will be a big part of his life because they have a daughter, but it still gets under my skin. I hate that it does, actually.

Paul jerks me from my thoughts when he asks, "And what did you ask Garrett to do for you? And why did he refuse? And why did he call me a stud muffin?" He grins and hitches a hip against counter.

"How did you hear all that?"

He shrugs. "Your volume was really loud." He stares at me for a minute. I'm pretending that I didn't hear him. He heaves a sigh and sings, "Fridaaaayy!" He waves his hands in the air wildly. "Earth to Friday."

"He calls you a stud muffin because you are one."

A dimple appears in his cheek. "Okay," he says. "And the rest?" he prompts when I don't say more. "What did you ask him to do?"

I look around the room. There's nothing I can use to distract him. "Is Hayley calling you?" I ask.

He rolls his eyes. "She's with her mom this week. But nice try."

He's not going to stop asking. "I asked him to help me with an art project," I say. I may as well have just spilled my guts out.

"What kind of art project?"

I shrug. "There's a contest going on at Bounce." Bounce is a local club, and all the Reed brothers have worked there at one point or another as bouncers, so I know he's familiar with the place.

"What kind of contest?" he asks.

"A paint contest?" I say. It comes out like a question, even though I didn't mean for it to.

"The fucking body paint contest?" Paul asks, and he slams his hand down on the counter. "Are you entering that?"

"I already entered. And I had a model for it, but then she backed out at the last minute. Her grandmother died or something. I don't know why her grandmother couldn't have waited until after the contest, but I guess I don't get any say-so."

He chuckles. "God, you make me laugh," he says.

I glare at him.

"So your model backed out and you were going to do what? Paint Garrett?"

"Umm, not exactly." I raise a finger to my lips and start to nibble the nail.

"Then what?" He throws up his hands.

"I was going to have him paint me." I look down the hallway. "Maybe Sam could do it. Is he here?" I start in that direction, but Paul grabs my arm and jerks me back. I fall against him.

"There is no fucking way any man, even Garrett, is going to paint your naked body. No. Absolutely not." He folds his arms across his broad chest and stares down at me like I've lost my mind.

"The entry fee was a hundred dollars and I spent a month working on the design. It's perfect, and I think I can win. And just when did you become my father?" I ask. I pull back from him.

"Trust me," he says. "The last thing I want to be is your father."

"Then stop acting like one."

He pulls me to him again, and I feel his dick pressed against my lower belly. "Trust me," he says again. "I don't feel like a parent when I'm with you."

"Oh," I breathe. My heart stutters, and I get this little flutter in my belly that only happens with him.

"Oh," he mocks. "I'm acting like a jealous boyfriend because I am one."

I close my eyes and say, "You haven't even kissed me since I told you about Jacob."

"You told me you needed time," he cries softly. "I've been right here waiting. Patiently, I might add." He chuckles.

"Well, quit being so patient!"

He brushes my hair back from my face with gentle fingers and doesn't say a word. He just stares at me, his eyes soft and full of something I don't understand. I wish I did. It would make this so much easier.

"So about this contest," he says.

"Reagan and Emily are both busy."

"There's no one else you can get to model?"

"There isn't enough time to teach them the position."

"Position?" He grins.

I shove his shoulder.

"I'll paint you." His eyes bore into mine. "I'll enjoy the hell out of it." His dimple grows deeper and even cuter.

"No." I shake my head. "You can't."

"Why not?"

"Because I'll be naked!" I cry.

"I know!" he yells back softly. "That's why I don't want anyone else doing it!"

# Paul

This is a really bad idea, and I know it before I ever step a foot into her bedroom. "Close the door behind you," she says. Her voice quivers, and I fucking love that she's this torn up over me painting her body.

"Nobody else is here," I remind her.

"Someone is always here, or on their way here, or thinking about coming here."

She's right, so I close the door. She has transfer sheets spread all over her bed. They're arranged in a weird pattern, and I can't quite make out what it is. "What are you going to be?" I ask.

She smiles and shakes her head. "You'll have to wait and see."

"What am I painting you with?" I ask, as she pulls her shirt over her head. My mouth falls open, but she just clutches her shirt to her chest and turns her back to me. She pulls her hair to the side.

"It's that really thick latex paint. It'll be like plastic when it's dry." She points to a sheet on the bed. "Let's start transferring."

This part I know how to do. She used the same transfer sheets we use for tattoos. So, I lay them on her body at her instruction, and then move on to the next one. I do her rib cage while she holds tightly to the shirt.

"Turn around," she says, making a rolling motion with her finger pointed down.

"Do I have to?" I pretend to sulk.

"Turn," she says again, more forcefully this time. I turn away from her and look toward her dresser. But she doesn't realize that I'm facing the mirror. She drops the shirt and lays the transfers over her breasts.

My mouth goes dry. I know I shouldn't watch her, but I can't fucking help it. She's perfect. Her breasts are big for her small frame but firm. Her nipples are hard and pointing directly out in front of her. Her areolas are as big as silver dollars and round and I want so badly to go to her and take one in my mouth. I want to hear her cry out.

She looks up, and I jerk my eyes from the mirror. "You can turn around now," she says. She lifts the shirt back to her chest. Such a shame. I swallow hard and try to push down the lust that's clouding my brain. She needs for me to paint her, not to fuck her.

Her brow furrows. "Are you okay?" she asks.

"Fine," I choke out. I clear my throat because my voice sounds gravelly. "Fine," I say again.

She shakes her head and turns her back to me. "All the spaces with a one in the center will be this fiery orange." She holds a tray of paint in her hand until she sets it on a stool right beside us. "Are you sure you have time for this? It's going to take a really long time."

"I can't think of anywhere I'd rather be." Friday is almost naked with me in her bedroom. I could stay here for days. I dip the brush and get it close to her back. It's almost a shame to cover up the phoenix tattoo. It's purple and gray and rising from the ashes. "Did you draw this tattoo?" I ask, as I start to swipe.

"Yes."

I keep painting. At least doing this, I get to explore all of her art. "It's pretty. And moving."

"It's me right after I met you," she says. Her voice is soft and curvy, just like her body. "Having a job and a family, even one that wasn't mine, made me stronger. I felt like I could finally carry on."

I explore the rest of her back as I paint all the ones. Then I move on to the two's, and they're purple. She smiles at me over her shoulder.

"You're doing great," she says.

"What's this one?" I ask. I point to a deck of cards with a clown on the front. There's a full house showing on the card faces.

"Life's a gamble."

"And this one?" I start to paint over her sailboat.

"Someday," she says quietly, "I'll sail into the sunset."

"There are wedding rings on the sail?"

"Yes."

"You want to be married."

"Yes."

My heart kicks in my chest.

"My back is my hopes and dreams. My front is my reality as I saw it at the time. Because I can face anything, as long as I let what happened to me push me forward."

Damn. I don't even know how to respond.

When her back is all covered, I scoot my chair to the side and she lifts her arm. "Just do the side. I can do the front."

I don't respond, because I'm not stopping.

She has a crashed sailboat on the front side of her belly. And right beside her pierced belly button is a deck of cards with a full house showing on the card faces. She had words like *faith*, *hope* and *charity* written on her back. And on her front, she has words like *loss* and a big *F* like you would see on a school paper. I don't comment on those because she's starting to squirm and I'm afraid she'll make me stop.

I hover over an empty bassinette. I look up at her and see that she has closed her eyes, so I paint over it.

"I can't figure out what we're drawing."

She grins. "I know. Isn't it great?"

I chuckle. "If you say so."

I paint up the side of her neck, where there's a turtle and skulls and other crazy shit that is so Friday.

When there's nothing left but her boobs, which are still covered by her shirt, she says, "My legs are going to be black."

"You're not walking out on the stage naked," I say. No way in hell.

"No, I'm wearing black bathing suit bottoms." She picks up a roller.

"Good." I'd hate to have to tie her to the bedpost. Well, actually, I'd love to tie her to the bedpost.

"I need to take my pants off," she says. Her face colors, and it's so damn pretty.

I set the paintbrush down and start to hum to myself as I reach for the button of her pants. She lets me, still clutching onto that shirt. She's wearing skimpy black bathing suit bottoms, and I whistle when I see them. She giggles, and the sound shoots straight to my heart. I shove her pants down, and she steps out of them.

I squat down in front of her, put one knee on the floor, and rest my elbow on the other. I look up and grin. "The view is nice from down here."

She grins and looks away.

She doesn't have a lot of art on her outer thighs except for a baby rattle that's encased in a spider web. It sweeps across her knee. I know what that one is about. I roll over it with black paint, and then cover all the way down to her toes. She giggles when I do the inside of her foot. "Ticklish?" I ask.

"Hypersensitive right now," she whispers.

"I need to get below your bottoms," I tell her, "in case they shift."

"Can you pull them down just a little?" she asks. "Not far."

I hook my thumbs in the hips of her bottoms and tug them down. She makes a whispery noise, and I look up to find her talking to herself. It sounds like she's saying, *Don't pass out, don't pass out, don't pass out*, but I can't be sure. I paint around her hips and her waistband and leave her bottoms turned down so it can dry for a minute. I lift her leg and rest her foot on my knee. I can see the inside of her thigh where her son's footprints are, along with his date of birth. I lean forward and kiss her there. I linger, taking in the sweet feel of her soft skin against my lips, and I stop to smell the overwhelming scent that's all Friday. Her leg starts to tremble so I roll it really quickly and lower it to the floor. I roll all the way up her thigh again, and then I look up at her and grin.

"Forgive me in advance for what I'm about to do," I say. I pull her bottoms to the side so I can swipe the brush up the crease of her thigh.

Holy Christ. She doesn't have a stitch of hair down there. Of course, I can only see the edge, but it's cleanly shaven, and I have to reach down and adjust my junk. I want to pull the suit back farther so I can look for her clit piercing, but I haven't been invited that far. Hell, I haven't been invited this far, either, but I'm here. Thank God, I'm here.

"You still okay?" she asks.

"Fine," I croak.

"Just checking, because your hand is shaking a little." Her voice trembles just about as much as my hand does.

"You're making me fucking crazy," I admit.

She sucks in a breath. "Sorry," she whispers.

"Don't be. It's a good kind of crazy." I grin up at her.

"I love those fucking dimples," she says. Then she presses her lips together like she said too much, which makes me grin even more.

"Don't say the word *love* around me yet," I warn playfully.

"Why not?"

"Because you make me hopeful," I say.

She steps back from me and looks down. "I think we're done," she says. She smiles at me.

"No, we're not."

I step toward her.

She takes a step back. "Yes, we are."

"No, we're not." I grab the edge of the shirt. "Drop the shirt," I say.

"I can do that part."

"I just spent two fucking hours painting your body, and you won't grant me the privilege of painting your boobs?" I ask, trying to look as dejected as possible. I lean close to her ear. "I just painted the left and right side of your pussy," I tell her. "I can paint your boobs." I tug the shirt, and she lets it drop. Her hands fall to her sides, and she closes her eyes.

"Go ahead," she says through clenched teeth.

I smile and start to paint. I work my way around her breasts until I get to the crest of the left one. I stop and roll her piercing in my fingers. Her breath hitches, and she looks down, her mouth falling open. She gasps out something I can't understand.

"We need to change these for something plastic," I tell her.

"On the dresser," she says. She closes her eyes and takes a deep breath.

"Can I do it?" I ask.

I do this all the time when I pierce people. Or when they need to take a piercing out for some reason. I replace the metal with something like fishing line that holds the piercing open until the metal can be put back in.

"You can do it," she says. She keeps her eyes closed, but she startles when I twist her piercing in my fingers, letting it roll again.

"That's not very nice," she says. But her eyes open and she watches me unscrew the end and pull the piercing free. I follow it with the plastic piece and secure it in place. I do the same on the other side, taking a minute to play with it. I can't help it. It's a fucking tit piercing. It begs to be played with.

When I'm done, I pick up my paintbrush and say, "Are you ready?"

She nods.

Then I let the paintbrush drag across her hard nipple. "Shit," she bites out.

"What?"

"We need to put the pasty things on."

"Not yet. I'm having fun."

"Paul," she protests, but there's no whine in her voice that's real. It's all pretend. Every little bit. I brush back and forth across her nipple. Her head falls forward, and then her mouth opens. She pants. God, she's going to make me come in my pants.

"I didn't expect them to be so big," I admit.

Her eyes fly open. "My boobs?"

I laugh. "No, I knew how big your boobs are. I've been staring at them for four years. I mean your nipples. They're big and perfect." I can see her pulse beating in her neck, as quick as my tattoo gun, almost.

I keep painting the one on the left and bend my head and slurp her right nipple between my lips. She cries out and reaches for the back of my head. "Careful," she whispers. "They're really sensitive right now. I didn't realize they'd hurt so much."

"I'm hurting you?" I ask around a mouthful of nipple.

"No, I mean, in general. Just being pregnant makes them hurt. What you're doing feels really good." I suckle her boob, plumping it in my palm. If I don't back up and get out of here, I'm going to disgrace myself. And her, too. "Really, really good," she whispers.

I stare up into her eyes. When I can't possibly take anymore, I drop her boob from my lips and paint around the edges and underneath, while I blow on the turgid peak to dry it. Her naked toes wiggle against the floor.

I step back from her, and she turns and puts pasties on, and then we paint over them. I'm glad she's not going to go out there with her nipples poking out. I wouldn't like the paint, either—you can see the curve of her boob—but it looks like she's wearing a latex body suit.

"I think we're done," she chirps. She turns to the mirror and raises her arms, spins around, and takes in the work. "You did a really good job."

I can't for the life of me figure out what she has designed, and I'm kind of curious what all the oranges and purples will form. "What is it?" I ask.

She grins. "I'm not telling."

She walks over to me and stands up on her tiptoes. She puckers her lips. I lean down and let her kiss me, and I fucking love that she initiated it. My heart soars.

"Thank you," she says.

"You're welcome."

"I need to do a few more things." She glances around the room like she's not sure what to do first.

"I'll wait for you in the living room." I open the door and go out it as quickly as I can. I stumble directly into Sam. "What the fuck?" I say. "How long have you been there?"

He throws up his hands. "I just walked in the door. I swear."

"You're sure?"

"Positive." He looks at Friday's door. "What were you doing? Do you need a condom?"

I shove him. "No, I don't need a condom."

He glances toward my lap. "You sure, 'cause…" He lets his voice trail off.

"Don't talk about her like that."

He grins. "Good."

"What's good?"

"You're protective." He nods his head. "I like it."

"So glad you approve."

I shove him out of my way, and he grumbles. I pay him no mind, though. Instead, I head into the bathroom. I strip down and turn the shower on the coldest setting. I step beneath the spray and let it wash over me. It's minutes before my dick softens. Minutes before the water becomes uncomfortable. Minutes before I can get the feel of her, the smell of her, and the taste of her off my mind.

But I don't want any of her gone. I want her here, every single day.

I get dressed and find her waiting in the living room. "Are you ready to go?" she asks. She's wearing a big button-down shirt and some oversized shorts. Her hair is loose around her shoulders, and she's made up softly. She's definitely wearing makeup because I can't see her freckles, but it's not the normal Friday get-up. It's different.

We get to Bounce with barely any time to spare. I see that Sam and Pete are already there when we arrive, and they're bouncing tonight. The band Fallen from Zero—the one Emily plays with sometimes—is on stage, and they finish their set. I have to say, they're not as good when Emily isn't with them.

They clear the stage, and the club's owner goes up to the microphone. I lean back against a speaker and watch. Painted people start to walk across the stage. Some are made up to look like they're wearing bikinis, and others are painted to look like they have on shirts. Some are superheroes and others are characters from books. No one is painted like Friday.

When it's her turn, I make my way to the front of the room. She walks out onto the stage, and the room goes quiet. The announcer says something about the paint, and she motions for him to wait. She sits down facing the wall, with her back to the audience. She puts one leg out to the side, and bends the other into a funny position. Then she bends her back, and her arm outstretches. And suddenly, I can see it. She's a butterfly.

She's a butterfly with a broken wing. The purples and oranges are the wings, and one is broken at an odd angle. She flutters her wings, and you can see the fucking art in the pose. The crowd goes crazy.

She's so fucking talented. She stands up and takes a bow, but the crowd is shouting for an encore. Hell, I want to see that beautiful art again, myself. This time, I drag myself out of my crazy stupor and snap a few pictures of her.

She wins, of course, and they hand her a check for five thousand dollars. She looks at me and grins, and then she jumps off the stage and straight into my arms. I squeeze her tightly. She had a wonderful moment, and then she looked for me at the end of it. My heart squeezes almost painfully in my chest as I hug her.

Someone passes her shirt to her, and I help her shrug into it. She's all smiles, and, I swear, she takes my breath away. My heart is fucking galloping in my chest. I can't stop it, and I don't want to.

She accepts congratulations, and she hands out business cards to people who want to be painted for the next competition.

All I can think about is getting her home so she can wash all that paint off her body. I wonder if she might let me help. There are a lot of places she can't reach. That'll be my excuse. But, in reality, I just want to love her. That's all. I just hope she'll let me.

# Friday

I can't wait to get Paul home. I want to get all this paint off and then shove him on the bed and ride him. My clit has been thumping ever since he painted me, and it's not getting any better. I'm glad I was wearing a black bathing suit, or people would have been able to see how wet I was.

We walk by Pete, who is checking ID's at the door. "Damn, did I miss it?" Pete asks.

Sam walks up beside him and holds up his phone. "Don't worry. I got pictures." He shakes the phone at Pete, and Pete grabs for it, but Paul gets to it first. He grimaces and talks quietly to himself while he does something to the phone. Paul gives it back and grins at him.

"What did you do?" Sam asks. He flips through his photos. "You big fucker," he cries. "You deleted my pictures!"

Paul keeps smiling and takes my hand. "You ready to go home?" he asks. His blue eyes are shining, and he winks at me. "I have a problem I need you to help me with," he adds quietly so only I can hear.

My heart thuds. I nod, and his eyes smolder.

He tugs my hand and doesn't say a word on the walk back home. I look up at him a few times, but he just keeps walking with his jaw clenched. Every now and then I see a tiny tic in it. "You're not mad at me are you?" I ask.

He looks down at me, startled. "Why would I be mad at you?"

"You're not talking to me and you're clenching your jaw."

He stares at me for a second. "I have a reason for not talking to you," he tells me quietly.

I stop walking. "Well, what is it?"

He looks down at me. "Every single thought in my head right now is about how much I want to fuck you. All I can think about is getting this paint off and then kissing my way down your body so I can taste that hood piercing of yours."

My clit thumps harder than ever. "Paul," I whisper.

"And then I want to take my time and play with those big old nipples." His thumb drags beneath my breast, right there in the middle of the crowded street, and my stomach jumps straight down to my toes.

"And then?" I ask.

"And I'm going to come in my pants right now if you make me keep talking about it." He pulls me against him and hugs me while he chuckles, then I feel him press a kiss to my forehead. "I want to throw you over my shoulder, but you're pregnant." He sets me back from him. "Wait!" he cries. "Can you even have an orgasm yet?" His eyes search mine.

I laugh. "I don't know," I say. I bite my fingernail and grin at him. "Depends on how good you are at getting me there."

He laughs and pulls me by the hand down the street. "I'll get you there."

I laugh and let him drag me. When we get to the apartment building, he holds the door open for me and slaps me on the ass after I go through it. I look back at him and start to race up the stairs. I think he's going to overtake me, and he nearly does, but only in time to open the next door for me. Then we go into the apartment and stop when someone walks through the kitchen.

"Em?" he says. He looks over and sees Logan sitting on the couch with the baby in a carrier at his feet. "Is everything okay?"

Emily looks from me to Paul and back again. "We just thought we'd come for a visit," she says.

I bite back my groan.

"A visit," Paul repeats.

I hit him in the shoulder. "They came for a visit. Aren't you glad?"

"Fuck, no, I'm not—" he starts, but I hit him in the stomach, and he clutches for it with a loud grunt.

"We're so glad you're here," I say, trying to sound excited. What I'm feeling is quite the opposite. I feel let down. I feel miserable. I feel like I will never, ever get to come again in my life.

"Shouldn't you be at home letting that baby sleep or something?" Paul asks. He stalks over to the couch, flops down across from Logan, and stuffs a pillow into his lap.

"That baby wakes up every two hours and can sleep just about anywhere," Logan tells him. He glances toward the pillow Paul shoved in his lap and raises his brow. He smirks. "Did we interrupt something?"

"No," I say.

Paul says, "Yes," at the same time.

Logan smirks and reaches for a can of nuts on the table. He puts his feet up and grins. "So, how was the contest?" he asks. He can barely chew around that smile.

"I won!" I cry, holding my arms up.

Logan and Emily both clap, but their little one startles in the car seat and lets out a cry.

"Uh oh," Logan says. "She's awake."

"Which means she'll want to eat," Emily says.

Logan picks her up and holds her until her face turns red and she's screaming. "She's definitely hungry," Logan says, holding their daughter out to Emily.

She reaches for her and turns to me. "Do you want to go in your room so I can feed her and we can talk? I still can't get used to the whole boob-out-in-public thing."

I look at Paul, who throws up his hands and then swipes a frustrated palm down his face. Logan chuckles.

"Actually," I say. "I need to soak this paint off. Can you talk to me from the bathtub?"

She nods, looking relieved that she won't have to feed her daughter in the living room. She gives me a minute to undress and climb in, and then she knocks. "Are you decent?" she asks.

"I'm in bubbles," I call back. I halfway pull the bath curtain so that only my head is exposed. "Bubbles that are quickly looking like black licorice."

She pokes her head in. "That's kind of gross," she says.

I rub a sponge over my body and let the water out, then refill the tub. This is going to be a multi-step process. It was a lot of paint.

Emily closes the lid of the toilet and sits down. Then she bares her breast, and the little one latches on to it with a smacking noise and a sigh.

"God, your boobs are huge!" I say. They are. Like fucking huge. Like melon sized but with a baby attached.

She laughs. "I know, right?" she says. "They're too big. Logan likes them, though." She smiles. "He keeps wanting to play with them." She grimaces. "But they hurt. I think I have enough milk to feed a small nation."

I agree; she could probably start her own dairy farm, but I'm afraid to say so.

"So, how is pregnancy treating you?" she asks. Kit sucks greedily at her breast, and my insides go all melty at how comfortable and secure they look together.

"I still wake up sick, but it's not too bad," I admit. "I can deal with it."

"Do you wish you hadn't done it, now that things are going the way they are with Paul?"

"No." Not for a minute. Garrett and Cody deserve a kid, and I am happy I get to help with that. "It kind of makes things different, but not bad."

Emily laughs. "I was horny as hell when I was pregnant."

"You and Logan went at it like rabbits from the beginning," I remind her.

"No," she protests. "He wouldn't even have sex with me until I told him my real name. And that was weeks later."

"You know what I meant." I roll my eyes.

The paint is coming off, so I change the water again. I hope Paul doesn't need a shower, too, because there's not going to be an ounce of hot water left.

"Speaking of Paul…" She grins. "Spill it."

"There's nothing to spill. We haven't done anything yet."

"Oh." She looks disappointed, and that makes me laugh.

"He painted my boobs for me today. He might be a boob man." I lower my chin and look at hers. "So, keep your humongous knockers out of his face."

"I could be the last woman on the planet and he wouldn't look at my humongous knockers," she tells me. "I know that much about him. It's a brother thing." She shrugs. "So, did we interrupt you guys when you came home? He looked like he wants to have you for dinner."

"It can wait. I had to get the paint off anyway. So, you're not delaying our fornication. Just our foreplay." I laugh.

Her face colors, but she laughs, too. "Well, good luck with that." She pops Kit off her left side and switches to the other. The baby pecks around until she latches on, and Emily sits back and takes a breath. "Logan is wearing me out," she admits quietly.

"What do you mean?" I stand up and start to actually soap myself now that most of the paint is gone.

"He's working really hard to make it easy for me, but I wish he'd just leave and go to work and let me try to do some of it. He holds her. He gets up for every feeding and sits with us. He changes all the diapers."

I stick my head out of the curtain. "Not necessarily a bad thing."

"It's like he thinks I can't do it. I'm capable. I'm strong. I'm not going to break." A tear tracks down her face. "Dammit." She swipes it away. "I can't stop crying lately."

"Pass me a towel," I say. I wrap it around myself and step out. "I think you have a really good thing going on," I tell her. "But you're tired and your hormones are going crazy and your tits are huge." I look at her boobs and shake my head, and she laughs. At least I can do that much for her; I can make her laugh. "It's going to get easier."

"I miss our intimacy," she admits. "It's like he's afraid to wrap around me because he doesn't want to wake me up when I do finally get to sleep."

"Did you tell him?"

"I don't want to complain. He's trying so hard."

"I'll take care of it," I say. I pat her shoulder and put a robe on. "Come with me while I get dressed, and then I'll give him a few pointers."

"No," she protests. But she gets up and follows me. "Let's talk about sex for a minute." She points to me. "Yours. Not mine."

I grin. "Okay." She follows me into the bedroom, and I shut the door behind us.

# Paul

Logan is such a little fucker. He looks at the pillow shoved in my lap and grins. "When are you going home?" I grouse.

He pops a nut in his mouth and talks around it. "Never." He smiles even bigger.

I throw the extra pillow at him. "Fuck you, asshole," I say. I jerk my thumb toward the bathroom. "Is Em okay? She looks stressed."

His head jerks around to look in that direction. "She does? I'll go get her." He gets up, so I flip the light to get his attention.

"Come back," I tell him. "Sit."

He flops down. I set my pillow to the side because Logan has effectively killed my hard-on. I have a feeling Friday can get it back, though. Just by looking at me, probably. "What's wrong?" I ask.

His chest fills with air as he sighs. "I try to help her. I try to do everything for her. But she doesn't seem to like it. I don't know what I'm doing wrong."

I wait for him to continue.

"And her boobs are like—" he makes a grasping motion in the air "—like huge. And I want to touch them, but she says they hurt, so I try to sleep on the other side of the bed when we do sleep. I miss her. I want to toss my leg over her naked ass and sleep wrapped around her."

"Her boobs probably do hurt." If I remember correctly from Kelly when she had Hayley, she said the same thing. But we didn't live together, so I didn't get immersed in it the way Logan is. "Rub her feet or something nice. Hell, pick anything else to rub."

His face lights up.

"Not that," I say with a laugh.

He waves a hand in the air like he's dismissing me. "That's not even the part I miss. I can do without that."

I snort.

"Don't get me wrong. I like that as much as the next guy, but I don't have to have it. It's her I have to have." He looks toward the bathroom, and we see Friday come out wearing a robe. I want to go with her. But Emily follows her into her room and they close the door. Damn. Cock blocked by the best friend and my brother. "You suck," I grouse at him.

He laughs. He nods toward Friday's room. "How's that going? Do I need to restock the condom drawer?"

"What do you think I'm going to do, get her more pregnant?"

He laughs, but it's a serious thing.

"We haven't done…that…yet," I say quietly. I can't believe I'm discussing this with my little brother.

"What the fuck are you waiting for?" he asks. He leans forward. I have all of his attention.

"I'm waiting for her to commit," I admit.

He sits back. "Oh," he says.

"I'm just not sure she's going to be here forever." I shrug. "That's all."

"I think you're right."

My gaze jerks up. I didn't expect him to agree with me. I expected him to reassure me. "What do you mean?"

"What are your intentions?" he asks.

"I want my fucking ring on her finger and my baby growing inside her." Damn, I just shocked myself. And I might have to pick Logan up off the floor. He chokes on a cashew.

He clears his throat and says, "Then you need to buy a fucking ring and get on one fucking knee."

"It's too soon." I look toward the bedroom to be sure the door is closed.

"If it's too soon for a ring, it's too soon to fuck her."

"Says the guy who got his girlfriend pregnant."

"But we didn't get married because we were lazy. It wasn't because we didn't want to be married. If Friday doesn't want to get married, then you need to reevaluate."

Logan is so succinct with his thoughts. I'm glad he dropped by, actually, because I was going to fuck Friday all night long. And let her fuck me. And then do it all over again.

"Bet you wish I'd stayed at home," he says.

I shake my head. "I'm actually glad you're here. Oh!" I interrupt myself. I pull my phone from my pocket. "If I show you a picture, can you look at the art of it and not at her body?"

A vee forms between his brows. "Whose body is it?"

"Friday's."

"Eww… Like I could look at her with lustful intentions." He pretends to gag and shivers dramatically.

"I want a tattoo that looks like this butterfly." I show him the picture, and he grins.

"Damn, she's good," he says. He keeps smiling. "Where do you want it?"

"That spot on my chest." I rub the place over my heart, which I know is bare.

He looks at me like I've lost my mind. "The one you've been saving?"

"Yeah." I scratch my head and wish he'd stop prying.

"Sure. I'll draw it up tonight." He sends the picture to himself.

"Can you ink it tomorrow?"

He nods. "You're sure, aren't you?" He grins.

A smile tips the corners of my lips. "Yes."

The door opens, and Friday comes out of her room. She's wearing a pair of baby-blue sleep shorts and a matching pajama top, and she looks so damn cute that I want to pull her into my lap. And then I want to take that outfit off her and suck on her titties until she squirms and begs me to fuck her.

Friday looks at Logan and signs something to him while Emily puts Kit into her car seat. I can't catch every word, but I think she just said something about cuddling. He shakes his head, and she argues with him in sign language. Suddenly, he grins and signs, *Thank you.*

*You're welcome*, she replies.

He hugs her and reaches for the car seat. "Thanks for letting us hang out," he says.

"Come back anytime," I reply. My voice is deadpan, but Logan can't hear the inflection, so I make sure to put on a sad face.

He laughs, and Emily hugs Friday.

The door closes behind them. "What did you tell him?" I ask Friday.

"I told him to strip her naked and throw his leg across her butt and sleep cuddled up with her like he used to because she misses it."

"Shut the fuck up," I breathe. "He just said the same thing to me."

She shrugs. "They're so busy, they're not talking to one another." She walks up to me and stands up on tiptoe to put her arms around my neck. "You ready for bed?"

I kiss her, and I rethink my decision to wait. It's hard with her pressed up against me. I set her back from me. "I...um...need to actually go to bed." I scratch my head.

She steps back, her face falling. "Oh. Okay."

"I'll...uh...I'll see you tomorrow."

She doesn't say anything and goes to her room. She slams the door behind her. I stand outside her door for much longer than I should. I want to go in. I want to open the door. Just as I start to walk away, I hear a noise from her room. It's a low vibration, and I press my ear to the door.

Suddenly, it hits me. She's getting off with a fucking vibrator. I pace back and forth up the hallway, smacking myself in the head with the heel of my hand. Stupid, stupid, stupid fucker.

It goes on for about two minutes, and I can't stand it anymore.

I open her door and go to the side of her bed. "Move over," I say.

The vibrator turns off. "Fuck," she breathes.

"Move over now," I say again.

"Fuck you."

"Fuck you. Now *move over*."

She doesn't move, so pick her up and shift her over. I get in beside her and reach for her hand, where I find a warm vibrator. It's hot because she was using it. And it was touching her. I raise it to my lips and lick across it, and she tastes as good as I thought she would. Like spice and heat and Friday.

I push my body between her thighs and slide down. She protests and grabs my hair, trying to pull me back up.

"Stop it," I say. I take her hands and pin them together in one of mine and rest them on her belly. She could easily pull free. But she doesn't.

I touch the vibrator to her pussy and keep pressing and searching until I find her slick hole. I slide it inside to get it wet and then move up, looking for her clit. She stops moving, and a noise escapes her throat when I find it. "Right there," she breathes. I turn it on, and she moans.

"Be still," I say, but her hips arch and press against my touch. She rocks against the vibrator, and her legs shake ever so slightly.

"You didn't want me," she says. "Why are you doing this?"

"I want you. I just can't have you yet. I need to fucking marry you first. So you can't run away from me."

She lifts her head to look down at me. I can see her face from the light in the window. "No fucking way."

"Yes fucking way." I press the vibrator against her and find a rhythm with it, and she starts to tremble. "I fucking love you, Friday. Let me fucking love you."

I don't give her time to think. I don't want her to think. Not about this. She cries out when she comes, and her body trembles and shakes. I let her hands go free, and she sinks one into my hair, gently tugging as the orgasm quakes through her body. Again and again, she jerks until she stills and pushes the vibrator away.

"That was the worst proposal ever," she says when she can finally breathe.

"I know. I'll do it again tomorrow." I toss the covers over both of us and reach for her.

She shoves me away. "Get the fuck out of my bed, Paul," she says.

"No fucking way. I make you come, I get to sleep in your bed."

"Get out, Paul," she says. But there's no heat in her voice. None at all.

"I'm staying." I pull her against me. She's wearing that pajama top and nothing on the bottom, so I pull the top over her head. She's naked in my arms, and she feels so fucking good. I snuggle closer so that my thighs cradle her bottom. I cup her breast in my hand, just because I can't get close enough to her, and she lays her head on my arm. I brush her hair down between us. "Let me sleep with you."

"Okay," she says quietly. She yawns, and I feel her warm breath on the inside of my elbow. Within seconds, the woman I love is asleep in my arms. And my dick is so hard it'll probably never go soft again.

# Friday

I wake up sweating, stuck against a man. I haven't been stuck like this to a member of the opposite sex in years, and it feels kind of foreign. Then the thoughts of yesterday seep back into my brain.

He painted my naked body.

He got all intimate with my nipples.

He supported my art project with lustful eyes.

He let me jump into his arms and pretty much promised me he was going to do amazing things to me last night.

He didn't kiss me back when I threw my arms around his neck.

He told me he didn't want to sleep with me.

He went to bed.

But he didn't go to bed.

He listened outside my door and heard my vibrator.

Then he took it from me and fucking made me come.

He told me he loved me.

Then he went to sleep.

In my bed.

With me in it.

Wrapped around me like he wanted to be with me for the rest of his life.

Did he mention marriage?

Oh, holy hell. He did mention marriage.

I roll over slowly, trying not to wake him. He's sleeping on his side, facing me, but his blond eyelashes flutter. I freeze, my nose a mere inch from his, and try to will him back to sleep. I want to look at him. I want to study his crooked nose up close. I think he got that hump when he broke it fighting with someone in the shop. They said something crude to Pete and Paul went after them. Not *him*. *Them*. He didn't think twice. He protects his family with everything he has.

He has blond beard stubble on his cheeks. I wonder if he shaves every day. He's always so fresh faced. His lip is pierced and so is his eyebrow. I look down and study the barbells that are in his nipples. Each one has a bulky bead on the end of it. One is an *R* and one is an *H*. Probably for *Reed* and *Hayley*? I'm not sure, and I don't know him well enough to ask.

Yes, I've known him for four years, but I had to set myself apart from them a little because no matter how much I wanted to be, I wasn't part of their family. I was just an employee. I couldn't get too comfortable because when I get comfortable, people leave. They let me down, every single time.

I lift my knee and brush against Paul's erection. Whoa. He was hard when I went to sleep last night. I know he was because I could feel it. He's wearing only boxers right now. He must have gotten up during the night to take his jeans and shirt off because I distinctly remember the feel of his clothing against my inner thighs when he was *down there*.

Still trying not to wake him, I pull the elastic of his boxers away from his stomach and look down.

Damn.

That man is way bigger than I would have even imagined. At the head, he has a piercing with a jewel in the center. It's a Prince Albert piercing. It makes me wonder who did it for him because I know I didn't. I don't like the idea of anyone else getting intimate with his dick. Hopefully, it was a guy who pierced him. But I highly doubt it.

His hips arch toward my hand. My eyes jerk back up to his face, and I see that he's still asleep.

I wrap my hand around him and give him a gentle squeeze. His dick pulses like it likes being petted. The purple tip calls to me so I scoot down in the bed and touch my tongue to the bead of pre-come that has beaded on the slit. I pull back. He tastes salty and clean.

I want more.

I bend lower and grab his dick at the base, then take the head into my mouth and close my lips around it. A flash of salty spray hits the back of my tongue as he pulses delicately. A breath escapes his lips, and I look up to find his mouth open and his eyes squeezed shut.

I take a little more of him, and he rolls to his back. His eyes fly open, and he lifts his head to look down at me, but I close my eyes and take him all the way to the back of my throat.

"Friday," he says softly, his voice rough, his tone nasally from sleep. "Stop."

I shake my head, and his dick moves back and forth in my mouth. He groans and threads his fingers in my hair. I suck harder. His dick is so hard I can barely pull it back from his stomach, so I get closer and take him deeper, shuttling my hand up the base. There's way too much of him for me to take him completely into my mouth.

"Friday, please stop," he says. He sounds like he's struggling, and I look up to find that he's watching me. "If you don't stop, I'm going to come in your mouth." He tugs on my hair, and I wince, but I don't stop. "Friday," he says a little louder. "Pull back."

I shake my head again and lock my mouth around his dick. I'm not popping off. I don't care if he gets up and moves; I'm going with him.

But he's not moving. He stays. He stares down at me. His blue eyes are intense and so fucking hot that I never want him to look away from me. "Please pull back," he whispers.

I say "no," but it comes out more as a mumble because I don't want to break suction. I can taste more of him now, and his salty essence tickles my tongue.

"Take it, then," he finally growls. Then he holds my head in place with his fingers tangled in my hair and pushes into my mouth. He groans, and his dick pulses, and he comes so much that it runs out the corners of my mouth because I can't swallow fast enough. "Take it," he says again, and he thrusts over and over, until he's done. "Take all of it," he whispers. I do. I suck him clean, and finally, he jerks away. "Enough," he says quietly. "Too sensitive."

I laugh. He wipes the corners of my mouth and pulls me up to lie on his chest. I turn so that my face is over his heart and listen to the beat of the blood racing in his veins. It slows, and he grows quiet, his hands swiping up and down my naked back. It's more fingertips than hands, and it tickles in the best of ways.

"I wish you hadn't done that," he finally says.

I turn so that my chin pokes into his chest. "Why?"

"Because every time I look at that pretty mouth of yours, I'll see you with your lips wrapped around my dick and my come leaking out the corners." He slaps me on the ass. "I won't be able to get you off my mind." He's quiet for a minute. "You didn't have to do that."

"I don't do anything I have to do," I remind him. It's true. I pretty much do what I want when I want. It's one of the benefits of being single and alone. One of the only benefits. "*Don't let me come in your mouth* is a stupid complaint for you to have, to be honest." I laugh against his chest.

A chuckle rumbles through him. "It's been a really long time."

"How long?"

"Months."

I snort. "Like you didn't use a little hand action."

He scoffs. "Men don't do that." He pauses. "But once or twice a day." I look up and find him grinning down at me.

He's silent for a moment.

Then he blurts out, "This doesn't change anything."

"What doesn't?"

"You ambushed me by taking my dick in your mouth while I was sleeping, but this doesn't diminish what we have. I'm still going to marry you. I'm not going to let you get out of it."

I sit up. "I don't think I said yes."

His gaze drops to my boobs, and he licks his lips. "You will."

I shake my head.

He sits up and cups the side of my face. "You don't want to be married or you don't want to be married to me?"

"It's not—" I stop. I don't know how to say what I want to say. "It's not you."

He tosses the covers back. "Oh, don't give me the it's-not-you speech." He mocks a female voice. "It's not you, it's me. I need some time to work on me right now. I need to focus on myself. I need you to get the fuck out of my life." His voice goes back to normal. "If that's how you feel, you should just say it."

"Don't put words in my mouth." I scramble naked across the bed trying to catch up with him, but he's already at the door. He closes it behind him. I lay my head against it.

The door opens a minute later, and his arm slides in. He's holding a can of ginger ale and a pack of crackers. "Eat and drink these quickly so you won't spend the morning puking."

"Are you still mad at me?" I ask as I take them from his hand.

"Yes." The door closes. Bile rises up my throat, so I take a quick sip of the ginger ale. This is usually how it goes in the morning as soon as my feet hit the floor. But the drink actually makes me feel better. Go figure.

I sit on the edge of the bed and fall back, eating a cracker and trying to be still for a few minutes.

The door opens again and only his voice comes in. "Glad it worked." The door shuts with a *click*.

I grin. I can't help it. He's taking care of me even though he's mad at me. And that scares me even more than it would if he ignored me and treated me like every other man in the world. Like I don't exist.

# Paul

Fuck, fuck, fuck, fuck. I shouldn't have let her do that. I had been lying there for an hour watching her sleep. She sleeps with her mouth closed, and she fidgets even when she's out cold. Maybe that was because I was in bed with her and that's new for her, but I'm not sure. Or maybe she's just always unsettled and fretful. That actually sounds more like her.

I closed my eyes when she opened hers and pretended to be asleep. But I could feel her eyes on my chest just like they were her hands touching me. And when she lifted the waistband of my boxers, I didn't want to stop her fingers from roaming. Maybe that makes me a bad person. Or maybe that makes me a really horny guy. Or maybe it means I'm in fucking love with her and want her hands all over me.

And when she closed her mouth around me, I couldn't stop her. I couldn't even try. Sure, I told her to pull back, but never, not once, did I really want her to. I didn't. I wouldn't. I needed her.

But.

But.

But.

Me getting off shouldn't be high on my priority list because it will mean nothing to her tomorrow that she swallowed for me. It won't cement her to me. It won't. I know it won't.

Fuck, fuck, fuck, fuck.

I shower, get dressed, and quickly, before she even comes out of her room, leave to go to work. Logan is going to meet me there at nine to put the tattoo over my heart. Her tattoo. The broken butterfly. My broken butterfly. I'm going to brand myself with something that is all Friday.

Logan is already there when I arrive, and he has already set up his station. He's even wearing gloves and has his machine prepped. He motions toward the chair, so I pull my shirt over my head and take a seat. Logan shaves the area really quickly.

"Did you forget how to talk?" I ask him. He has an excuse not to use his hands, but he can use his voice. Unless he doesn't want to.

"I was thinking," he says, and he transfers his stencil onto my chest.

"Thinking about what?"

He shakes his head. "Did you want to see it before I start?" He waits with his gun poised over my chest.

I shake my head and get still. If Logan drew it, it's fucking perfect. I have no doubts about that.

Logan watches what he's doing closely, so he can't look at my lips to see what I'm saying. I sit quietly with my eyes closed until he's done. Sometimes being with Logan makes me feel quiet and peaceful inside. But there's something on his mind, and I want to know what it is.

He's finished and lifting his gun away from my skin when Friday walks into the shop. She's all decked out in her retro gear, and she's wearing four-inch-high heels with laces that wrap around her naked legs. They stop with fat bows on the backs of her thighs. If I can see her bows, her dress is too fucking short. She's wearing bright-red lipstick and heavy eyeliner, and she's so fucking pretty. No. She's fucking hot. Smoking.

Logan preps my new tattoo for wrapping. "Do you want to see it?" he asks, holding a piece of plastic up.

"No, just cover it," I tell him.

He puts the wrap on and affixes tape, and I pull my shirt over my head. I am dying to see it, but I want to keep Friday from seeing it for now. I'm sold on her, but she's not so much on me. I don't know how she'll take it.

I go into my office and pull out a piece of paper. On it, I draw little hearts around the edges, because I know she likes them. Then in big block letters I write:

WANTED: WIFE
TERMS NEGOTIABLE
ONLY BEAUTIFUL LITTLE
BOMBSHELLS NEED APPLY
PREFERABLY ONES NAMED FRIDAY

I tack it to the bulletin board and go to my office to wait for her to find it.

A knock sounds on my door, and Logan sticks his head in. "What did you think of it?" he asks.

"Close the door," I reply.

He closes it behind him and leans against it. I go to the mirror and lift my shirt, and then peel back the plastic. He reads my lips in the mirror. "It's fucking beautiful," I say. "You changed it?" I look over at him and he shrugs.

"It needed changing."

I don't understand. "Why?" It was her. She's the butterfly.

"She's not broken," he says. "So that didn't fit her."

I scoff. "Okay."

"That's why she's pushing you away, you idiot," he says.

I don't understand, so I throw up my hands and wait.

"You see her as this broken little thing that needs you to take care of her. She doesn't need that. She might have been broken at one time, but she's not fucking broken now. She's put it all back together. She's made a life for herself, and you're trying to change it. It's kind of like she's built this fortress around herself, brick by fucking brick, and you might think a fortress is too much, but it's not. Do you know why?"

I can only sit and stare at him.

"Do you want to know why?" he asks.

I nod. My heart is in my fucking throat.

"Because she fucking lives there, Paul. It's home for her. It's safe and it's secure and it's hers. And she built it with her own two hands. So for you to swoop in and not only try to move her out of her fortress but also to tear it down, you're fucking up everything she's worked for. And that's why she's rejecting you. It's not because she doesn't love you, because I believe she does. It's because you need her to change for you, and she's too smart for that."

I cough into my fist because words won't come to me.

"Do you understand, now?" he asks. When he came in, he was all protective and confrontational, but now he's softening, and he's looking at me with those blue eyes that look so much like our mother's.

"I get it," I say.

He walks toward me and slaps me in the forehead. "You dumb fucker," he says. But he laughs and pulls me against his chest and pats my back. He sets me back and looks into my eyes. "Now figure out what you need to do."

Suddenly, my door flies open, and Friday walks in. She slams the fake advertisement I'd made down on my desk, her palm flat as it strikes the wood. I jump. I can't help it. There's no one else in the world who can do this to me.

"What the fuck is this?" she bites out.

Logan steps around her and closes the door on his way out.

I sit back and rest my elbows on the arms of my chair. I want to reach for her, but I know that would get me nowhere. Instead, I slide the paper from under her hand and tear it slowly into two pieces. I let it fall into the wastebasket.

She steps back and puts her hand over her heart. "Why did you do that?" she whispers. "I liked it."

My heart leaps. "It wasn't the right thing to do," I tell her.

"Why not?" she asks.

I scrub a hand down my face. "Will you let me move into your fortress with you?" I blurt out.

Her brow furrows, and she looks so damn cute that I want to kiss her, but I know I can't.

"What?" she breathes out.

I get up and walk to her. "That fortress where you reside? Will you let me live there with you?"

"What the fuck are you talking about?" she asks. She puts her hands on her hips and glares at me.

"I don't want to blow all your walls to bits," I say. She has a piece of hair stuck to her lips, so I pull it away and tuck it behind her ear. "I just want to live inside them with you. Fuck," I say, throwing up my hands. "I fucking love your walls. Every single brick. But let me move in. Let me be there with you. Then you can find out if you love me, and you can invite me to stay if you find out that you do. Just let me inside."

I take a deep breath and watch her.

"Did you hit your fucking head on the way to work?" she asks.

I laugh and rub my forehead. "No, but Logan just slapped some sense into me."

"Then what the fuck is wrong with you?"

"I'm in fucking love with you, Friday!" I cry. "I fucking love you, you irritating, obnoxious, sexy-ass woman that I can't get out of my fucking head." I hit myself in the head with my fists like I'm knocking. "I'm in love with you."

I drop down onto my knees in front of her, and she steps back, so I inch forward until I can pull her belly to touch my forehead. "I'm in love with you." I look up at her. "I'm on my knees, and I'm not going to try to get you to marry me or make you do anything you don't want to do. Just let me in, and I'll be happy with it."

"So, you don't want to talk me into marrying you?"

I shake my head, staring up at her like a puppy.

"You're not going to hold it over my head and refuse intimacy until I cave to what you want?"

"No."

"You're not going to keep asking me again and again?"

"No."

"You're going to stop being stupid?"

I grin. "I don't know about that one."

"You have testicles," she says, and she shrugs. "I can't have it all, can I?" She sinks down onto her knees in front of me. She bites her lower lip and stares at me.

"Say it," I coax.

She goes back to glaring at me. "Say what?"

"Whatever you're thinking."

"I'm thinking that my knees are uncomfortable on this fucking floor, and I'm wondering how long you're going to fucking make me stay down here."

I laugh. God, she's so contrary!

She takes my face in her hands. "Tonight, can I make you dinner?" she asks.

My heart does that pitter-patter thing again. "Like a date?"

She rocks her head back and forth like she's weighing her words. "I guess you could call it a date."

"Then yes, I'd love that." Then I remember. "But I have Hayley tonight."

She brightens. "Good." She kisses me quickly and grins. "Because that's about as close to a threesome as you'll ever get with me." She points to the floor. "Can I get up now?" she asks.

"Get the fuck up," I growl. I get to my feet, too. She falls against me and wraps her arms around my waist.

"So does this mean that you don't want to marry me?" she asks, her voice muffled against my chest. Her words touch the tattoo I just got, and it stings a little. But I don't pull back. I don't want her to see it yet.

"I didn't say that."

"You didn't say the opposite."

I set her back a little and look down into her upturned face. "Are you telling me you do want to marry me?"

She shakes her head and jabs a finger at me. "But I want to leave the door open."

Oh, holy hell. She's opening a fucking door and I didn't even have to threaten her or withhold anything or torment her in any way. I might pass out.

"Okay," I say.

"And Paul," she says. "Don't ever do that on-your-knees thing again unless you're down there licking my pussy because it weirds me the fuck out."

A grin tugs at my lips, even though I want to look fierce. Finally, I have to toss my head back and laugh.

She squeezes me one last time and walks back into the work area. I see Logan reach up and high-five her.

"What was that for?" she asks.

Logan grins. "I got cuddled last night."

"Because I rock," she says, and she high-fives him again. He grins at me at the back of the shop and shakes his head.

He jerks his thumb toward her and signs to me, *She's a good one.*

*I saw that!* Friday signs dramatically at him.

*I meant for you to!* he signs back with just as much force.

# Friday

I like bustling around Paul's kitchen. And I like it even more when he walks up behind me and wraps his arms around me while I'm standing at the stove. He pretends like he's going to try to steal a piece of chicken from the pasta, but he presses his lips to my shoulder and lingers, his hot breath blowing across my neck. I reach up and wrap my hand around his neck and bring him down so I can kiss him. Then he pops the chicken into his mouth and grins.

"That's pretty good," he says, nodding.

I roll my eyes. "Glad you like my chicken."

"Oh, I wasn't talking about the chicken," he says, letting his eyes roam up and down my body. My nipples go hard, and my heartbeat thrums.

The door opens, and he doesn't spring away from me. He stands beside me like he belongs there. Hayley comes running in the door wearing a pink tutu and ballet slippers with some awesome pink tights. She launches herself into Paul's arms, and he dances around the kitchen with her. I love watching him like this.

Kelly comes in last, and she looks a little harried as she blows hair out of her eyes. "I'm in a big hurry," she says, throwing Hayley's bag down. Her gaze meets mine, and she smiles. "Oh, hi, Friday," she says. "I didn't know you'd be here."

Paul talks around another piece of chicken that he stole. "She lives here," he says. "Like my girlfriend." He winks at me. "All the time."

My face goes hot. A cloud passes over Kelly's face, and she turns and smiles at me again. I can tell she doesn't want to, but she does try. "So happy for you," she says. She motions Hayley forward, and she gives her a quick hug. Suddenly, she stands up and puts her hand on Hayley's head, petting her like she's a dog. "Someone got in trouble at ballet for dropping the f-bomb," she says.

Paul's face falls. He looks over the counter and into his daughter's face. "You dropped an f-bomb?"

Hayley looks up into Kelly's face, her brows furrowed. "I didn't drop a bomb. I just called the teacher a fu—"

Kelly slaps a hand over her mouth. "You don't need to repeat it. We get the idea." She looks at Paul. "Talk to her?"

"We'll talk about it," he assures her.

"Oh, and she has a recital next week!" She rushes out the door.

"I'll be there," Paul says to her back. The door closes, and Paul sits down on his haunches in front of Hayley. "What did we say about that word?"

She hangs her head and goes into her room. She comes back with a quarter and holds it up. Paul takes it and puts it in a jar on top of the fridge. I give him a crazy look.

"The swear jar," he whispers. "Every time she says a bad word, she has to put in a quarter. And if she catches me saying a bad word, I have to put in a quarter." I see a ten-dollar bill in there. He laughs. "Sam paid in advance."

"I'm going to go broke," I say. I do watch my mouth around Hayley, although that's really the only time I even think about what a potty mouth I have.

"Probably." He laughs and sets the table. Hayley climbs in a chair, and he fixes a plate for her. We all sit down and have a really nice meal, and Hayley chatters with him about her week. I watch the two of them together, and my heart twitches and my insides do that melty thing they do when I'm moved by the awesomeness that is Paul and Hayley

"You okay?" he asks after we clear the table and put the dishes in the dishwasher. Hayley runs to play in her room for a few minutes, and we move to the couch. He sinks down beside me and drapes his arm around my shoulders. It's nice, so I lean into him.

"I'm great." We sit silently for a little while, and then I have a thought. "Can I show you something?" I wince to myself because I am not sure what he'll do with this situation.

"You can show me anything you want after Hayley's in bed," he says quietly. My tummy drops toward my toes. He kisses the tip of my nose.

"No, it's not that," I say. Although I plan on showing him some of that later, too. Now that he's not going to hold his love hostage, I'm ready to take him inside me. And I think he's ready to be taken. "It's something else. Are you up for it?"

He nods, looking at me curiously.

I go to my room and reach onto my shelf, taking down a small shoebox. My hands tremble as I lower it. I'm afraid. I'm terribly afraid. But I take it down, tuck it under my arm, take a deep breath, and go back out to the living room. I sit down next to him, and he eyes the box with a worried expression.

"What's this?" he asks, sitting forward.

I remove the top off the box and take out a pile of pictures. I hand him one. "This is Jacob," I say. My eyes fill with tears, and I don't even try to blink them back. I let them fall over my lashes and onto my cheeks. Paul brushes them away, but I really don't want him to. I want to feel all of this because I have forced myself not to feel it for so very long.

"This is when he was born." I point to the squirmy little ball of red skin and dark hair. Paul looks from me to it.

"He looks like you," he says.

I shake my head. "He looks more like his dad, I think." These fucking tears keep falling. I'm not crying. It's like someone opened an emotional dam in me and I can't get it to close. I don't want it to.

"What happened to his dad?" Paul asks.

"He died," I say. I have to stop and clear my throat. "Drug overdose a few years after Jacob was born. I read about it in the paper."

"I'm so sorry."

I sniff. "I am, too." I feel like I need to explain, and for the first time ever, I want to. "We were young, and we played around with marijuana and stuff. But I cut it all out when I found out I was pregnant with Jacob. He didn't. He wasn't able. It was really sad when I couldn't be with him anymore. I didn't have anyone else. But I didn't really have him, either. The drugs had him, you know?"

He nods. I hand him more pictures, and he flips through them. I have looked at them so much that they're dog-eared in places. He holds one up from when Jacob was about three. "You can't tell me he doesn't look like you. Look at those eyes! He's so handsome."

My eyes fill with tears again, but I smile through them. He *is* perfect. And I should be able to hear someone say so.

"Look at that smirk!" Paul cries when he sees the most recent one. "That is so you!"

I grin. I guess he's right.

"Where is your family, Friday?" he asks.

"I don't know," I tell him. I lay my head on his shoulder and watch as he takes in the photos over and over, poring through the stack so he can point out ways that Jacob looks like me. "They kicked me out when I got pregnant. Terminated their rights."

Paul presses his lips to my forehead and doesn't say anything.

"I thought I knew everything back then." I laugh and wipe my eyes with the hem of my dress. "Turns out I didn't know shit."

"Do you ever think about looking for them?"

I shake my head. "No. Never." I point to special pictures of my son. "His mom—her name is Jill—she sometimes sends me special milestone pictures. This is his first tooth he got and the first tooth he lost. And this one is from his first step. That wasn't even part of the agreement. She just does it because she wants me to know how he's doing." I try to grin through the tears. "He's doing so great. He's smart. And they can send him to college and to special schools. He takes piano, and he plays sports. And Jill says he likes to paint." My voice cracks, and I don't hate that it does. I just let it.

"Of course, he does. You're his mother."

"I just wanted to do what was best for him, you know?" This time, I use Paul's sleeve to wipe my eyes. I blink hard trying to clear my vision.

"That's what parents do. We do what's in the best interest of our children." He kisses me softly. "Thank you for showing me these."

"Thank you for looking at them." I reach into the box and pull out the letters. "She writes me these long letters. Do you want to read them?"

He looks surprised. "Do you want me to read them?"

I nod. "If you want to." My heart is aching so fucking much right now, and I feel like I'm hanging out there on a tightrope, just waiting for a stiff wind to send me careening into a ravine full of vipers and alligators.

"I want to."

He grabs my tightrope and steadies it, like I need him to do, with just a few simple words. *I want to.* "I'm going to go play with Hayley," I say.

I get up and go to Hayley's room, and as I turn the corner, I can hear the first envelope crinkle. I have read them a million times. I know every word by heart.

I don't know why I wanted to share them with him, except for the fact that he loves me. And since he loves me, I want to let him inside. He promised not to tear down my walls, but he wants to come inside with me. And since he does, I'm going to let him.

His voice calls me back. "Friday!" he yells. He looks at one of the envelopes.

"What?" I ask, turning back to face him.

"Your real name is-"

"Don't say it!" I cry. "I never want to hear that name again." That person no longer exists.

He grins at me. "I'm just honored that I get to know the person you were." His face softens. "And the person you are."

I shake my head and flip him off. I can hear his laughter all the way down the hall.

"Hey, Hayley," I say as I sit down and pick up one of her action figures. She has Barbies, too, but she would rather play with her Legos and building blocks. Maybe she'll be an engineer one day. Or maybe she'll be an amazing tattoo artist like her dad. I make her action figure kiss her Barbie, and she giggles. "I think they're in love," I whisper.

"Like you and my daddy," she says back quietly.

I nod. And emotion clogs my throat again. I turn my head and cough, and then I dump a box of Legos on the floor. "I think Barbie needs a fortress," I say.

She nods, and we start to build a plastic fortress together, because sometimes a girl just needs a fucking fortress.

# Paul

I'm surprised to find that two hours have passed when I finally close the lid of Friday's box of secrets and push it to the side. I rock my head back and forth and crack my neck, stretching because I have been sitting in one place for way too long. But once I started reading, I just couldn't stop.

Jacob's adoptive mother, Jill, had poured her heart out on the pages in more than one letter. There was no doubt about it: she wanted Friday to be a part of her son's life. If she didn't, she wouldn't have reached out to her with the heartfelt emotion that she did.

Jill had been married for ten years when she and her husband adopted Jacob. He was their first and only child. For years, Jill frantically reached out to Friday, begging her to come visit with Jacob. She wants Friday to meet him. She made no mistake at all in the words. Jill is his mother and she always will be, but she firmly believes that Friday can have a place in his life, too. I happen to agree with her.

I get up and go to check on Friday and Hayley, but I stumble to a stop when I turn the corner into Hayley's room. They're both asleep on the bed on their stomachs with an open book in front of them. Friday has changed into her pajamas and it looks as though she was reading to Hayley when they both fell asleep. But what kills me is that their noses are turned toward one another, so close they're sharing breaths, and my daughter's hand is tucked into Friday's.

I take a mental picture, because I never, ever want to forget what this feels like. Click! Click! Click! I cement it in my head, because my heart is so happy it's ready to burst, and I don't want to let this moment go.

I don't wake them up. Instead, I pick up some of the toys Hayley has left lying around the room. I put her dolls on the top shelf, and her trucks and matchbox cars go in the bucket at the foot of her bed.

I laugh when I see they built a big house out of building blocks and they put one of her male actions figures in there with Barbie. I look closer. Are their faces pressed together? It looks almost like they're kissing. Leave it to Friday…

Friday sat and played with my daughter for two hours, and then she read to her and she fell asleep on her bed. I want to see this every night for the rest of my life. I want to wake Friday up and take her to my bed, but there's something I need to do first.

There's a possibility she'll hate me for it, but it needs to be done. I go into the living room, pull out my phone, and search the web. It's a huge violation of Friday's privacy, I know, but I can't help it. She has a son out there, and she needs to know him. And he needs to know her just as much. It only takes two wrong numbers before I find her.

"Hi, is this Jill?" I ask.

"Yes," the lady says.

"Do you have a son named Jacob?"

"Yes," she replies, but this time, there's a question in her tone. "Who is this?"

"My name is Paul Reed, and I'm a friend of Friday's. Well, she's my girlfriend. I'm going to marry her if I can ever get her to say yes."

The line goes silent.

"Are you still there?"

"Yes, I'm here."

"I was hoping that maybe we could talk."

"Yes, I think we should," she replies, and my fucking heart soars.

####

I hang up the phone and swipe a hand down my face. Either I just sealed my fate and made it so that Friday will never marry me, or I made her love me a little more. I won't know which until tomorrow.

I go back to Hayley's room and stare down at them for a little longer. They've rolled now so that they're facing one another on their sides, and Hayley's hand is still tucked in Friday's. Click!

I bend over and run a hand down Friday's hair. She stirs, her eyes opening slowly. She blinks up at me and smiles. "We fell asleep?" she whispers.

"Yeah." I extricate Hayley from Friday's grasp and slide my daughter under the covers. Hayley could sleep through a tornado as long as it's still dark outside, and I don't worry about waking her up at all. Friday leans over and presses her lips to Hayley's cheek.

"I had fun with her tonight," she whispers.

I jerk my thumb toward the big house they made. "I see you were busy."

"We made a fortress for Barbie."

That word makes me smile. "Did Barbie need a fortress?"

"All girls need a fortress. Barbie doesn't have a dad, so she needed one more than most." She shrugs. "Hayley and I discussed all this when she tried to convince me that girls with strong daddies don't need big walls." She lays a hand on my chest and looks up at me, blinking those green eyes. She's so fucking beautiful. "You'll always protect her heart. And if anything ever happens to you, you have four brothers who will do the same. So Hayley won't need a fortress."

I get it. I so get it. "You guys went that deep?"

She nods. "We did. It's a kick-ass fortress, don't you think?"

I kiss her forehead. "Badass. Just like you."

She leans her head on my chest, and I palm the back of her head. "I'm not, though, Paul. I'm afraid every single day. I just hide it well."

"Do I scare you?"

"Sometimes."

"How about now?" I ask.

"I'm not afraid right now." Her voice is so soft I can barely hear it.

I scoop her up, and she wraps her skinny arms around my neck.

"How about now?"

"Nope." She grins at me.

We walk toward the door. "Light," I say.

She flips the light off, and I carry her into my room.

"How about now?" I ask.

"No," she says quietly. I let her legs drop, and she slides slowly down my body. "I want what you want," she whispers.

I freeze. I take her face in my hands, and she stares up at me, my palms bracketing her cheeks. "Are you sure?"

"Yes."

I kiss her. Kissing Friday isn't like kissing any other woman in the world. She tastes like everything I've ever wanted, and I drink her in. She pushes back against me, wrapping her arms around my neck as she puts her tongue in my mouth and tangles it with mine.

"God," I breathe out, and I have to set her back from me for a second so I can get a breath.

She smirks and pulls her pajama shirt over her head. She's not wearing a bra, and it makes my mouth water. But before I can touch her, she's shoving her pajama bottoms down, too. Then she's naked, and I was right. She's almost completely shaved down there but not quite.

"What's wrong?" she asks, her eyes following mine toward her tiny little landing strip.

"You're just so fucking pretty," I tell her. "And I love you so fucking much."

Her gaze drops for a second, and she climbs onto my bed, her round bottom up in the air for a second. I reach forward and slap it, and she squeaks in protest.

"I cannot believe you did that!" she cries, looking affronted.

"Oh, believe it." I strut over to the bed and shove my jeans down over my hips. Her gaze goes to my dick, and she licks her lips. I came in her mouth this morning, and I want to come inside *her* this time. "Do I need to get a condom?" I ask.

"You think you're going to get me more pregnant?" she asks, her lips tilted in a quirky grin that's a-fucking-dorable.

"No," I grunt out. "I just didn't know if you'd be worried about other stuff."

"I've seen your test results and you've seen mine," she reminds me.

We work in a business where plasma sprays into the air, so we have to get tested regularly for everything.

"I haven't done it without one in a really long time," I admit. "I might not last for shit."

She laughs. "Then we'll have to do it twice."

Hell yeah. "If you insist." I chuckle as I climb over her and prop myself up on my elbows on each side of her head. I look down into her face and I know, inherently, in my soul, that I'm going to be with this woman for the rest of my life. I'm going to climb into her bed every day until I die. And when I'm too old to be able to fuck her, I'm going to hold her. And she's going to hold me. Forever.

"What are you thinking?" she asks.

I brush her hair back with my thumbs. "Are you sure you want to know?" I'm not sure she's ready for shit to get real.

But she nods. "Yes."

"I was thinking about how I want to climb on top of you when we get old and do awesome things to you." So, I edited. But who cares?

"What if I don't want your old ass crawling on top of me?" she asks. I freeze, because I'm suddenly scared. But she takes my face in her hands and forces me to look at her. "What if I want to get on top, instead?"

I chuckle and bury my face in her neck. The scent of her almost overwhelms me, and I lift my head and kiss her. "You can get on top anytime you want."

"Except today," she breathes.

"You want to get on top today?" I ask. Hell, I'll roll over and pull her on top of me. Won't hurt my pride at all.

"No," she whispers. "I want you to carry me away. Take me with you where you're going."

"Don't want to go without you," I say.

She points between us. "Then you better get busy, big guy. You got some work to do."

God, she makes me laugh. I look down at her boobs, and she's put her piercings back in so I wrap my lips around her left one and roll it with my tongue. She pants and palms the back of my head to pull me closer to her. My dick is sitting right at the apex of her thighs, and I can feel her heat all around me, so I notch it in her cleft, where my piercing will thrum against her clit, and she nearly comes up off the bed. I kiss her breast and lick over it and under it and around it, and goose bumps rise along her arms and neck, and I fucking love that I can make her come apart like this. She has fine lines up both sides of her stomach, probably from her first pregnancy, and I tongue them gently. I like that I get to see this part of her because it's all the scars that make up a good part of who she is.

"Paul," she says quietly.

I lift my head and look up at her.

"I'm officially afraid," she says.

I stop what I'm doing. "Of me?"

She snorts. "No, I'm afraid you're never going to get to my pussy with all that licking you're doing everywhere else," she cries, and she shoves my head toward her heat with an impatient hand.

"God, you're so fucking bossy," I say, but I slide down, wiggling until her thighs part so I can settle between them. I rock from side to side and push her open wide. "Give me some room," I say. "I have broad shoulders."

"I'm not a contortionist," she huffs, but she pulls her legs farther apart. Her pussy is wet and glistening, and I can see the little piece of gold sticking out from between her folds where she has her hood pierced. And she has labia piercings, too. I have honestly never kissed a pussy with so much metal on it. But good God, I'm willing.

Since she's giving me a hard time, I don't even go easy on her. I suck her piercing into my mouth and give it a tug.

She cries out, and she rocks into my mouth. I hook the piercing with my thumb and very gently hold it out of the way, and then I suck her clit. She fists the sheets in her hands and closes her eyes and bites down on her lower lip.

She's already close, so I slide two fingers into her heat and tip them up, making a come-hither motion against that spongy little spot inside her that I hope will make her go crazy. She stills. "So it does exist," she breathes.

I laugh against her clit, and she growls.

"Do that again."

I hum, sucking in gentle strokes, and suddenly, her body bows. She grabs my head and pushes my face into her pussy, and I lick and suck until I can barely take a breath, until I get every quiver from her arching body. I pull my fingers from inside her, and she watches as I stick them in my mouth and lick them clean. She's so fucking wet that there's a puddle under her on the sheets, and I love that I just did that to her. I wipe my face on the sheets and climb up her body until we're nose to nose. I'm just going to rub noses with her because I just ate her out, but she takes my lips and kisses me solidly. Her tongue slides in my mouth, and she touches me in ways no one else ever has before.

"Fuck me," she says. I look into her eyes. I want to correct her and tell her that I want to make love to her, but I know that will get me nowhere. She fists her hands in my hair, and I've just about had enough of that. I made her come buckets already, so I deserve to have a little of what I want. I take her hands in mine and anchor them against the bed sheets with my weight. She struggles for a moment, and then she whispers, "Okay." She stills beneath my weight.

"My way," I say.

She shivers. "All right."

Her gaze lands on my chest, and she sees the butterfly. "When did you get that?" she asks.

"Today."

"Why?"

"Because I love you and want to keep you close to my heart."

"The butterfly is not broken."

"Neither are you."

Her breath escapes her in a huge rush, and tears fill her eyes. I don't let her wipe them away. I hold on to her hands and press against her slick hole, nudging just barely inside.

"You're so fucking tight," I say, my voice guttural and harsh.

I kiss her, just because I can.

I push and meet resistance. "Relax and let me in." She's so fucking wet that she's slippery. "Let me in, Friday," I say.

She turns her head to look away from me.

I whisper in her ear. "You don't have to tell me you love me back. I can wait. I'll still love you no matter what."

She whispers something, but her eyes are jammed shut and she has her head turned away from me.

"What did you say?" I stop pushing, stop trying to get inside her.

She tips her face up to mine. "I do," she says quietly.

"You do what?" I whisper back. I can feel her heat wrapped all around me, but I'm not in fully. Will I ever be?

"I do love you," she says. She tips her hips, her body relaxes, a smile breaks across her face, and I sink inside her to the hilt. "I do love you," she says again. She wiggles her palms from under mine and takes my face in her hands. "I love you, Paul."

I'm in her, balls deep, but I can't move. I can just stare into her face because I've never seen such acceptance and trust in her green eyes. She's usually so wary, but she's open under me, allowing me inside her in every way possible. I let her hands go, and she wraps them around my neck. Her feet rest on the backs of my calves and she's so open and so trusting.

"I'm in."

She nods, and a tear slides down the side of her face toward her hairline. I catch it with my lips, the salty taste of her like the sweetest essence against my lips. "You're in."

Then I move. I slide out of her, her wetness slathering me, and then I push back in. Her hips tilt so she can meet me, and I sink all the way in. I sit up a little so I can look down between us, and I watch her take me inside. When I pull back, my dick is all creamy, and she feels so fucking good.

"I can't last long."

"Make love to me, Paul," she says. And she looks into my eyes. I slide my arms under her shoulders and pull her to me, and then I do as she requested. I make love to her. I fuck her. I pound in and out of her, and her cries spur me on. She murmurs sweet words of love and affection in my ear, and I close my eyes and try to hold out a little longer, but she's so fucking tight. It's like a hot, silky, buttery glove wrapped around my dick, squeezing me so tightly.

She comes undone around me, her walls squeezing me even tighter, and I stop moving so I can ride it out. I feel her quake around me, and without even another push, I come inside her. I soak her walls, pushing so deep I'm afraid I'll hurt her, but she just whispers, "More," in my ear. "More, Paul."

My dick is so sensitive that I have to stop moving. I look down at her and say the only thing that pops into my head. "Wow." I can barely breathe.

She giggles, and I slide out of her. I wince because her sheath surrounds me until it doesn't, and the wet friction makes the glide almost painful.

"You okay?" I ask.

She nods and buries her face in my chest, suddenly shy.

"You sure?"

"Yeah. Just feeling kind of exposed. That was pretty intense."

I fall onto my back and pull her forward to lie on my chest. "I've never had sex like that."

My breaths are still ragged and so are hers. She rests her chin on her hand and draws a circle around my tender tattoo. "I really love this," she says.

I don't say what I want to say because I'm afraid she won't say it back when she's not in the throes of passion. I don't tell her I love her.

"I meant it," she suddenly blurts out.

I look down my nose at her. "Meant what?"

She hides her face, but I can hear her. "Everything I said. I meant it."

"I know." I chuckle and kiss her forehead. "I know you did."

She would call me a pussy if she looked up and saw my eyes glistening the way they must be right now.

I know she meant it, and that's what makes what I'm going to do her tomorrow all the more scary.

# Friday

Paul wakes me up the next morning before the sun comes up. He's tucked in behind me, and my butt is cradled by his thighs. He cups my breast, squeezing my nipple between his thumb and forefinger very gently while he kisses the back of my neck and across my shoulder.

"You awake?" he asks softly, lifting his lips for only a moment, and then he puts them back on my skin, right back where I want them.

"I am now." I cover his hand with mine and show him that he can apply more pressure. He's so careful. I guess it's because I told him my boobs are tender.

I can feel him behind me. He's hot, hard, and ready, so I lift my leg a little, giving him some room, and he slides inside me in one warm, wet, completely full stroke. He grunts and says, "So good," right beside my ear. It's more moan and breath than talk, though. "I like waking up with you in my bed."

I close my eyes and let him fuck me slowly, feeling him move in and out, the base of his stomach bumping my ass every time he fills me.

"God, Friday, I can't last for shit when I'm inside you."

His hand slides down my belly, and his fingers press insistently against my clit, and he rubs back and forth, his finger gently manipulating my piercing, putting just the right pressure on it.

He grabs on to my top leg and rolls me to my back without pulling out of me. He lifts my legs over his thighs and spreads me open wide. He rubs my pussy while he fucks me. He pulls my hand to my breasts and says, "Play with them so I can watch." He sits up on his elbow, and his gaze falls to my boobs. He licks his lips. He doesn't stop his slow slide inside or his nimble fingers that are carrying me higher and higher.

He smirks at me when I look into his eyes and rub my thumbs across my nipple piercings. It doesn't take much. That's enough to send me over. I come, trembles overtaking my body as he pushes me through the orgasm, his fingers quick and sure as he strums my clit. He wrings every last tremor from me, and then he lifts up, pushes my knee toward my chest and puts his weight on it, and he fucks me harder. I cry out, but his lips cover mine, and he whispers, "Shh."

I try to hold it back, but I can't. So, he keeps my mouth busy with his tongue as he pumps in and out, his movements suddenly frantic and quick.

"I'm going to come inside you."

I nod. I have kept my eyes closed because the sensation of him moving inside me is more than I can bear. But when I open my eyes and find his boring into mine, my breath leaves me and a warm wash of pleasure takes me over the top. It's nothing like the clitoral orgasm of moments before, but it's pleasant and so fucking hot. And only then, when I am spent and lax beneath him, does he finally come.

"I'm coming," he warns. "Coming inside you." His eyes close, and he grunts, his dick pulsing inside me almost painfully, but it's a good bite. Definitely not a bad one.

He lets my leg drop, falls onto my chest, and kisses my shoulder, the weight of him so welcome that I never want him to move. But he pulls back. I grab for him, and he dodges my hands, saying, "I'll be right back." He kisses my cheek and moves away. I see him slide on a pair of boxers, and he dashes into the bathroom. He comes back a minute later with a warm, wet washcloth, and he cleans me up. "Sit up just a little," he says. He pulls one of his T-shirts over my head and then slides my panties on me. It's like he's dressing a doll, but I'm totally worthless for at least the next few minutes. "I like you fuck drunk," he says with a grin.

"What the fuck are you doing?" I ask, my voice groggy and thick.

"Hayley will be up in a minute."

I toss the covers back. "I should go to my room."

He pulls the covers back over me and climbs in with me. "No," he says. "Stay."

I am too well worked to protest. I can barely think, much less complain. I roll over, and he tosses his leg over my bottom and pulls me against him. His fingers tickle up and down my back as I fall back asleep. Quiet comfort overtakes me, and I welcome it.

I feel a tap, tap, tap on the side of my nose and open my eyes to find blue eyes just like Paul's staring into mine. "Hayley," I say. I wipe my eyes. The sun is just barely up.

Paul sits up on his elbow and looks over me. "Go back to sleep, Hayley," he says.

"The sun is shining," she says.

"No, it's not," he tells her. Then he reaches over me, grabs her, and pulls her over my body. She lands between us and snuggles into the spot. She closes her eyes and yawns. "Go back to sleep," he tells her again.

She rolls onto her side, facing me, and she looks at me for a second, her gaze curious but not at all sad or mad or any of the things I had been worried about. Her little-girl breaths are close enough that they fall on my chin and make me feel all warm and melty inside.

Paul's toes tangle with mine, and he pulls my foot to rest between his down at the bottom of the bed. He's touching me. He wants to touch me. I extend my hand toward his head, and he adjusts my palm to rest beneath his cheek and closes his eyes. There's a slight smile on his face as he falls back asleep.

And there's one on mine, too. It's an almost giddy feeling of peacefulness. I never imagined peace to come with quite so much bemusement. But it has. And I like it.

###

I wake up to find a foot shoved hard against my forehead. I open my eyes and see that Paul has one shoved into his stomach, but he's sleeping through it. Hayley has turned herself around and is facing the end of the bed.

I move slowly, trying not to wake her as I adjust her foot, but the minute I move, her head jerks up, and she says, "The sun is shining."

Paul chuckles. His voice is nasally from sleep, and he grunts when Hayley's knee pokes into his groin. "Be still," he warns. He looks at me. "Sleeping with Hayley is like sleeping with an octopus wearing sneakers that has really knobby knees. I should have warned you."

Hayley sits up, and she's absolutely adorable with her hair sticking out in all sorts of directions. She looks like she's been tumbled in a dryer. Her cheeks are pink, and her eyes are bright and shiny. She is all things beautiful and innocent, all wrapped in one adorable little package. I can't help but wonder if I was ever that naive, that trusting.

Probably not.

"Can we go get waffles?" Hayley asks.

Paul looks at me and arches a brow. "Waffles?"

"With strawberries and chocolate chips and whipped cream." She licks her lips. "Then we can go to the park."

Paul's eyes cloud for a moment, and I can't help but wonder what that's about. But Hayley starts to wiggle her feet in excitement, so I grab one of them and tickle her toes. She laughs and falls back onto the bed squealing.

"Waffles?" Paul asks. He plumps his pillow under his head and stares at me.

I nod. "Waffles."

"The park?" he asks. He doesn't look me in the eye when he says that, and it's odd. Maybe he's just distracted by Hayley being in bed with us? I don't know.

"Sure." I toss the covers off and stretch.

"You got panties with flowers on them," Hayleys says, as she eyes the hip of my undies. She looks up at her dad. "Can I have some panties with flowers on them?" She pulls her pajama pants down at the waist and shows me hers. "Mine just have stripes." I pull my shirt down over my hips.

"What did I tell you about showing your panties to people?" Paul asks.

She rolls her eyes at him. "Friday's a girl," she says.

I bite back my snort because Paul isn't laughing. I look at him over my shoulder, his eyes meet mine, and they go hot. And so do I. "I know she's a girl." His eyes roam up and down my back. "Most definitely a girl."

"We need to get you some waffles," Hayley says to Paul. "Because you look hungry." She says it very matter-of-factly, and I can't keep from laughing this time.

Paul shoots me a look of warning, and I throw my hands up. "What?" I cry. "I can't help it."

But now that I'm sitting up, nausea hits me. I flop back onto the bed.

"Go get Friday a can of ginger ale," Paul says to Hayley. "Her tummy hurts."

Hayley runs out of the room and comes back with a cold can as Paul said. She opens it up, takes a sip, and hands it to me. She grins and wipes her hand across the back of her mouth.

"What did I tell you about drinking out of people's drinks?"

"It's just Friday," she says. She blinks those blue eyes at me. I'm just Friday. I'm just Paul's girlfriend, which makes me something serious in her life. It's kind of scary, knowing I'm something to her. But in a good way, for the first time ever.

"Is your tummy feeling better?" she asks.

"Not yet."

She sits cross-legged in front of me. "Maybe you just need to go poop," she says, looking at me very seriously.

Paul falls back on the bed, clutching his gut as he laughs. He laughs until he has tears rolling out of his eyes. He wipes them and goes to get me some crackers, laughing all the way down the hall.

Sam stops and pops his head into the room. I'm glad I'm wearing one of Paul's really long T-shirts. Sam grins at me. "Maybe you should just give it a try," he says, "just in case you need to poop." I throw a pillow at his head. He ducks, and it flies over him. He mocks an affronted look. "You didn't throw a pillow at Hayley."

I grab her toe and tug it. "Because I like her." She grins at me and looks smugly at Sam. He scrunches up his face like he's upset.

"I like you, too," Hayley says quietly when Sam steps out of the doorway.

I could get used to this family thing.

Paul comes back with a pack of crackers, opens them, and hands me one. I nibble the edge of it.

He leans down and kisses my cheek. "Just so you know," he says softly, "I've never had a woman sleep in my bed when Hayley's here before."

My heart squeezes in my chest, and my belly flutters. I know this much about him.

"So no matter what, don't break her heart, okay?" he asks softly. His blue eyes stare into mine. "You cuddled with her daddy and with her, so that makes you special. Keep that in mind, no matter what."

There's something almost ominous about his tone, but I have no idea what his reticence is about. I wish I did.

###

I sit down on a park bench so full of waffles that I will probably never move again. I might have to get Paul to carry me back to the apartment.

Hayley runs off to play, and Paul calls out to her, "Stay where I can see you!" She rolls her eyes at him, and he grunts. "I have a feeling I'm going to have to break her from that habit before she becomes a teenager."

I laugh. "Good luck."

He takes my hand and grips it tightly. He holds it so long that our palms get sweaty and stick together. I extricate mine and pull back. "Sometimes I feel like I can't get close enough to you," he says. He's not looking at me. He's looking toward where Hayley is climbing on the monkey bars.

I scratch my head. "I don't think we can get much closer than we were last night."

He shakes his head. "Sex is easy. It's the rest of it that's difficult."

I look at his profile because he's still not looking at me. I pretend to make light of his comment and scoff. "I wouldn't say that I made sex easy."

His gaze suddenly jerks to mine. "We didn't have sex."

I hold up one finger and grin. "I distinctly remember—"

But he cuts me off. "I remember it, too. I remember telling you that I loved you and you telling me you felt the same way. And we made mad, passionate love. Crazy good love like I have never had before. And then we did it again. And then we pulled my daughter into bed with us and that was the best fucking part about the whole thing." He turns to face me. "I want a family, Friday. Not just a fuck. Tail is easy to come by. You, on the other hand..." He lets his voice trail off. "You're one of a fucking kind, and I want you to be mine so badly I can taste it.

And I'll still be tasting it next week, next year, and every day following that."

"I'm with you," I say hesitantly. I don't know how much more of a commitment I can offer him. I've already offered more than I ever thought I would be able to offer anyone.

He leans over and hovers over my lips. "I love you so fucking much," he says. "Just remember that." He stares into my eyes for a minute, and then he goes to Hayley and races her to the sliding board.

I watch them playing and am just about to get up when a woman drops down beside me. "Beautiful morning, isn't it?" she asks. She sighs heavily, but it's a nice noise. It's not frustrated or confused. It's just comfortable.

I look up at the blue sky. "Such a pretty day," I say. I smile at her. She isn't looking at me, so she doesn't even see it.

She points toward Hayley. "Is that your little girl?"

I nod. Then I startle because she's not. But she so is. "My boyfriend's little girl."

"She's adorable."

A grin tips the corners of my lips. I can't take any credit for her, though. "Thanks."

I see a little boy with brown hair run over and talk to Paul. "Is he yours?" I ask.

She nods. "Yes."

"He's adorable, too." He is. He's tall and slim. Then he looks up, and his eyes meet mine. I gasp. I know those eyes. I have seen them before. It was only once in real life, but I will never, ever forget them. My gaze jerks to the woman beside me.

"Please don't be angry," she says. "I talked your boyfriend into it."

My heart is so tight in my fucking throat that I can't get out a sound, not even the sob that's buried deep within me. I sit forward, balancing on the edge of the seat, because now that I've seen him, I can't look away again. He grins, and I can see his dad's quirky smile, the one he had when I met him, and I know, without a shadow of a doubt, that this little boy is my son.

"Are you all right?" she asks quietly. She turns to face me on the bench. "Please don't blame your boyfriend. I just wanted to meet you. Jacob doesn't even know who you are, and he won't, not unless you tell me you want that."

I can hear her talking, but I can't speak. I get up and walk very slowly over to where Jacob is standing with Hayley. I feel like there's a magnetic tether between us, and I couldn't stay away from him even if I wanted to. I want so badly to touch him. I want to feel the heartbeat in his skinny little wrist and watch his chest go in and out when he breathes. I want to take off his shoes and count his toes because I never got to do that. I really wanted to do that.

I stop beside him and squat down. "Hi," I say quietly. I'm surprised that noise crept past the emotion in my throat because I still feel like it's going to choke me.

"Hi," he says quietly. He looks over at Jill, and she gives him a thumbs-up. She doesn't get up, though. I see her wipe a tear from her cheek.

"Did you meet my friend, Hayley?" I ask.

He nods. Paul keeps trying to catch my eyes with his, but I won't let him.

"I'm Friday," I say. *I'm your mother, and I love you more than anything, anywhere, anytime.* The words rush to my lips, but I bite them back. "What's your name?"

Jacob runs over to his mother and says something to her. She reaches into the big bag at her feet and takes out a box. She hands it to him, and he runs back over. He never did tell me his name, but that's okay. I'd rather he have a little stranger danger. And I'm a stranger, after all.

Jacob sits down on the sidewalk and opens his box. He takes out a clunky piece of chalk and says, "Do you want to draw with me?"

I sit down beside him and say, "What color should I use?"

He gives me a blue piece of chalk. "This one."

So I sit for hours and draw with my son in chalk on the sidewalk. We draw rainbows and dragons, and we even make some flowers for his mom. I look around and see that the sidewalk is completely full of our art. There's not an available space to be had.

"You're a really good drawer," he says. He grins up at me, and I see the space where his missing tooth should be.

"So are you." I reach out a tentative hand and touch the top of his head. I close my eyes and breathe, letting my hand riffle through the silky strands. I pull back way sooner than I want to because he's looking at me funny.

I look over and see Paul sitting and talking quietly with Jill. He gets up and yells over to us. "We're going to get some lunch! We'll be right back!"

I give him a thumbs-up and get up to chase Hayley and Jacob over to the swings.

"Push me!" Hayley cries.

"Push me!" Jacob calls at the same time. He laughs, and I put my hand in the center of both their backs, standing between them, and give them both a shove.

It's only a minute or two later when Paul and Jill come back carrying hot dogs and drinks. The kids race to the table. I jam my hands into my pockets and walk over a little more slowly. Paul and Jill sit side by side on one side of the picnic table, and Hayley and Jacob sit on the other.

"Sit beside me!" Hayley cries.

"No, me!" Jacob says. I put my legs over the bench and sit between them, and Paul hands me a hot dog. Jacob scoots so close to me that I can feel his thigh against mine. The heat of his little body seeps into the cold of mine and warms me everywhere.

I close my eyes for a moment and just breathe, enjoying the feel of having my living, breathing child pressed into my side.

The kids inhale their hot dogs and are ready to go back and play. Paul gets up with them and follows, leaving me with Jill.

"You don't look anything like I expected," she says quietly.

"What did you expect?" I take a bite of my hot dog.

She grins. "Something less colorful."

I put a hand in front of my mouth and talk around my food. "Color's not a bad thing."

She heaves in a sigh. "I expected some washed-up, downtrodden girl who regrets her life. I'm glad that's not what I found." She closes her eyes and waits a beat, and then they fly back open. "So glad that's not what I found."

"Sometimes, that's still me." I look over at Jacob, and he grins in our direction.

"Sometimes, it's all of us." She covers my hand with hers. "Can I tell you something no one else knows? Well, except for my husband."

"Please do."

"When I was twenty, I got pregnant."

All the air in my body whooshes out of me, and I choke on my hot dog. I cough into my fist, trying to clear my airway.

Before I can speak, she holds up her hand to stop me. "I had to make a very difficult decision. And I had an abortion. I wasn't in love with the father, and I didn't think I could do it on my own."

"Wow." I don't know what else to say.

"What you did took so much strength." Her eyes fill up with tears, but she blinks them back, waving a hand in her face.

"So did what you did." I mean that with all my heart.

"We do what we have to do to survive."

I set my hot dog to the side because I couldn't swallow it even if I wanted to.

"I thought for a long time that not being able to get pregnant was my punishment for having the abortion."

I can understand how she might feel that way. But it wasn't the case. The universe doesn't work that way.

"Jacob is the best thing that ever could have happened to us. We love him so much."

I still can't get over how beautiful he is. He's standing looking up at Paul with his hands on his hips, and Paul is glaring playfully down at him. I can't help but grin, too.

"Don't be too mad at him, okay?" she says. "He loves you so much."

I nod. I know he does. And I haven't had enough time to process what he did today.

"I'm sorry we ambushed you." She looks sincere. But I can tell she's happy about the way it turned out. I kind of am, too.

"Did he call you?" I ask.

She nods. "Last night, actually."

After I showed him my box of secrets, he used the information and found her. My gut clenches because I can't help but feel betrayed.

"Can we see you again another day?"

I nod. Now that I've been this close to Jacob, I don't think I could stay away. It was almost easier not knowing where he was or what he was doing or what he looked like or what he smelled like or the way he smiled.

"He looks like you," she says.

"He looks like his dad, too."

"Do you have any pictures of him? I'd love for Jacob to see them when he's ready."

I look at her. "He knows that someone else gave birth to him?"

She lays a hand on her chest. "He knows he grew in my heart while he grew in someone else's belly."

I like that. I like it a lot.

"I want you to have whatever place you want to have in his life. You can just be the really sweet lady we met in the park one day, or you can be the woman who gave birth to him. It's completely up to you."

I nod. I am suddenly choked with emotion. A hot tear rolls down my face, and I brush it back. "I'm pregnant," I say.

Her eyebrows arch. "Congratulations?" she asks. She looks from Paul to me and back.

"It's not his. I volunteered to be a surrogate for some friends of mine."

Her gaze gets soft.

"So, it might be best to wait and decide what to tell him later. I don't want him to think I just give up all my babies." I lay a hand on my stomach.

"When will you be done torturing yourself?" she asks. She lays her chin on her upturned palm and gazes at me. "We do the best we can with what we have."

I nod and get to my feet. I walk around the table, and she stands up in front of me. I open my arms, and she hugs me tightly, and then whispers in my ear. "Thank you."

I don't know if she's thanking me for coming today, or if she's thanking me for giving her my son, or if she's thanking me for something else I don't understand. "You're welcome," I grunt out.

"Jacob!" she calls over my shoulder. "It's time to go."

Jacob runs over, and he stops at my feet. He looks up at me and smiles. He holds up a purple piece of chalk. "Do you want to keep the purple?" he asks. "It's my favorite color."

I take it from him and squat down. "Thank you so much," I say. I desperately want to hug him. But I am afraid to.

Suddenly, Jacob launches himself at me and wraps his arms around my neck. I fall back gently onto my butt, and we roll to the ground. I can't keep from laughing as he hugs me. I wrap my arms around him and bend my head so I can smell his hair. He has that little-boy smell that reminds me of the outdoors and purple shampoo.

Finally, he squeaks and starts to squirm, and I realize I've held him too long so I let him go. It wasn't nearly long enough, though. Not even close. He steps back and wraps his arms around Jill's legs. "Can Friday come over and play with me one day?" he asks.

Jill nods.

"Call me," I say.

They walk off together hand in hand, and I watch them until they disappear from sight. Paul comes toward me from the other direction with Hayley's hand in his. "How angry are you?" he asks. He cocks his head and looks at me like an inquisitive puppy.

"I'm not angry."

I touch the top of Hayley's head and tell her, "I'll see you later, Hayles, okay? I have some errands I have to run."

She nods, and I walk away.

"Friday," Paul calls. But I don't turn back. I can barely see for the tears blurring my eyes, but I'll be fucked sideways before I'll let anyone see them fall.

# Paul

Shit. I fucked that all up. It was going so well and she looked so fucking happy. Watching Friday with her son was like watching chocolate being poured over ice cream. It was warm and soothing, and they just belonged together. The two of them in the same place—it was magical. It was meant to be. My only regret is that I didn't warn her. I didn't give her notice that we would be meeting them. But she might not have come if I had told her. I run a frustrated hand through my hair.

Hayley pulls on my hand. "Where is Friday going?"

As far from me as she can get, I'd imagine. "She said she had to run some errands. I don't know."

She blinks up at me, her blue eyes big and wide. "Is she coming home later?"

I don't know. "I think so."

"Why is she mad at you?" She's all innocence and wonder.

"What makes you think she's mad at me?" I narrow my eyes at her.

"She looked like she was going to cry."

Fuck. She did. I pick up my phone and call Matt. "Hey," I say.

"What the fuck do you want?" he replies. But he has that playful tone in his voice that's all Matt.

"Hayley wants to come over and touch Sky's belly."

"Oh," he says. He puts his hand over the phone and says something to someone. "Bring her over. Sky's belly will be waiting."

I wait a beat.

"What's wrong?" he says.

"I think I messed up."

"Friday?"

"Yeah."

"Bad?"

"Yeah."

"You want us to watch Hayley so you can go talk Friday down off the ledge?"

"I just want to climb up with her and hold her hand." I scrub my palm down my face.

"How far away are you?"

"Five minutes."

He hangs up on me. I hate it when he does that; I taught him better manners.

I look down at Hayley. "You want to go touch Matt and Sky's babies? See if they're kicking?"

She puts her hands on her hips. "You're despecting."

I sputter. "I'm what?"

"Despecting. Making me think about one thing when I want to think about another. Like why Friday is crying."

I scratch my head. "Despecting?"

"Despecting," she says again. She puts her hands up like she's blocking karate chops. "Despecting."

"Oh, deflecting!" I laugh. "Yeah, I'm deflecting. That okay with you?"

"Do I still get to go see Sky's belly?"

I nod, and she grins. Apparently, deflecting is okay as long as Matt's babies are involved.

I knock on Matt's door when we arrive, and it opens to a little girl wearing a pink-and-purple tutu and nothing else.

"Hi," Mellie says.

Hayley looks at me, rolls her eyes, takes Mellie's hand, and leads her to her room to get dressed.

Matt is in the kitchen making an early dinner. "Where's Sky?" I ask.

"Taking a shower." He dumps hot pasta into a colander.

"One of your children just opened the door wearing nothing but a tutu."

He grins. "As long as it wasn't Seth, I don't care." He thinks about it for a second and then adds, "And if it was Seth, I hope he'd pick one with fall colors to match his eyes."

"Dude, I am so taking your man card."

He laughs. "At least I'm getting laid."

Heat creeps up my cheeks, and I look away.

"Oh," he breathes. "That's what's up."

I pick up the salad bowl and toss the salad with a pair of tongs, pushing the carrots to the bottom because I hate carrots and don't think they should be in a salad.

"Sorry, didn't mean to kick you in the vagina," Matt says to me.

I growl and finally raise my eyes.

"How was it?" he asks softly. He doesn't want details. He just wants to be sure we're okay, and I know that.

"Earth shattering." I groan and throw my head back. "Fucking perfect." I close my eyes and let my head hang there.

I hear feet pitter-pattering across the floor and open my eyes to see Sky walking into the kitchen. She wraps her arms around Matt's back and squeezes him. She can't wrap around much of him with that belly in the way, but it's sweet to watch. He kisses her over his shoulder.

"Hey, Paul," she says. She walks by me and runs her hand through my hair. Then she tips my head back with a quick, soft jerk to my hair. She kisses my forehead, which makes me smile. "What's up?" she asks.

Matt cups his hands around his mouth and whispers, "He and Friday bumped uglies, and then he opened his mouth and did something stupid. He hasn't told me what yet."

She sits down and glares at me.

"We did not *bump uglies*," I grumble.

She tilts her head and grins at me. "But you did something stupid."

"What makes you think that?" I grumble.

"Because you have testicles." She throws up her hands. She picks up the salad bowl and stares into it. "What happened to all the carrots?" she asks.

Matt barks out a laugh.

"So what did you do?" Sky asks, and then she digs until she finds a carrot and pops into her mouth.

"I overstepped," I say quietly.

Sky looks at Matt and arches a brow. He gives her a subtle nod. "Is this about one little secret?" She points to her belly.

I shake my head. "I don't care that she's pregnant." Well, I care because I kind of wish the kid were mine. But that's the only reason.

"Who's pregnant?" Seth asks as he comes into the room and takes out a bottle of water.

Matt grins at him. "As long as it's not you, I don't care."

Seth rolls his eyes and walks back to the living room.

"So it wasn't about the surrogacy..." Sky prods.

I shake my head. "It's about something else. And I kind of stuck my nose in where it didn't belong. But she really needed for it to be done."

"Maybe she wanted it done on her own schedule," Sky says softly.

"Now she's mad at me, and I don't even know where she went."

Matt jerks a spatula toward the door. "Go see if you can fix it. We'll let Hayley play with Sky's belly for a while."

Sky grins and shakes her head. "Something about twins," she says.

I get up and push my chair in. "I won't be gone too long," I say. "You sure you don't mind?" Like they need another kid.

"What's one more?" Sky says. She waves a breezy hand around. "After a while, you just stop counting them. One of them will scream when they want something. Or when someone is bleeding. It all works out."

"Mine's blond," I say. "She'll stick out in your crowd." For now at least.

"Oh, good to know. Maybe we'll feed that one." Sky looks at Matt and nods. "Look for the one with yellow hair. Feed it. We got this." She claps her hands together like she's coaching a team.

I laugh. They're just too damn cute together.

I kiss Hayley, show her Sky's belly, and take a minute to feel for double kicks myself, and then I leave. I go by the shop, but Friday's not there. I go to the apartment, but she's not there, either. I stop in her doorway and look around her room, startled at the lack of her things on the dresser. She did have makeup and other oddities there, but now there's nothing. I go to the closet and open the door. Her suitcase is gone. I slam my fist against the wall, feeling like someone just kicked me in the gut.

She's gone. Completely and totally gone.

I call all my brothers, and no one has seen her. I call all their girlfriends and wives, and they haven't seen her. I call Garrett and Cody, and they haven't seen her, either, but now they're worried. So are my brothers. They want to go out looking for her, each of us taking a different part of the city. But there's one thing I know for sure. She won't turn up until she wants to be found. No doubt about it.

# Friday

I roll my suitcase right into the cemetery. I know it's weird and I don't know where I'm going after this, but I couldn't wait one more minute to come here. I know he's here, but I don't know where. I have to stop at the office, which is a little building surrounded by flowers. I open the door and step inside. It's cool in there, which is nice. A lady looks from me to my suitcase and back. "I'm sorry, but you can't move in if you're still breathing, and you're definitely still breathing," she says. She snaps her gum at me, and I like her immediately.

"I need to find a grave, and I'm not sure where to look." I step nervously from side to side and have to force myself to stand still when I realize it.

She goes to her computer. "Do you have a name?"

I nod. The name is sitting there, right on the tip of my tongue.

"Do you want to tell me what it is?" She waits.

"His name is Travis Conway." That's the first time I have said that name in a really long time.

"Are you a relative?"

"Does it matter?"

She smiles. "No, I was just being nosy."

She jots something down and walks over to me. She pulls out a map and draws lines and arrows around the cemetery so that I can find the plot. "If you have any trouble, just let me know."

"Thanks."

"You can leave that here if you want." She looks at my suitcase.

I unzip it and take out my shoebox. "You sure you don't mind?"

She pulls it behind her desk and I feel like it'll be safe. I walk out of the office with my shoebox under my arm and the map in my other hand. I open it up and follow the arrows. It's actually a pretty long walk, and then I realize that he had a state-funded funeral, so he's in a crowded section. He doesn't even have a headstone. He has a little piece of weathered plastic poking into the ground with stick-on letters.

I walk over and sit down beside his little piece of poor plastic. "Hey, Trav," I say softly. The wind blows and lifts my hair, and I close my eyes. He had this thing he would do when times were good: he would walk behind me and lift my hair and place a tender kiss on the nape of my neck. It was sweet and kind and made me feel so loved.

It's easy to think that he's letting me know he's still here, but it's probably just the wind. I know that. It's the most basic human need—self-comfort. I want to think he's there and safe. So I do.

"I brought something to show you," I say. I open my box and take out the pictures I have looked at so fondly through the years. My heart clenches as I shuffle through them, looking at them like I have never seen them before. "He's so beautiful," I whisper, and my voice cracks. "We did something so right, Trav." I look toward the sky and wait. Then the wind picks up my hair again, and this time the hair on my arms stands up.

"I met him today. I didn't even know it was going to happen. I went to the park with my boyfriend, and he had orchestrated this whole meet-and-greet with our son. My boyfriend's name is Paul, and he's pretty fabulous. He has a daughter and a family he loves more than anything." I take a breath. "Anyway," I say, "I met our son today. And he looks a lot like you. I can see your smile in him and your sense of humor. He snorts when he laughs kind of like you did."

I drag my finger down the edge of the plastic sign and wish it didn't have to be this way.

"I'm sorry I never came when you died. I read about it in the paper. I don't even know if you were in pain or if it just happened and, poof, you were gone. I guess that's a good thing. They say the truth is better than not knowing, but sometimes I think not knowing trumps it. It lets you believe what you want. And I choose to believe you're at peace. Does that make me naive? It probably does. But I don't care. No matter what, you're not here anymore, and that's just a tragedy all by itself."

The wind stirs again my hair lifts.

I throw up my hands and sniffle. "I get it!" I cry. "You're here!" My eyes fill with tears, and they finally spill over. It's a shoulder-shaking, can't-catch-my-breath cry, and it goes on way longer than I should let it. But I can't seem to stop. It's just too hard.

When my tears are spent, I touch the little homemade sign again and think about everything he needs to know.

"Our son's name is Jacob, and he has a great mom and dad. Her name is Jill, and I don't even know what his dad's name is yet. Jacob's artistic and he plays sports and he likes music." I point to my forehead as though he can see me. "And he has your cowlick! Oh my gosh, it was so fucking adorable. You have no idea how beautiful he is."

I wait a beat and take in the beautiful day and the people milling around.

"I just wanted to tell you that he's okay. That's all. I thought you deserved to know. No matter what happened with us, he was yours, too, and you didn't get any say about what happened to him, because after a while, I couldn't find you." I point to my chest and then thump it hard with my fist. "I did the best I could. I really did. I did everything I knew how to do! I wanted him to be taken care of. I didn't even know where my next meal was going to come from most days, and I couldn't do that to him. I know you might not like my choice, but I had to make one, and I had to make one that was in his best interest. I wanted him. But I wanted him to be safe more. Does that make sense?" I talk to him like he's here with me. It's stupid, I know, but I *need* for him to fucking be here so much that I'll set aside everything else. I'll chuck my pride. I'll throw all of it away because I need for him to hear me. More than anyone else, I need for Travis to hear me.

"I love him," I say. "And I know you love him, too. They want me to come back and see him another day, and I'm going to do that. They're even willing to tell him who I am and let him know me as the woman who gave birth to him. I still can't get over that part. They're good people. And he's happy."

I stop because I don't know what else to say.

"He's happy, Travis. He's happy and healthy, and we made something so wonderful. He will go on to do brilliant things. And I just wanted to tell you that. That's all." I get up and dust off the butt of my jeans.

I stare down at Travis's final resting place, and a weird sense of peace envelops me. My hair lifts again, and this time, I swear that I feel his lips touch the nape of my neck. The hair on my arms stands and a shiver slides up my spine, but it's a good feeling.

"Thank you," I whisper to the wind.

I go back to the office to get my suitcase, and the girl behind the desk chirps, "Did you find what you were looking for?"

I nod. I found that and more. "What would it take for me to get a gravestone for him?" I ask.

She snaps her gum. "Just stone and brass?"

I shrug. "Something nice."

"About two thousand." She looks closely at me. I reach into my purse and pull out my checkbook. I did just win five thousand dollars, after all. Jacob might want to come here one day to visit, and I don't want him to see that crappy sign. And Travis, all by himself with no thought to Jacob, deserves better.

She slaps an order form in front of me. "I can fill out the dates. Just put your information and what you want it to say."

I think about it for no more than a second. I write the words, "Beloved father and friend." Because that's what he was. He was beloved. By me, most of all. He was valuable. We all have intrinsic value, just because we exist, don't we? I like to think so.

I write the check and hand her the order form. "Please let me know when it arrives?"

She nods, and I roll my suitcase out the door and down the sidewalk.

"Friday," I hear someone say. I look up and find Henry walking out the same gate as me.

Henry is a friend of the Reeds'. He was the doorman in Emily's building, and his wife had a stroke. Not long after he met Logan and Emily, all the Reed boys went and moved his furniture so he could bring his wife home from the rest home. She died last year, and he was left alone. He has children and grandchildren, and his granddaughter Faith is expecting his first great grandchild. Through it all, Henry never wavered. He grieved, but his faith never faltered.

"Henry," I say. I lift my arms and hug him, because you just have to hug Henry when you see him. "What are you doing here?"

"I was just visiting my Nan," he says. He looks at my suitcase with a curious eye. "What about you?"

"Unfinished business," I say.

He takes the handle of my suitcase and starts to pull it down the street.

"What are you doing, Henry?" I ask. I race to catch up with him.

He looks back at me over his shoulder. "It looks like you have a good story to tell, and I just happen to love a good story."

"But," I sputter.

"I'm a lonely old man," he says. "Humor me."

"Henry," I protest.

"I have an empty house and a lot of time." He puts his free arm around my shoulders and pulls me close to him. "Make me happy and come have tea with me."

"Just tea?" I ask.

"Oh, the tea is for in the morning. Tonight, we'll have popcorn and a movie." His eyes twinkle. "I'll let you sit in the massage chair Faith got me for Christmas."

I raise my brow at him.

"Oh, fine, I'll sit in it." He waves a hand like he's swatting the idea away.

"Henry," I say softly. "I can take care of myself."

"Never doubted it," he says sternly. "I'm a lonely old man. Come and keep me company for a day or two."

"Are you sure?" I watch his face closely to be sure he's one-hundred-percent certain he wants me to go with him. What stares back at me is that he does. Wholeheartedly. He wants me.

"I want to hear everything," he says. "I adore a good love story."

I snort. "What about a bad love story?"

He looks sad all of a sudden. "There's no such thing," he says. Then he grins. "I'll let you pick the movie."

I go with Henry, because there's really no place I'd rather be right now.

Suddenly he turns to me and says, "Do I need to go and bash Paul's head in? He didn't do anything stupid, did he?"

I laugh. "No. I just needed some time."

"Time is the only thing we can't grow more of," he says, his gaze wistful. "Just keep that in mind."

I will. I really, really will.

# Paul

It's the middle of the night, and I can't sleep. Friday has been gone for five days. Sure, I know where she is. Henry called me. But he also warned me that he would bash my head in with a baseball bat if I dared to even knock on his door. He's a sweet old man, but I think he was serious.

I know Friday has talked to Emily and Reagan, and she had lunch with Matt one day this week. But none of them would tell me what happened or what was said. They're all fucking traitors in my book.

Friday hasn't even been to work all week. I have no idea what she's doing, but she's not talking to me, that's for damn sure. I deserve it. I know I do. I should have talked to her instead of taking the choice out of her hands. She's a fucking adult. I should have waited for her to say she was ready. She had opened up to me about her kid and my fucking heart soared and I knew she had a problem. I thought I could solve it. But I should have let her do it herself. She has every right to be mad. I just hope she settles it soon because I miss her like crazy.

Not having her in my shop every day makes me feel like somebody has stolen my heart right out of chest. She's not flitting around, charming people, or drawing anything beautiful that makes my customers smile.

She's just gone.

I pull out my phone and text her really quickly.

Me: *Hayley has a recital tomorrow. She wants to know if you're coming.*

I wait with my fingers poised over the phone.

Nothing. I get nothing.

I lay it down on the bed and pound my fist into my pillow, jamming it into a ball beneath my head.

Suddenly, my phone dings, and I reach for it like I'm an addict reaching for a fix.

Her: *Don't use Hayley as collateral.*

Me: *I'll use anything I can.*

Quiet. No response.

Me: *Please forgive me. Come back home.*

Her: *I don't think that's a good idea.*

Me: *I think it's the best idea I've ever had.*

Her: *What time is her recital?*

Yes! Thank God!

Me: *Seven. Will you come?*

Her: *I'll come. But only because Hayley asked me to.*

I take a deep breath because I suddenly can. I feel like the belt that was wrapped around my chest just loosened.

Me: *I'll take you however I can get you.*

She doesn't send more messages and my eyelids are getting heavy, so I send one last message.

Me: *I've been taking care of people my whole life. My job was to solve everyone's problems and make sure that everything was okay. You weren't my responsibility, and I should have realized that. I want you to be my equal, not someone I have to take care of. I promise not to do that again. And when I make a promise, I mean it. I'll talk to you and listen when you talk. I won't always do what you want. But I'll try not to steamroll you again.*

She's not going to reply. I knew that before I sent the message. I tuck my phone under my pillow, just in case she does, and I close my eyes. I dream about her red lips and that perfect smile. And for the first time all week, I don't wake up grasping for something I don't have.

# Friday

Henry keeps strange hours. It's two in the morning, and he's down in his shop working on clocks. Faith was here until around midnight working with him until her husband, Daniel, came to take her home.

I skip down the stairs and stop at the bottom. Henry has spread out pieces of a clock, and the tiny gears are all over the table in front of him.

He grins at me and shakes his head. "My Nan used to skip down those stairs just like that. She brought me coffee and snacks because I sometimes got so engrossed in my work I forgot to eat."

"What are you working on?" I ask, handing him a cup of coffee.

He takes a sip and smiles at me over the rim. "Thanks," he says. His eyes twinkle. He motions to what's in front of him. "This clock is not cooperating," he says. "It's a stubborn bastard, but I refuse to let it win." He laughs and picks up a tiny gear and shows it to me. "Do you see that? Sometimes it's the smallest things that can set off a whole slew of symptoms. You have to dig really deep to find it, and you almost have to dismantle the whole thing. But if you're willing to dig deep enough, you'll almost always get there."

He starts to put the clock back together. He's wearing thick magnifying glasses that make his eyes look huge.

I sit down beside him and pick my feet up, spinning my chair in a circle like a child. He shakes his head. "Faithy used to do that when she was little. She still does, when she's in a quirky mood. It's usually a signal that she wants to talk."

I lean forward, rest my elbow on the counter, and put my chin on my upturned palm. "What do you miss the most, Henry?" I ask softly.

He doesn't even look up. "I miss the noise," he says. "My Nan used to chatter like a magpie. She talked all the time. The woman never shut up. I used to have to kiss her so that I could get her to be quiet long enough to get a word in edgewise." He takes a deep breath. "Yes. I miss the noise the most." He looks up at me finally, and smiles. "It's been really nice having you here this week," he says. "A little noise in the house is a good thing."

"Thank you for letting me hide out."

He snorts. "Let me guess. It's time for you to go back to your family."

A smile tips the corners of my lips. "Paul just texted me."

His brow arches. "Oh yeah?" He grins. "What did he have to say?"

"He pretty much said he's a dumbass and he won't be one again."

Henry laughs.

My voice goes quiet. "He really said he's been taking care of people his whole life, and it's always been his job to solve everybody's problems. It's a hard habit to break." I spin my chair around again. "What do you think?"

"I think he loves you." He looks up and shrugs. "That's all I think. He loves you. You love him. That much is obvious. What else do you need to know?"

I draw in a deep breath and spin.

"You need to know he won't leave you? That he won't betray you? That he won't leave you all alone? That he'll love you until the end of time?"

I stop spinning, but I can't open my mouth because everything in my head seems stupid, even to me.

Henry lays his tools down. "I'll tell you one thing. I'd take five minutes with my Nan over never having had her at all. If I had five wonderful minutes and then it all went to hell, I'd remember the five minutes just as much as the part that was shot to hell."

I watch him. He doesn't look sad.

"People keep the bad things in their heads, but let me tell you, pretty lady, when you're as old as me, you learn to shove all that shit to the back of your mind and relive the good times. All the five minutes are what stick in your head. They give you strength. They keep you going."

"I've been stupid, haven't I?"

He shakes his head. "You've been careful."

I bared my soul to Henry that first night he brought me home with him. We never did watch a movie. We sat up for hours, and he listened to my whole story. I told him things I never told anyone. I told him things I didn't even know were buried deep in me until they started to roll out my mouth.

"Paul has been raising kids since he was one," Henry tells me. "He grew up quick. But inside, he's still a stupid young man, just like all of us are at one time." He grins. "And you can tell him I said so."

"He hasn't even tried to come and see me once."

Henry's face flushes. "That might be my fault."

"What do you mean?"

"I might have threatened his life with a baseball bat." He scratches his bald head.

"Henry," I scold, but I like that he's taking care of me. I like it a lot, and it makes me feel all warm inside.

"You needed time to get through all that crying." He waves a hand through the air as though he's brushing a bug from his face.

"I think I might go home soon. What do you think?"

"I think that's the best idea I've heard all week." He grabs the edge of my chair and spins it for me, and I laugh as I go around in a circle.

"Do you want to be my date for Hayley's recital?"

He rubs his hands together. "Can't wait. Little girls tripping over one another wearing funny shoes and little, fluffy skirts. What could be better?"

I get up and press a kiss to Henry's weathered old cheek. "I wish you were my grandfather, Henry," I say to him.

"Someday, when you get married, I get to walk you down the aisle. So reserve my space."

"You got it, Henry."

I go and pack my things because, very soon, I'm going home.

###

Henry and I make a stop on the way to the place where the recital is being held. My nerves are right on the surface as I ring the bell. Henry puts his hand on my shoulder. "Chill, dudette," he says. He grins. "Did I say that right? I learned it from Pete."

I shake my head. "You really shouldn't repeat what Pete says, Henry. It's not healthy." I laugh at his crestfallen expression.

The door opens, and Jacob stands in the doorway. His mom is right behind him. Jacob sees Henry and steps behind Jill's leg, and he wraps his arms around it, hiding his face.

Henry reaches into his shirt pocket and pulls out a piece of candy. He holds it out to Jacob. He looks up at his mom, and she nods. He reaches out and takes the candy, and Henry has made a friend for life that quickly.

"Thank you for letting me take him," I tell Jill.

"Thank you for calling. I was worried that we would never see you again after Saturday." She blows out a heavy breath.

"You can call me if you get worried," I say. "I promise to keep my phone on."

"I have a date planned," she whispers loudly and dramatically. "I sincerely doubt I'll call you for anything. But you can call me if you need me."

I hold out a hand to Jacob, and he fits his tiny one into mine. I close my eyes and take a deep breath. He still doesn't know who I am. He thinks I'm just a friend of Hayley's, and he wants to go with me to watch Hayley dance. He has no idea that he grew inside my body, that he's a part of me. But I'm closer to being able to tell him than I have ever been.

I take the bag that Jill hands me, and she bends down and kisses Jacob on the forehead. She lingers over him, and I'm guessing she's taking in that little-boy scent just like I did at the park.

But then she steps back, waves to us, and we walk off hand in hand. My son has his hand in mine and we are walking down the street together like we're just two people walking down a fucking street.

Henry dances a jig on the sidewalk beside us, and he teaches it to Jacob on the way to the auditorium. By the time we get there, they have become fast friends as they dance side by side. Jacob giggles, and Henry guffaws, and I am so damn happy that I could just burst.

Then I see Paul.

# Paul

I look out at the audience through the curtain on the stage.

"She here yet?" Matt asks from over my left shoulder. He sets his chin on it and looks out, his face really close to mine.

"Get the fuck off my shoulder," I grouse.

He steps back. "I guess that's a no," he says. "She told you she was coming, right?"

I nod. "For Hayley, though. Not for me. Because I made her feel guilty."

"Hey, whatever works," he says. He grins at me.

"Fuck you," I say.

Hayley runs up to me from across the room and tugs on my pant leg. She holds out her hair bow. "My bow fell out."

"Where's your mother?" I ask.

She points toward the audience, and I see that Kelly is sitting with her fiancé. She looks anxiously toward the stage, her foot tapping.

I take the hair bow and fix Hayley's hair, clipping it into place. I am a dad, but dads can fix hair. I just wanted her to find her mother so that I could keep looking for Friday. But I quickly realize how selfish that is and do what needs to be done. I've been fixing Hayley's hair since she was a baby, and I still do it now, particularly when something goes wrong. Fuck gender stereotypes. Dads rock.

I know I give Matt a hard time about turning in his man card, but the true definition of manhood is doing what needs to be done when it needs to be done. It doesn't matter if it's fixing hair, changing the oil in the car, or washing dishes. If it needs to be done, it gets done. That's manhood. It's instilling in our daughters that dads can and will do anything that needs to be accomplished.

I want to be the be-all and end-all when it comes to my daughter. I want to be the man that every other man has to look up to. I will treat her like a princess because if I don't, she might go out and latch on to the first man who does. So yeah, I open car doors and I take her on dates and I buy her flowers for no reason. Because I want her to know she's worthy of all of those things. And I fix hair.

I pop her on the bottom, and she scowls at me before she smiles and runs back over to her friends. They're all dressed in pink tights, tutus, and pink leotards. They have pink hair bows, and it's like a pink elephant threw up all over the room. Except it's really busy pink. Really busy. They're so excited that they're spinning around the room. Pink in motion.

I hear the dance teacher get up to start her first speech. Matt looks at me and wrangles his two girls—they're also dressed in pink and performing tonight—into the groups where they're supposed to be. I shift the edge of the curtain and look out. Then I see her, and my heart fucking stops.

Friday is sitting with Reagan and Emily. And next to her is Henry. On her other side is… Who is that? Oh my fucking God. That's Jacob. My heart soars, and I feel almost giddy. She brought her son. She brought Jacob. That must mean that things are going well.

"Is that him?" Matt asks from right beside my shoulder. His chin is almost resting on my shirt, and I don't try to move him away.

"You know?" I ask.

He nods. "I've always known."

"What?" The breath that I was holding escapes me in a rush.

"Friday and I used to spend a lot of time alone together in the shop." He shrugs. "We talked."

"About that?" I can't believe she told him.

"When Pete did her tattoo," he says. He looks at me sheepishly. "We both knew. We didn't and still don't know details, but we knew she had a kid."

"Why the fuck didn't you tell me?" I'm irked. I can't help it.

He shrugs. "Wasn't my story to tell."

I wish someone had fucking told me.

"You were so busy trying to get into her pants that you didn't really get to know her. Not the real her."

"That's not true," I sputter.

"Yes, it is."

"No, it's not."

"Yes. It. Is." He glares at me. "You saw the glam girl that everyone else sees."

"There's so much more to her than just that."

"You were fucking Kelly, so you didn't really have room for anyone else."

He's right. I scrub a hand down my face. He's so right. "Okay," I say.

"He's cute," Matt says. He nods toward the audience. "Her son. He looks like her."

"He's a lot like her. In a lot of ways."

"Is he the reason she stopped talking to you?" Matt asks.

"Sort of." I scratch my head.

"You think she'll talk to you today?"

"I'm not going to give her a choice."

He squeezes my shoulder. "Good." He looks at me for a minute, blinking those blue eyes at me. "Anything worth having is worth fighting for."

I fake a punch to his shoulder. "I'm coming out swinging," I say.

He grins.

The music starts, and the curtain opens. Matt and I step back and out of the way. Pete, Sam, and Logan are helping, too. We're all waiting on the stage so we can move props around between sets. Seth is in charge of the music, and he's standing there with headphones on and his sound mixer in front of him.

Matt watches the dancing closely because Mellie is in the first number. She dances, but it's more like jerky running around than dancing.

"I think my kid is the best one out there," he says. He's smiling so broadly that I can see every tooth in his mouth.

"Until one of your other ones gets out there. Then that one will be the best." I chuck his shoulder.

"Damn straight," he says.

Matt's the best dad I've ever seen. So much better than ours ever was. Ours couldn't even tell Pete and Sam apart most days.

"Where'd you learn to be such a great dad?" I ask.

His gaze jerks to meet mine, and he doesn't look away. "From watching you, dumbass."

# Friday

I sit with Reagan and Emily, and Kelly and her boyfriend are right in front of us. She introduces me, and I like him. I like him a lot. I don't particularly like that she was fucking both him and Paul at the same time, and I can't help but wonder if he is aware of that little fact. Not my business, I guess. But he probably deserves better.

Jacob is being really good, and he sits on the edge of his chair when the recital starts. "I can't see," he complains.

Next thing I know, he's crawling into my lap. He sits his skinny little body right on top of mine and leans back so that his head is resting on my shoulder, and he snuggles in. He still smells like the outdoors and purple shampoo, and I want to hold him like this forever. Tears fill my eyes, and I blink them back furiously. Henry reaches into his pocket and hands me his cotton handkerchief. I wave him off. I'm going to keep it together, I promise myself.

"Can you see now?" I ask Jacob. He nods, and his cheek brushes mine. I close my eyes and drink in the feeling.

I see one of Matt's girls, the older one, and she dances with the second group. I point her out to Jacob and tell him who she is, and he claps for her when I do. God, she's so adorable. She trips over her own feet a couple of times, and one time, she lands on her face in the middle of the floor.

I gasp and Jacob sits up. She looks like she's about to cry. But Matt dashes out onto the stage, picks her up, dusts her bottom, and he starts to do the routine with the little girls, and Mellie jumps up and gets back into it quickly. He looks ridiculous, this great big tatted-up guy dancing with all the pink little girls. But he does it, just because she needs him to. He backs away as soon as she gets moving again and fades off the stage.

Sky claps and shakes her head. She loves every second of it, I'm sure.

Hayley and Joey, Matt's oldest daughter, are in the same class, since they're the same age, so they dance at the same time during the next dance. I can see Paul lingering by the curtain, and just the sight of him makes my heart thump in my chest. I've missed him. I've missed all this. I've missed having a family.

Their last dance is next, and while they're still sort of clumsy, they have so much more form than the younger group that it's kind of artsy to watch. I need to ask them next year if I can paint their backdrops, because they need something a little more creative.

Next year? Am I really planning for next year with Hayley and Paul? I suppose I am.

Jacob seems to be pretty content sitting in my lap, and I love having him this close to me. I never dared to dream that I could have a life this wonderful. I was homeless, pregnant, lost, and fearful. Now I have Henry, an honorary grandfather figure by my side, my son in my lap, my boyfriend and his daughter on the stage, and all of his brothers and their girlfriends and wives. My fucking cup is running the fuck over. And I wouldn't change a thing.

When Hayley is done, I set Jacob to the side so I can give her a standing ovation. I put my fingers in my teeth and whistle, and I hear a whistle from beside me. I look down and see that Jacob is doing the exact same thing. He whistles loudly. Kelly covers her ears in front of us.

"Do it again," I whisper with a grin. He does, and Kelly scowls. "That's enough for now," I say.

I sit back down, and he crawls back into my lap.

The teacher comes to the microphone and makes a quick announcement, thanking the girls. After some of the older, much more talented students have danced, she tells us there's one more performance.

She grins. "We had to convince these guys to perform, but they were easy to win over." She points to the curtain, and it opens slowly. "I give you the Reeds, performing to Taylor Swift's 'You Belong with Me.'"

The curtain opens, and Paul, Matt, Logan, Sam, and Pete are all standing in a line. They're all dressed in jeans and sleeveless T-shirts, and you can see all their tattoos and they're so fucking handsome that I can't even believe they're mine. I see Hayley, Joey, and Mellie standing on the side of the stage, all waiting anxiously to watch their daddies and uncles.

Seth starts the music, and he's underlaid some kind of hip-hop track beneath the beat, but you can still pick out the music. It's a song about unrequited love and realizing that what you wanted was right there in front of you the whole time, but you were being too stupid to see it. It's told from a girl's point of view, so some of the words don't exactly fit the boys, but it makes it all the funnier.

The Reeds have moves. Serious moves. I think everyone woman in the auditorium sits forward in her seat so she doesn't miss seeing the shaking hips and flexing muscles. Paul even picks Matt up and spins him around one time, and Sam does the same to Pete. I can't stop laughing. Even Logan dances, and I can imagine the kind of work it took for him to learn this routine when he can't even hear the music the same way everyone else can. He can appreciate music, just in a different way.

As the song starts to close, Matt, Pete, Logan, and Paul all point out at the audience when the words, "You belong with me," play. Matt points to Sky. Pete points to Reagan, and Logan points to Emily, who is holding the baby in her lap. And Paul points in my direction. Those four men jump off the stage and come toward us. They sing and dance all the way down the aisle.

Out of the corner of my eye, I see Kelly get up to intercept Paul, but he doesn't even notice her. He points past her, and sings out the last line, "You belong with me," in my ear. He picks me up and spins me around, and I have never felt more happiness in my whole life.

The music stops, and everyone looks to the stage. Sam has sat down on the side of it, and he looks pretty dejected. He's holding a sign above his head that says, *Available*.

After this, he won't be available for long, because every woman there now has a crush on all the Reeds, and he's the only one who isn't taken.

I love that they can be so silly, and so loving, and so...them. They don't hide it. They don't make a game of it. They just love. They love hard.

"I love you so hard," I say to Paul.

His eyes jerk to meet mine, and he almost looks surprised. "You do?" he asks.

I nod. "I do."

"Will you come home tonight?" he asks quietly.

I nod.

"Good. That's where you belong."

# Paul

I've missed having her in my arms so much. I swing Friday around and clutch her tightly. I want to squeeze her ass and hoist her against me, but there are too many people around. I lift up the edge of my T-shirt and wipe my brow. "You belong with me," I tell her, as the song dies down.

She does. She belongs with me, and I never, ever want to let her go.

I reach out and give Jacob a gentle fist bump after I put Friday down.

"I have to stay and help put away the props," I tell her.

"That's okay. I have to take Jacob home."

I brush a lock of hair from her temple and tuck it behind her ear.

"Then I have to go get my suitcase from Henry's."

"Then you're coming home." I say it again because I like the way it sounds on my lips. Home. Our home.

"Yes, I'm coming home." Her face colors, and I can't help but wonder if she's thinking what I'm thinking.

I feel a squeeze on my arm and look up. Kelly is standing there, and she doesn't look very happy. "Can I talk to you?" she asks. She taps her foot and blows out a breath. Her fiancé has left, apparently, because I don't see him anywhere.

"Can it wait?" I ask.

"Wait?" she asks, her voice growing louder. People turn to look at us. "I'm the mother of your child, and you want me to wait?" She points to her chest and looks like I just struck her across the face.

"God, Kelly, can you cut the theatrics? Just give me a minute." I tip Friday's face up and kiss her really quickly, and when I raise my head, Kelly is rushing toward the stage where Hayley is standing. She's not even waiting for me.

"You better go and deal with that," Friday says.

I heave a sigh. "What do you think that's about?"

She pinches her lips together so hard that a white line forms around it. "She's nearly green with envy," she tells me.

"No, not Kelly," I protest. Kelly doesn't get jealous. We've both been fucking other people for years and that never even bothered her. But she did have her jealous meltdown at the apartment the other day. Maybe?

Friday points her finger in Kelly's direction. "She's jealous. Mark my words."

"Fuck," I say.

"Go talk to her and get your props done. I'll see you at home." She steps up on tiptoe and kisses me again, and it feels so good that I never want to stop. But at least I have her to look forward to. Now and forever. She leaves hand in hand with Jacob. Henry goes with them.

I can't find Kelly so I go and start loading the props into the storage room, and my brothers help me. I'm alone in the storage room, bent over picking up a piece of paper when I feel a hand on my back. I immediately hope it's Friday and that she's come to find me because she can't be without me. But when I stand up, Kelly is suddenly in my face. Her lips touch mine. Actually, her lips crush mine, and I grab for her shoulders and push her back.

"What the fuck, Kells?" I say. I push her back again, and she looks at me like I've lost my mind. I wipe my mouth with the back of my hand. "What the fuck was that for?" I really want to wash my mouth out and spit because all my kisses are reserved for Friday now, and I feel like she just fucking spoiled my kisser. "Why did you do that?"

"I think I made a mistake, Paul," she says. "I know I probably caused this when I agreed to marry my boyfriend and told you about it and it pushed you away, but I ended that tonight." She wrings her hands in front of me.

"You ended what?"

"The engagement, silly," she says. She laughs like I should have a chance in hell of knowing what the fuck she's talking about. "I ended it."

"Why would you do a stupid thing like that?"

"I saw the way you were looking at me during that song," she says.

"I wasn't looking at you."

She puts her hands on her hips. "You looked me right in the eye. You were singing directly into my heart, and it made me realize what a fool I have been. I can tolerate your brothers. I can. I will."

"I wasn't singing to you, Kells," I say. "I was singing to Friday. All that was for her."

"No," she whispers. She points to her chest. "It was for me."

"No," I say strongly. "You and I are done. That was all for Friday. I'm sorry you misunderstood."

She steps back. And this time, she does look like I slapped her. "Why her?" she asks.

I shrug. "Because she's Friday." I don't know more than that.

"But what's special about her?"

"Everything."

She glares at me. "Give me a list."

"I don't need to give you a list."

"Give me reasons."

"Why are you jealous?" I finally ask.

"We were good together," she says quietly.

"Yeah, we were good until we weren't. You really should go and catch up with your boyfriend."

She shakes her head. "That's over."

"Good," I say.

"What do you mean?"

"The whole time you were sleeping with him, you were telling him you love him and then sleeping with me, Kells. He deserves better than that. He should have a woman who loves him so fucking much that she would never think about sleeping with another man. And if she did think about someone else, it better be a fucking fantasy she comes home and lets him play out with her." I shake my head. I don't even know how to give voice to my thoughts. "I'm sorry you misunderstood."

"I was hopeful. I guess I read it wrong."

"You're not in love with me. You want what could have been."

She nods, and her eyes fill with tears. "Just tell me why her."

"She loves me. She loves my daughter. She loves my family. She loves my business and my work. She loves the hustle and bustle of my life. I can see my life with her fifty years from now. That's why her. So, don't kiss me again." I scowl at her.

"I'm sorry," she says.

"We're friends, Kells," I tell her. "But don't ever hope I'll fall out of love with her and into bed with you because it'll never happen. And don't come between us. You understand?"

She nods. "I get it."

"Good." I adjust my shirt for lack of anything better to do. "One day, you're going to meet the right one. And when you do, you'll see fucking sparks. You'll feel it from your head to your toes."

"And you feel that for her."

"Yes." I don't even need to think about it.

"Okay," she says. "I'm going to go home and be embarrassed all by myself."

"No need to be embarrassed." Well, there sort of is. But it is what it is.

"You'll forget this happened, right?"

"Already forgotten."

"Are you going to tell her?"

"Yes." I won't keep secrets.

"Okay." She sighs heavily.

She turns on her heel, tips her chin up, and walks out of the room.

What the fuck was that?

###

I let myself into the apartment, and Hayley runs in ahead of me. She's still in her tutu and she's hungry, so I make us quick sandwiches and wrap one up for Friday because she should be here soon. It's either really sad that I'm so excited about it, or it's really wonderful, and I'm leaning toward wonderful.

Hayley eats her sandwich and some chips, and I send her to take a bath. She's tired, so I read her a quick story afterward and tuck her into bed, but as soon as I do, there's a knock on the door. I hope it's Friday and that she's just forgotten her key, but I open the door to find two police officers with their hats stuck under their arms.

Oh fuck, which one of my brothers did something now?

"Mr. Reed?" one of them asks. He looks down at his notepad.

"Yes." My heart starts to thump. What if someone is hurt? What if someone was in an accident?

"Mr. Paul Reed?" he asks.

I nod because I doubt a squeak could leave my throat.

"May we come in?"

I step to the side, and they enter the room. They walk to the sofa and take a seat. One of them holds out a file and opens it up. He looks at me. "Can you confirm that you are the son of Mr. Max Reed of this address?"

"Yes. But he wasn't of this address. He's been gone a long time."

He gazes at me warily. "But he did once live here?"

"Yes, he's my father."

The man's gaze turn sympathetic. "I'm very sorry, Mr. Reed, but we have unfortunate news. There was an old warehouse on the other side of town that was being demolished, and your father's body was found inside."

I fall into my chair because my legs won't hold me up. "What?" All this time and he has been in the same city?

"We were alerted that there was a body that was found during demolition."

I scrub a hand down my face.

"How long has your father been gone?"

"Years."

"That makes more sense then," he says. "The coroner says the death happened years ago." He pulls a picture from the stack and shows it to me. I avert my eyes because I've seen enough. I remember that shirt like I just saw it yesterday. It was his favorite. He wore it all the time, and my mother hated it because it had a curse word on the back of it with a picture of someone flipping the bird.

"He was wearing that shirt the day he left." The day I kicked him out. I jab the heels of my hands against my eyes and scrub.

"He most likely died around that time. Maybe even the same day. It's hard to say. His body was fairly well preserved as he was stuffed into a freezer in the basement of a building."

Oh holy hell. I get up and start to pace. Bile rises up my throat, but I swallow it back.

"Would it be possible for you to come to the station with us?" he asks.

"I have a daughter," I say.

"Is there anyone you can call to come and stay with her?" He looks kind but firm. I get the idea that this isn't a choice.

I nod and pick up the phone. But I can't call my brothers. If I did, I'd have to tell them that Dad died the day I kicked him out. I let them think he left all those years ago. But he didn't. I threw him out. And now he's dead.

I dial. "Hey, Kells, can you come over and get Hayley?" I ask. "I have to do something."

"Why?" she asks.

"It's an emergency."

"Why me?"

"Because you're her fucking mother and I need for you to come and get her," I say. "Take her home with you."

"I'll be right there."

Fuck, I'm opening up a whole can of worms, but I can't tell my brothers yet. I just can't.

# Friday

The feeling is sweet when Henry and I go and drop Jacob off. Henry taught him the slap game, and they played it on and off all night. Jacob was actually pretty good at it and learned to flip his hands quickly. I'd like to think I have something to do with what a good kid he is, but I'm not sure that's the case.

When we drop him off, I can hear Jill run down the stairs and her hair is all messed up so I can just imagine what kind of "date" she had tonight. I just hope they had a good time, and I'm happy to see that they have such a good relationship. She takes Jacob from me and invites me to come back another day, preferably one when her husband is home and not in bed so I can meet him, too. I agree. I'd love to.

Then Henry and I go to his house. He crooks his arm, and I slide my hand into the vee he made for me. He smiles down at me. "When I met Nan, she made my heart go pitter-patter just by doing what you're doing," he tells me softly. "She would touch me, and it was like someone shot me with a lightning bolt."

"I'm sorry I make you remember," I tell him.

He *pffft*'s me. "Oh, I love the memories. They keep me going." He taps the end of my nose, and I close my eyes and laugh at him. "When you're as old as me, I hope you have half as many good memories."

"I plan to."

"It's good to have plans."

We walk quietly to his house, and I gather my suitcase. "Thanks for taking care of me, Henry," I say quietly, and I step up to kiss his cheek.

"Thanks for giving me something to worry about," he says. "Sometimes it gets lonely when you're old and by yourself. It's good to have a problem to work out in your head."

"Particularly when it's not yours." I laugh.

"I'd rather it be mine," he says, and I believe him.

"I love you, Henry," I say.

"I love you, too, kiddo," he says. He grins at me. He pulls me toward him and hugs me tightly, holding on to me just long enough. Then he sets me back. "Go find your future," he says.

So I do.

I'm almost giddy when I get to Paul's apartment. I let myself in and roll my suitcase into the room. But I stop short when I see Kelly standing in the kitchen wearing nothing but one of Paul's T-shirts. What the fuck?

"Hey, Kelly," I manage to say.

She smiles at me over the top of a cup of coffee.

"What are you doing here?"

"Oh, Paul called me. He said he needed me." She smiles again, but it's acidic and almost painful to look at. "Then he left."

"Why are you wearing his shirt?"

She shrugs. "I'm spending the night."

"Where did he go?"

"He left with two policemen. It was kind of scary."

What? "And you just let him leave?"

She shrugs again.

"Who the fuck *are* you?" I ask. "You just let him leave?"

"He needed me to be here for Hayley." Suddenly, the grin falls off her face, and she looks worried. "Fuck," she breathes. "I was so damn excited that he called me, of all people, that I didn't even question why."

"You just let him leave with them?" I am shrieking by this point, and I force myself to gentle my voice so I won't wake Hayley.

I'm already dialing the phone. "Matt," I say. And I tell him what I know, which is nothing. "Meet me there," I tell him.

"I cannot fucking believe you didn't get any information," I tell Kelly.

But I'm already running out the door and she's looking a little chagrined behind me. I catch a cab to the police station, and all the brothers and their girlfriends are pacing outside. Matt must have left his girls with Seth because they're not there. Logan has Kit in her carrier. We all head inside together, and Matt goes to get the story.

He comes back, and he's a little shell-shocked. He sinks into a chair. "It's about Dad," he says. "He died."

"Where is Paul?" I ask.

"He left." Matt shrugs.

"Dad died?" Sam says.

Matt nods. "The officer said Paul was really upset. Blaming himself."

"Why would he do that?" Pete asks.

Matt shrugs again.

"Who's with Hayley if we're all here?" Reagan asks. She looks from one brother to another.

"Her mother," I say. "I just left there."

"She's at Paul's?" Matt asks.

"He called her."

"Why would he call her instead of one of us?"

"What the fuck happened?"

"Where is he?"

They're all talking at once, and I can't hear any of them.

"We need to split up and go find him," Logan suggests.

Matt nods.

"I know where he is." I get to my feet. "I'll go and get him."

"Where is he?" Matt asks.

"I'll go and get him. Don't worry."

"You have to tell us something," Pete says.

"I'll bring him home. You can go there and wait." And I leave them all and hail a cab. I know exactly where he is.

# Paul

The projector is harder to work than I remember it being. But after a few busted knuckles and even more curse words, I finally get it started up. The theater is completely dark, except for the screen, and it casts a small glow on the room. This particular movie theater is small, and it has old wooden chairs with barely any cushion on them. But this is the only place that my dad and I ever went to be alone.

We would sneak in here in the middle of the night when the other boys were in bed, and we would watch old films together. Sometimes, we would pop popcorn and bring it from home, and we would sit all night and watch film after film. I go and sit down in one of the seats in the middle.

I don't think anyone has been here in a really long time, if the amount of dust on the seats is any indication. I don't care. I sit down anyway and watch the screen flicker. There's no sound because I couldn't figure out how to turn that on. But I can watch the movie and remember. My dad wasn't always bad. He was forgetful and he was never serious enough, but my mother was the opposite so they complemented each other really well. Where he didn't care, she cared too much, and vice versa. After my mom died, though, there was no one to balance him out, which made him seem like a deadbeat. He wasn't though, looking back on it. He was lonely. He was alone.

I hear the door open behind me, and the hair on the back of my fucking neck stands up. It's her. I always know when it's her. Her scent hits me before I even see her, and she doesn't say a word when she sits down beside me.

She's quiet, and she just watches the movie with me. When the reel stops, the room goes a little brighter because the lamps are still on.

"That was fun. What's up next?" she asks. Her voice echoes in the open room, even though she's speaking quietly.

"Why are you here?" I ask.

Her hand covers mine. "Because you needed me." She squeezes my hand gently.

"Go home, Friday," I bite out.

But she doesn't. She just sits there, quietly. "Why don't you start another movie?"

"I don't want to watch another movie."

I lay my head back and close my eyes.

"Why didn't you call me?" she asks quietly.

"I couldn't figure out how to tell anyone."

"Even me?"

"Even you."

"Why?" Her voice is soft.

"Because I feel so fucking guilty that it's like somebody is taking a knife and stabbing me in the gut over and over and over."

"Guilty about what?"

"I lied, Friday. I fucking lied, okay?" I lied to the people I love, and they'll probably never forgive me.

"Lied about what?"

"Dad didn't leave. I threw him out." I pick at a piece of lint on my jeans.

"Why did you do that?" Her voice is so quiet that I can barely hear her.

"It doesn't matter."

"Yes, it does." I feel her shift, and she climbs into my lap. She straddles me, one thigh on each side of my hips, and I reach for her bottom and jerk her against me. She yelps because I move so fast I scare her. But I need her. I need to feel her against me. I need her on top of me and fucking me. I need her. "It does matter." She takes my face in her hands. "Why did you kick him out?"

"I came home in the middle of the day and found him in my mother's bed with another woman. He was really careful not to bring women around us, and I had heard he was dating someone, but he hadn't told us. But I walked in and found them together. I wasn't supposed to be there."

"Keep going." She touches the pad of her thumb to my lower lip, and I chase her thumb and try to bite it. She smiles and rests on my chest on her elbows.

"Mom had been gone for a year, but I felt like he was taking a knife to her memory."

"I can understand that."

"I got mad, and I was bigger than him, so I jerked him out of bed. He tried to explain, but I wouldn't listen. I kicked the woman out, and he was really angry. He swung at me, and he missed, so I punched him in the stomach. Then I hit him in the face. I threw him out. I tossed him out like garbage. I didn't even let him get a change of clothes. Nothing."

She doesn't say anything.

"Then I told my brothers he left."

"Oh, Paul," she says quietly.

"They showed me the picture of his dead body. On his cheek is a slash. It's from where I hit him with my fist. I was wearing my new class ring. I had just gotten it. I saw it across his face when I hit him. I saw it that day, and I saw it today. So, he died right after our fight."

"Paul." She shakes her head. "It's not your fault."

"It is my fault. I thought he would get over being mad and that I would, too, and then he would come back, but he never did. So I blamed him. And all that time, he was dead. Dead. Gone. Never to be heard from again. Not until someone found his fucking dead body in a freezer."

A tear rolls down my cheek, and she catches it with her lips. She swipes my face with her thumbs to wipe my tears away.

"I kicked him out. It's my fault. And now I have to tell my brothers that I did it. That he never left. That it was all because of me."

"It's perfectly natural to want to protect your mother's memory. You didn't kill him. He was a grown man. We have no way of knowing why or how he ended up in a freezer, but you didn't put him there."

"My last memory is a fight with him."

"No, it's not. If it was, you wouldn't be here." She looks around us. "This is your last memory, this perfect place, Paul, and those perfect times you had with him. You know that."

"Friday," I say. "I don't know what to do."

"You do what you always do, dummy." She laughs. "You proceed with honesty and integrity. That's what's in your heart."

"I have to tell them the truth."

"Yes, you do."

"Come here," I say. I pull her against my chest. "I love you so much."

We sit like that until I feel her lips on my neck. She purrs against my skin and nips me playfully.

"You fixed me," I say.

"You weren't broken."

"I wasn't whole until you, either."

"Neither was I."

"I want you."

"I'm yours." She sucks my earlobe into her mouth and nibbles it with her teeth, tonguing my piercing and rolling it gently. My dick starts to throb and presses insistently against my jeans.

She's wearing one of those dresses she likes so much, so I lift the skirt and settle my hands on her hips. I bend my head and lick across the exposed flesh of her boobs. "I want to get to these," I say against her skin.

She shrugs and her straps come down, and she shoves the dress down below her boobs. With my hand at her back, I pull her toward me, and she lifts up a little so that I can get to her tits. They're so fucking pretty, her skin alabaster white in the soft light of the room. She mewls when I take her into my mouth.

My hands sink into her panties to cup her ass and draw her forward. "You're going home with no panties," I say next to ear. She shivers and nods. I rip her panties at the hip and pull them out of my way. I need to be inside her. I need in her now. I can't wait. I can't stop.

I unbutton my jeans and shove them down just far enough, along with my boxers. She takes me in her hands and squeezes my shaft. I hiss out a breath. "Fuck me," I say. "Fuck me now."

She lifts up and positions me at her center. Then she sinks down slowly. I arch my hips, pressing deeper inside her. I can't get deep enough, so I use my fingers to spread her open and push farther.

"God, you feel so good," she whispers. "So big like this."

"Am I hurting you?" I stop and let her rest on me, her silken walls sheathing me.

She bounces, and I sink in to the hilt.

"Fuck," I breathe. "Be still for a second."

"How many times did you jack off while I was gone?" she asks against my lips.

"None."

She laughs and squeezes me inside her. "Are you telling the truth?"

"You're going to find out when I shoot off like a sixteen-year-old if you don't stop doing that." She's squeezing me inside her, and I feel like I'm going to come undone.

"Doing what?" she whispers. She squeezes me again.

I grab her bottom and tip her forward so that with every retreat, she rides the ridge of my dick.

She cries out my name. "Paul! God, Paul!"

She's so fucking wet that my balls are slick, and I don't let up. I continue to pull her forward and back, holding tightly to her bottom. "God, Friday. I need for you to come."

She looks into my eyes, adjusts our bodies, and leans back so that she's resting on her hands, with her weight on my knees. I look down between us and I can see where I'm buried inside her as far as I can go. My dick is shiny in the dim light, and her cream coats me. Her legs are spread wide and I can see her hood piercing, so I cover it with my thumb and start to massage it as she bounces on my dick. I have to close my eyes because I can't watch her tits move. I can't watch her mouth fall open. But even then I can feel her breaths, hot and humid.

She rides me, taking me hard, and I massage her clit. Her legs begin to quiver, and her arms start to shake. Her rhythm falters, and I know she's close.

"Come for me," I say. "Please."

She cries out. Then she stills and her walls milk me, clenching tightly as I rub her clit in small, tight circles the way I know she likes. She comes hard, and I let her ride it out until she shoves my hand away.

She sits forward. "Now you," she says.

She rides my dick, taking me in her slick hole over and over, and I push through it, holding off for as long as I can. I can hear the smack of our bodies together, all tight and wet and hot.

Suddenly, she pulls my hair. "Open your eyes," she says. "Look at me."

I open them, and it's like I can see her soul looking back at me.

"I fucking love you so much," she says.

"I'm going to come inside you," I warn.

"I know."

Suddenly, she grows even wetter, and her mouth falls open, and I realize she's coming again. She's coming on my dick, and I join her, pumping all the way through the orgasm as she looks into my eyes.

"I fucking love you," I tell her as my dick begins to go soft inside her. She falls onto my chest and collapses there. I wince as I slip out of her tight little body, and I'm already thinking about how soon I can get back in there.

"I don't think I'm ever going to want to start using condoms after this baby gets here," she says.

"Good. Because I'm going to get you pregnant as soon as you have this one."

"Okay," she says. And I can feel her smile against my chest.

I palm the back of her head and tug her hair so she'll look up at me. "Okay?"

"Yes. Get me pregnant. Please. Make a baby with me. Make our family bigger." She throws her arms open wide. "I want it to be fucking huge."

"Okay," I whisper.

"You're in, Paul."

"Yes, I'm in." I'm further in than I ever dreamed she would let me be.

We sit there for I don't know how long. But finally, we have to move. "I need to go and talk to my brothers," I say.

"I know." I use her torn panties to clean us up, and we fix our clothing. I go and turn off the projector, and we sneak out the same way we sneaked in. Only this time, we're hand in hand.

We get to the apartment, and I'm not surprised at all to find all my brothers and their partners there. They're quiet as we walk in the door.

Friday goes and changes into her pajamas, since she's not wearing panties, and I go to my brothers. They deserve an explanation.

"I'm sorry," I say.

"For what?" Matt bites out. I can tell he's angry.

"For making you wait. They gave me the news, and I freaked out a little."

"Why?" Logan asks.

"Guilt."

"For what?" This time, it's Pete.

"He didn't leave," I blurt out. "I kicked him out."

"We know," Sam says. They all look at one another. "We've always known."

"What?" I jump to my feet. "How the fuck did you know?"

"Sam was home that day," Matt says. "He skipped school, and he was hiding in the closet. He heard the whole thing."

"You knew."

"Yes," Sam says.

"You always knew."

"Yes," he repeats.

"I'm sorry," I say. "I didn't mean to get him killed."

They look at one another. Finally Matt speaks up. "Just how do you think you killed him?"

"I threw him out. Then he died. If I hadn't tossed him out, he might still be alive."

"Fate's a fickle bitch," Matt says. "If anyone knows that, it's me."

"You don't honestly think you have enough power to cause the fates to take him out. You're not quite that awesome," Logan says. He laughs.

"But—"

"But nothing," Matt says. "You didn't cause it. That's the end of it."

"You're not mad at me?"

They all get up and wrap their arms around me. They squeeze and jostle me around until I laugh and cry out, "That's enough."

They step back, but they're never far away. I know that.

"I'm going to have Dad buried beside Mom," I say.

"Let's plan a service and everything," Matt says.

"Okay." I smile. I feel like the weight of the world has been lifted from my shoulders.

My brothers and Emily, Sky, and Reagan leave. But as the three girls are walking out the door, I hear Friday ask them, "Wait, where's Kelly?"

Emily snorts. "We threw the bitch out. She was walking around like she owned the place wearing one of Paul's shirts. Fuck that."

Friday high-fives them both, and I have to shake my head at their antics. And at the fact that Kelly lingered instead of taking Hayley home with her immediately.

Friday tangles her fingers with mine and pulls me toward the bedroom.

But just as we're settling into bed, the door opens and Hayley jumps in the middle. "The sun is shining," she says.

"No, it's not," I tell her. "Go back to sleep." She snuggles between us and gets comfortable. Friday reaches a hand toward me, and I flip her palm up and lay my cheek on it.

*I love you*, she mouths at me.

"I love you, too," I say out loud.

"Me, too?" Hayley asks.

"You, too," I say. I kiss her cheek and snuggle into Friday's palm.

I'm in.

# Quite some time later

# Friday

The apartment is so full that we can barely move. All of Paul's brothers are here and their wives and girlfriends. Cody and Garrett are here, too, along with their baby girl, Tuesday. Hayley and Joey are fighting over who gets to play with her first. But Matt says, "There are enough babies to go around." He points to his own. One is little Matty, his son, and the other is Hope, his daughter. They call her Hoppy most of the time because she's much more active than Matty is. Matty and Hoppy are almost eighteen months old, so they're into everything.

We're all together to watch an episode of "Reeds," the new reality show based on life in the tattoo parlor. We've seen a few episodes, and this is the one when Tuesday was born. She's exactly one year old today, so this was filmed a while ago.

I already know that this is going to bring up a shit ton of memories for me, so I have a box of tissues ready. And I have Paul. I always have Paul, no matter what.

A knock sounds on the door, and the members from Fallen from Zero, Emily's band, walk in. They're in this episode, too, since I just happened to be watching them all record when I went into labor.

Fallen from Zero is an odd group of women. The only thing they have in common is that they all grew up in the same foster home. Emilio and Marta Vasquez took the kids from group homes who no one else wanted. They took the ones who had the most damage and the most to work through, and they tried to help them. They couldn't help everyone, but they did help a lot of people.

Sam opens the door and steps back to let them in. I watch as his eyes fall on the drummer's ass. He bites his lower lip and makes a noise, and Logan punches his shoulder. *Cut it out*, Logan signs.

Sam signs back to him. *Damn, Logan. That one's got a swing on her back porch that I could swing on all day long*, he signs.

*Dude, shut up*, Logan says, his hands flying wildly.

*I know, I know*, Sam signs. *It's rude to sign in front of people who don't know what we're saying, but did you see her thighs? I want her to wrap them around me.* He draws an hourglass figure in the air with his hands. *Introduce me*, he says. *She's got enough ass to hold on to. I bet she'd like a cupcake.* He shoves Logan's shoulder again. *I want to meet her.* He points like he wants Logan to get her attention. *Please.* He puts his hands together like he's pleading.

I watch all this from the couch, and it's like watching a train wreck. Sam hasn't met these girls yet, not any of them, but the rest of us know them pretty well. We know that Peck, the girl who has gotten his attention, is not someone he should fuck with.

Logan taps Peck on the shoulder. Then he signs to her. *Peck, I'd like for you to meet my stupid brother, the dumbest man on the planet.* He waves at Sam, and Sam's mouth falls open.

"Oh, fuck," Sam says. "She's deaf."

*Not deaf*, she signs back. *I can hear.*

*And you can sign.*

*Apparently.* She grins at him.

*I'm Sam. I'm an idiot. And I like your ass. And your thighs.* He jerks a thumb behind him. *Do you want a cupcake?*

His face is red, and the whole room bursts out in laughter.

She pulls her drumsticks out of her pocket and taps them lightly on the counter. Then she opens her mouth and says hello. It's a Peck thing. Sam watches her sticks while she speaks to

Reagan and Emily. When she's done talking, her sticks stop moving.

Sam has been gone. He started playing pro football right after graduating from college. So while we have spent time with Wren, Finch, Lark, Star, and Peck, he hasn't.

*You should tell her how you play pro ball and make a shit ton of money. That's the only thing that would save you now*, Logan tells him. He laughs.

Sam flips him the bird. *Fuck you.*

Sam flops down on the floor beside the couch. Paul is sitting at my feet with my leg over his shoulder. He rubs my instep, and I fucking love that he still likes to do this.

"The episode is starting," I cry. I turn the TV up loud, because no one can hear over all the children.

The tears don't start until halfway through the episode, and they're mainly from Garrett and Cody. We watch as Tuesday comes into the world. We let the cameras into the room, but they had to stay up by my head. So, when they pick her up and lay her on my belly on the TV, I can almost feel the weight of her on me now. I close my eyes and I'm right back there, right back to the day that Tuesday was born. I held her for a moment while Cody and Garrett cried on each other, and then I handed her over. She wasn't mine.

They now had their family, and they were happy. So was I.

We all laugh at some of the outtakes in the shop that the cameras caught. We never know what the final cuts will look like, but so far, they have been a lot more about the customers than about us.

Our business has gotten so busy that we bought the shop right next door to ours, added eight more booths, and hired a slew of new artists. People wait months for appointments with us.

The episode is over, and everyone hangs out. No one is in a hurry to go home. They never are. The apartment is always full, and there are so many babies here that it never seems to quiet down. But we love it this way. We don't want to change it. Ever.

People start to mill around, and Sam keeps trying to get close to Peck. I watch him from across the room. She sidesteps him and shoots him funny glances. She's in her element here because everyone signs, so she doesn't have to talk unless she wants to, which is almost never.

Suddenly, Sam is beside me. "So, what's up with the tapping?" he asks.

"I don't know what you mean," I say crisply.

He rolls his eyes. "Yes, you do."

Suddenly, Peck is right behind him, and she taps him on the shoulder. She doesn't stop her finger from pecking as she speaks. "You could just ask me," she says quietly.

He stands up. "I keep fucking up," he says.

She nods.

"I was being really rude. It's none of my business."

She nods.

"What does Peck stand for?" he asks instead.

She taps the table and makes a sign for the word bird.

"Woodpecker?" he asks. "Peck is short for woodpecker?"

She nods and smiles. With her brown hair and brown eyes, she's stunning. Absolutely stunning. And when she smiles, she lights up a room.

He looks to her band mates. "So you all have bird names."

She nods. "We got them when we fell out of the nest—Fallen from Zero," she says. She taps the whole time she's talking. When she stops talking, the tapping stops. "You want to know what the tapping is about, right?" she asks. She rolls her eyes and blows out a frustrated breath.

Sam smiles. "I don't particularly care what the tapping is about if you'll keep talking to me."

Tap. Tap. Her eyes narrow. "Does it bother you?"

"I fucking love it," he says.

She blushes.

That's the beauty of the Reeds. They look beyond the surface. They always have.

Sam and Peck go off to a quiet corner to talk. I see her refuse cupcakes a few times, even though he keeps trying to feed her. It makes me laugh.

"What's funny?" Matt asks as he drops down beside me.

"Your stupid brother might have just met his match." I point toward Sam.

He raises his brow. "That one might be a challenge."

I grin. "It'll be fun to watch."

Suddenly, pain shoots from across my belly. I clutch for it, and Matt sits up. "Oh shit," he says. "Paul!"

Paul is standing across the room, and he runs over. He takes Matt's spot beside me and puts his hands on my huge belly. I'm a week overdue and have been having pains all day. I thought it was just Braxton-Hicks, but I think I was wrong.

"Is it time?" Paul asks.

"I think so." I've done this twice already, so I have a pretty good idea of what's happening. "We should probably hurry."

When Tuesday was born, I was in labor for an hour and a half. That's it. Just an hour and a half. I'd really like some drugs this time, though, so we should probably go.

Logan tosses Paul his keys and goes to scoop up his daughter. Emily gets my bag, and we all file into the hallway as one big unit. Even the Zero girls come, because they're nosy, they say. But they're quickly becoming family, too.

Paul takes my bag, and we go to Logan's car. "I feel bad taking Logan's car," I protest. Another pain hits me, and I feel like I need to double over.

"He'll find his way there," Paul says as he buckles Hayley in. She's been waiting for this baby. She loves her cousins, but I have a feeling she's not going to let any of them be the first to hold her new baby brother or sister. We still don't know what we're having. We didn't want to find out.

We get to the hospital quickly, and Pete and Logan pull up right behind us. Logan takes his keys back and goes to park the car. Emily gets Kit from her seat, and we all walk in together. Emily kisses my cheek. "Go get settled. We'll see you in a little while." She takes Hayley with her, even though Hayley protests.

The nurse scowls at the number of people we've brought with us. Even Garrett and Cody came with Tuesday, and the room is absolutely packed. This is my ragtag family, though, and this is what we do.

I change into a gown, and Paul sits down beside me. He was with me during Tuesday's delivery and held my hand through it, but this one is different. This one is ours.

Suddenly, a little brown-haired boy pokes his head into the room. "Hi," Jacob says. Jill walks in behind him and comes to kiss me on the cheek. "We came to see the baby." He touches my tummy. "I grew in there, too," he tells my stomach, his lips really close to my hospital gown. He looks up at me and grins. He lost another tooth last week, and he lost it when he was at our house. So, I'm getting to experience some of his milestones. Jill and I are really good friends.

"Yes, you did," I say. "I think this one is ready to come out."

He steps back. "Right now?"

I nod.

"Ewww," he says. "Where's Hayley?" He scampers off to find Hayley. Jill waves to me from the doorway as she goes after him. I didn't know they were coming, but I should have known.

"Did you call them?" I ask Paul.

He shrugs. "Maybe."

I lean over and kiss him. "I love you so much."

I'm barely hooked to the monitors when I feel the need to push. "I think it's time," I say.

Paul jumps up and calls for a nurse. The room is suddenly filled with doctors and nurses and the real work starts. Paul talks me all the way through it, never leaving my side. He's my rock. And I think I'm his.

This one is going even faster than Tuesday's birth. Holy fuck, it hurts.

"You're almost there," Paul says.

"I wish you would shut the fuck up," I say.

"Fuck you," he tosses back as he wipes my brow with a damp cloth.

"Fuck you," I say to him.

The nurses look at one another with concern, but this is who we are. This is who we have always been.

"There's the head, Dad!" the doctor says.

Paul doesn't let go of my hand but looks down to watch his baby come into the world. His eyes shimmer with tears, and I push. I feel like I'm going to push forever, when finally, the pain and the pressure ease. I open my eyes, and they lay a bloody, purple mess on my belly.

"It's a boy," the doctor says.

Paul leans into me and presses his face into the side of mine. "Our boy," he says. "He's ours."

I nod. I know he is. Paul cuts the cord, and I lay my hand on our son and he looks up at me. Then he starts to scream. They reach to take him from me. "Just a minute," I say. I look down into his eyes, and I know this one gets to stay. The weight of him on my belly is so different from the weight of him inside me. He blinks up at me, and his skin turns even more purple as he screams. I count his fingers and toes, just because I can. "Okay," I say.

They take him from me and clean us both up.

"He's perfect," I say.

"So are you." Paul drags his nose down the side of mine, and I feel the hot splash of one of his tears as they hit my chin. He wipes them away.

# Paul

I have a son. I dry my eyes with my shirt and walk out into the waiting room. They all sit forward. When did our numbers grow this big? Even Henry is here. Hayley runs to me and jumps into my arms. "It's a boy!" I tell them all. "Eight pounds, nine ounces, twenty-four-inches long, and he's here!" PJ. Paul Junior. Our son. We decided on both a girl name and a boy name months ago. We just didn't know which one we were having until now. I have a son. Holy fuck.

Hayley squeals, and everyone claps. I give Hayley to Emily and go back to be with Friday because there's nowhere else I want to be. After they're all cleaned up, the nurses let Hayley and Jacob in for a few private moments. Then they let the family in, and they hand the baby around to everyone. Friday is tired, but her labor was pretty quick. She hasn't been sleeping well, though, so she's probably exhausted.

People start to file out as soon as they've had a turn with the baby. Matt and Sky take Hayley home with them, and when the room is finally empty, I sit down with Friday and put my arm around her in the bed. We're alone, but we're not. I'm surprised she's not an emotional wreck; she's pretty calm and cool. She's done this twice but never with a baby she would be taking home. "I want to learn to breastfeed," she says quietly. "I can do that, right?"

"You can do anything you want to do."

She nods. "We did a good job." A tear slides down her cheek, and she doesn't brush it back. Friday still busts my balls, but she's also more open and honest about her feelings than she was for a long time. Or at least she is with me.

The lactation consultant comes in and teaches her how to feed the baby. I've never seen anything sweeter than the sight of her with my baby at her breast. She flinches and says it's harder than Sky and Emily made it look.

"You'll get the hang of it," I tell her.

"You promise?" she asks. She smiles at me.

"Have I ever broken a promise to you?"

She shakes her head. "Never."

She promised me she would love me forever when we got married. She promised me we could weather any storm that comes our way, and we have. She can't promise me perfect, but she promised me her, and that's all I need.

She closes her eyes while our baby suckles at her breast. I notice that her breast is plumped around his nose, so I reach over and dimple it with my finger, making some breathing room. She opens her eyes. "You're still taking care of me."

"You let me live in your fortress, Friday. I'll protect it until the day I die. I promise." I kiss her softly and watch our baby as she feeds him for the first time. I take a mental picture of it—Click! Click!—but I won't share it with anyone. This picture is only for me.

Also from Tammy Falkner

**The Reed Brothers Series**

Tall, Tatted, and Tempting

Smart, Sexy, and Secretive

Calmly, Carefully, Completely

Finally Finding Faith

Just Jelly Beans and Jealousy

Maybe Matt's Miracle

Proving Paul's Promise

Zip, Zilch, Zero (coming winter 2014)

**Regency Fantasy**

A Lady and Her Magic

The Magic of I Do

The Magic Between Us